# NOTHING LEFT

## A JACK WIDOW THRILLER

## SCOTT BLADE

Black Lion Media

Published by **Black Lion Media**.

# CHAPTER 1

wo cops. Both dead. Murdered by twenty-six bullets between them. Twenty-six shots fired. Twenty-six shell casings ejected. Twenty-six bullet holes suggest they were killed with extreme prejudice. Without remorse. Without hesitation. Without fear of consequence. But also, without experience. Without planning. Without expertise. Because the whole scene was overdone. Overreach. Over-stated. Overkill.

The shooter wanted to kill them, resurrect them, and kill them again.

The corpses were slumped over the front seats of an unmarked white Ford police cruiser, like deflated tires. Blood dripped off the driver's side door panel. It dripped slowly off the steering wheel, like a loose bathroom faucet. The blood soaked everything. Broken glass littered the interior and the ground around the vehicle. Fluids leaked from the car's undercarriage and pooled in the dirt. Dust clouds lingered in the air like a car had just sped off, and I missed it.

Someone shot both cops in their heads, shoulders, necks, and chests—straight through the driver's side windshield. Large sections of the windshield remained intact. But other sections were broken and gapped and scattered about where glass used to be. Jagged edges of broken glass on the ground reflected the moonlight, the clouds, and the stars.

Bullet holes riddled the remaining glass, the hood, the metal, the dash, the seats, and the rear bench. There were probably spent bullets in the trunk. Countless veiny cracks splintered across the windshield, fracturing off in thousands of directions, like an infestation of spider webs. The windshield slowly cracked in places. I heard it under the wind. It sounded like someone tiptoeing over broken glass.

I stood in the middle of nowhere, about sixty yards off an old road in the distance behind me. It was a forgotten two-lane highway, just a line on a map with no real interest to anybody but the people who passed through, like an abandoned tunnel or an ancient bridge. It wasn't used all that often anymore because newer interstates and roads emerged and took away the need for it.

Besides the locals—which there weren't many of—this road was mostly used as the *scenic route*. Some travelers are into that sort of thing. No one stopped to see what was in the middle of it. They just passed through it as fast as they could and went onward to their final destinations.

I was in the middle of New Mexico, on the Great Plains. Low hills rolled in all directions. Huge mountains loomed in the distance. Billowing Indiangrass stretched out for miles. To the west, a herd of huge, shadowy objects moved like slow-rolling boulders. It was a herd of grazing buffalo. The highway and the police cruiser were the only signs of human existence for a few miles, with one exception.

Hovering over me, and all around me, were huge wind turbines. They spread out for a hundred thousand acres. They towered over everything at around five hundred feet high. The long blades *whooshed* and spun, like enormous heli-copter rotors. They looked pretty new. My guess was less than five years old. Some were only months old, maybe. They were all well-maintained. I must've been surrounded by a giant wind farm. Some kind of multimillion dollar project to cheapen power for the state, as well as help the environment.

I *was* headed to Roswell, hunting for aliens—the little green men, not the migrants. It was a simple curiosity, one of those things where the stars aligned.

This morning I stopped at the Four Corners Monument, a quadripoint where four states merge at a crossing with four perfect right angles. You can stand in two states at once, one foot in each. You can step from one state to the next and twice more, a total of four states. Crossing the borders of Arizona, Colorado, Utah, and New Mexico in a single second. I saw younger people trying to time each other to see who could traverse the four states the fastest. It was like a kids' game. It was one I'd seen before. Only, that game is drawn on a street with chalk. There are squares and each player hops on one foot to the next square. The young people seem to enjoy it. I think it's called Hopscotch.

I'd never been to the Four Corners before. That's where I met a young couple who were on their way back to wherever they came from. They drove an old Bronco covered in alien and UFO bumper stickers. One sticker was of a UFO beaming a man up. It read: *Get in Loser*.

There was a mural painted all over the Bronco. It was like a collage of alien stuff. There were little green men, UFOs, and drawings of space. The couple smelled of marijuana. I was looking for a ride, which they offered me, but they were headed north, and I was headed southeast. Although, I could've changed my direction. I was headed down toward

Texas for no particular reason. Like the wind hitting sails on a boat, I could change course. No problem.

We got to talking, and they told me all about how much fun they had doing an alien tourist thing down in Roswell, New Mexico. I asked if they had tried Area 51, in Nevada. There's a small town there, not even sure if it's a town, more like a settlement. The whole thing is built around the allure of Area 51. There's an alien diner, alien museum, and a mysterious black mailbox where visitors can leave mail for the aliens. It's not marked on any map. It's a big black mailbox stuck on the side of the road. It's easy to miss. They told me they had been to Las Vegas many times and visited all that stuff before. But this was their first time in Roswell.

I'm not a believer in aliens or past visits. But I also can't rule it out. This couple got me curious, but the thing that pushed me to decide to stop here was what happened this past summer. The U.S. Navy released a report that admitted to more than a dozen cases of pilots coming across UAPs over the ocean. UAP stands for Unidentified Aerial Phenomena. The powers that be renamed the technical term from UFO to UAP. There are plenty of conspiracy theories about that too. It's the official position of the Navy that these flying crafts, or whatever they are, can't be determined. But several retired pilots—men I never met, but respected—have come forward and described things that sound an awful lot like aliens. This public admission has caused quite the fervor in the alien community, in an *I told you so* kind of way. But it's also affected regular people as well. The whole planet talked about it. So I decided, why not follow in the footsteps of my new acquaintances and pass through Roswell?

It was at a gas station close to the state border that I got a ride from the woman who later abandoned me. I passed through an abandoned town, with empty rundown buildings and one major intersection with half of a stoplight dangling from a cable.

And that's how I ended up here.

Roswell, New Mexico was more than twenty miles southwest, but less than fifty, from where I ended up. The driver who abandoned me had overshot Roswell. So I had to backtrack, which was what I was doing now. I had hitched a ride with the mission of discovering aliens. Instead, I found two dead cops.

Two hours ago, the driver who picked me up had dropped me off without explanation. Right at that moment, she was blasting Sheryl Crow on the stereo. Ironic.

The driver's decision had been a last-minute sort of thing, like she just changed her mind about me suddenly. It was bad luck for me, because we were outside the realm of civilization, and it was after nightfall. In hindsight, she ditched me. Maybe she suddenly didn't like the look of me. Or maybe it was something I said, or didn't say. Either way, it's fine. That's part of the road, part of the rules of nomadic life. You take your chances, like Sheryl Crow said: *Every day is a winding road.*

*You got that right, Sheryl.*

So I walked a while and ended up here—lost. I saw the unmarked police cruiser's faded red brake lights in the distance. I stepped off the main road to check it out. I thought maybe there was someone here who could help me out. Maybe someone who could give me a ride to a service station. I expected to discover some campers, or a couple of teenagers out here drinking and thinking they wouldn't be bothered. Instead, I stumbled upon two dead cops. But they wouldn't help me. They wouldn't help anyone. Ever again.

The wind blew around me, turning the massive turbine blades. They droned with each rotation. The grass *whooshed* and rustled. Darkness surrounded me. Nighttime prairie sounds thrummed across the landscape. It was quiet, but not silent. Crickets chirped all around me. Coyotes, or wolves, howled far off in the distance. A rattlesnake rattled somewhere between the howls and where I stood, somewhere off in the tall grass. Nightbirds fluttered their wings overhead. Their flight path was below the massive blades. I couldn't see them. Judging by the sounds, they were probably birds. But they could've been bats. I prayed they were owls.

Above, the moon was full. Heavy clouds streamed across the sky quickly, like time was fast-forwarding. There was still plenty of moonlight to see, clouds or no clouds. I could see the scene pretty well, even without a flashlight. The nearest city lights were faint on the horizon, but the darkness was soft enough and the moonlight bright enough to make the visibility pretty good.

I concentrated on the dead cops and examined the murder scene. Bullet holes honeycombed the cruiser's hood. Thin plumes of smoke wafted out of the bullet holes, like parts of the engine were smoking. *Hopefully the thing wouldn't catch fire.*

The front tires were flat from bullet punctures. Water from the radiator leaked out under the car and soaked into the soil.

Gunfire smells lingered in the air. I smelled blood on the wind. The whole thing smelled like it went down not that long ago. Tire tracks were smeared back down the track. The killer peeled out before speeding away. He left behind all kinds of tire tracks, and probably rubber from the tires. There were clear skid marks all across the highway, which would be easier seen in daylight.

The cruiser's headlamps were off, but the brake lights were lit up, tinging the hills behind the cruiser in a low red hue, like faded blood. The cruiser was in park, but the driver died with his foot on the brake pedal, and it stayed there after he was dead. Thus, the lingering brake lights.

I was the only living person around in the nighttime gloom. I looked around in all directions, and saw no one else. No signs of other humans. No traces of anyone else, except for the aggressive tire tracks the killer left behind, the looming city lights of the nearby town, and, of course, the giant rotating wind turbines.

I leaned over the open driver's side window, careful not to touch the corpse. A coffee napkin from my pocket made a great tool to cover my fingerprints. With the napkin covering my hand, I reached in through the window and shut off the ignition. Then I grabbed a knob and twisted it for the headlamps. They flickered on. Dust hazed through the beams. I leaned back out of the car and walked around the cruiser's nose, out several yards to the killer's tire tracks.

I knelt and studied the tire tracks in the dirt. I was no expert on tires, but I knew the FBI could easily identify everything about them from these. I stood up and turned back to the police cruiser. I saw the dead cops as dark figures, staring back at me. They looked more like heaps of bones and skin than humans.

I stayed where I was and scanned the ground between the killer's vehicle and the police cruiser. Instantly, I realized I had missed the shell casings on the ground. But I saw them now. Luckily, I hadn't stepped on them. Out in front of the cruiser's headlamps there were numerous shell casings. They littered the ground. I counted them up, as I had the bullet holes. I accounted for twenty-six, matching the number of bullet holes.

I crept closer to them, squatted, and looked, staying careful not to step on them. The killer's footprints were right there with them, several feet away from me. His gun had spat out the bullet casings in the same direction, indicating one firearm used.

I inched closer again and looked at them. The bullet casings were all the same. I recounted them and stared at each to be sure of the number and caliber. I got twenty-six again. Near the shooter's footprints, I found one empty magazine, from a Glock. It was too dark to count the notches, which marked how many bullets each magazine held. The killer was sloppy, leaving the magazine behind. Criminals forget to pick up their casings all the time, but a magazine? That was dumb.

The same gun fired them. There was one shooter. I dared not get any closer. I didn't want my footprints mixing in with the shooter's. So I stood up and retreated to the cruiser.

I got close to the dead cops, but touched nothing. Like my fingerprints, I didn't want my DNA on any part of the crime scene. Using the napkin again, I reached in and shut off the headlamps. I didn't want anyone to mistake me for having any part of it. I studied the dead cops from an observer's distance. Their wounds appeared to be scattered kill shots. They weren't random, but they weren't professional either. It was just sloppy work. Plain and simple. The shooter knew how to fire a gun. Probably because he had seen it on a bad prime-time cop show. But he wasn't a trained professional. My guess was that he had fired a weapon before, but had zero training. This was no assassination for pay. No professional hit. It was just a run-of-the-mill criminal homicide, except the victims were cops.

There are a few things that really piss me off. One is injustices, like when bad guys get away with bad things. The second is cop killers. The same goes for anyone who kills our military service members. Cop killers, and enemy combatants who kill service members, struck a vengeful nerve with me.

The cruiser was unmarked, but I knew it was a police car because there was an array of antennas sticking up along the trunk lid. The kind police needed to stay in contact with dispatch, especially when driving out in the middle of nowhere.

Both dead bodies had that cop look about them. They wore street clothes, but were definitely off-duty cops, or federal agents in plain clothes. They could've been on a stakeout, or having a clandestine meeting with an informant, or doing any of those things that cops do.

I've spent the last several years hitchhiking from one state to the next, never stopping for long, and never getting too used to staying in one place. I started drifting after I left my under-cover job in the NCIS. And I'm addicted. Not unlike a drug or alcohol addict, but my addiction isn't going to kill me—probably.

I'm addicted to two things: coffee and nomading. My addic-tions have no cure. Not that I'd want to cure them. I love them both. Why live paycheck to paycheck? Why stay in one place your whole life? Why work for someone else, paying taxes, paying rent, paying bills? Why settle for any of that? Why settle at all? I didn't get it.

I love not knowing what's around the corner. You never know what the tide will bring. Sometimes that's a good thing and sometimes it's a bad thing. On the road ahead of me, there could be anything. I could meet a beautiful woman. I could meet a stranger with a gun. I could run into danger. I could run into adventure. That's the magic. The spontaneity. The improvisation of life. The unknown. That's what I love.

But, right then, all of those things happened to me all at once, like some kind of twisted ambush.

Right then, a pair of headlights appeared in the darkness. A car approached from down the two-lane highway. I froze where I was and watched it. It grew larger in a long moment as it headed in my direction. *Was it the killer? Was he returning to the scene of the crime?*

At first it passed by, but then the brake lights came on. And the driver slammed to a stop. The tires skidded, and the brakes howled. Dust rose behind the tires.

Once the headlights had passed, I got a better look at the vehicle. And it was bad news for me.

*Shit,* I thought.

The oncoming car was another police cruiser, but a regular one, not an unmarked one. I could tell because the light bar on top lit up and blue lights washed through the darkness, over the terrain. The blue light bounced off the nearest wind turbine's white base, illuminating a wide stretch of ground beneath it.

The driver left the siren off. The car reversed, and the engine whined until the cruiser made it back to the track I stood on. The car stopped, and the engine whine died away as the driver switched the car into drive and turned onto the dirt track. The cruiser sped up as fast as it was safe to. The headlights bounced up over dips in the track.

The cop must've seen the lights from the dead cops' car. Not knowing what to do, I froze. Technically, I didn't kill them. There was nothing for me to fear. But in my experience, I had been arrested more often than your average drifter, for crimes I didn't commit. It was mostly because of how I looked and partially out of convenience.

I was six foot four, two hundred and twenty pounds of concrete muscle mass. And I stood over two dead cops in the middle of nowhere. *What would this new cop think when he saw me?* He'd arrest me. No doubt about it. I'd do the same thing if I were in his shoes.

I could run. So far, he hadn't seen me. Not from the highway. *But where would I go?* There was nothingness in every direction. Plus, running would get me more than arrested. It'd probably get me beaten with nightsticks in a room with no cameras and no witnesses. It'd get me charged and probably stuffed into a jail cell. In some rural areas, in some states, it'd get me killed. Cops don't like cop killers. Even though I had killed nobody. At least not in New Mexico. Not yet.

I stayed where I was.

The newly-arrived police cruiser continued up the track. As it got closer, I got a better look at it. The cruiser was old, but had once been a state-of-the-art machine. The driver must've spotted me, and spotted the bullet holes in the police car in front of me. Maybe he saw the two dead bodies inside because he buzzed the siren, not turned it on, just blipped it, like a warning to me to stay put.

The cruiser swayed and bounced as it sped toward me from out of the darkness. A coyote howled somewhere behind me. The giant wind turbine *whooshed* overhead. The police cruiser slammed to a stop again. The tires screeched, and the brakes squealed as the thing came skidding to a stop ten feet from where I stood. The rear of the car skidded clear across the dirt. Dust sprayed up into the air behind it. The wind gusted a huge dust cloud out past the cruiser. It engulfed both of us for a moment, before dissipating into the gloom.

The siren blipped again, and the blue lights lit up the low, hilly grassland around me, like little blue lighthouses on the sea. The night sky brightened and the beams from the light faded into hazy clouds. More dust rose up from the tire skid, but this time slow and somber.

The headlamps washed over me, and stayed there. But the light stopped at my neck, just below my chin. My head and face remained in darkness above the beams.

I stayed where I was.

The cop inside threw the car's transmission into park. The driver's door burst open, and the cop jumped out and pulled a department-issued Glock on me. The cop had excellent moves. It all went down as I had predicted. Except I was wrong about one important detail. The cop wasn't a he. He was a she.

She steadied her arms over the top of her car door, the Glock held out and pointed directly at me. She locked her arms straight out and stood strong—textbook stance. She aimed her weapon at the dead center of my chest. There was no laser sight, but I felt it. This cop was well-trained.

I didn't know if it was bad luck on my part that she appeared out of nowhere or if she'd pulled up to answer a distress call from the two dead cops. I hadn't thought to check the police radio, or look to see if their hands were empty. It was plausible. Maybe one of them stayed alive long enough to radio for help. Maybe the radio was still in the palm of his hand.

What I knew for sure was, to this cop, I was a total stranger. She was a cop staring at a police cruiser with two dead cops in it, and me, a stranger, standing over them. Not a dream scenario. To her, I was just a giant hitchhiker with black clothes on.

Factor in the black clothes, my large stature, and the middle-of-nowhere scene, and she probably looked at me and saw the thing from outer space from many eighties alien invasion/horror movies. One of those movies where a giant alien, who never dies, hunts man for sport. The kind of giant alien who keeps returning from the dead after being shot with shotgun rounds, nine-millimeter parabellums, or whatever else the local cops could throw at it.

The policewoman aimed down the barrel of her Glock at me, and shouted, "Hands up!"

Without objection, I raised my hands high above my head and kept my fingers limp and still. As my arms went up, she followed them with her eyes slowly. Like uniformed sailors watching a flag rising up a flagpole in front of them. It was a long route. Her eyes flicked back down to my face. I doubted she could see much detail because of the darkness.

She shouted, "Keep them up!"

Her voice was calm, yet firm. It was a seasoned cop-voice. She had used it hundreds of times, maybe thousands.

She shouted, "Turn around! Face the other direction! Do it slow!"

I turned around, slow and calm. My head pivoted back to look over my shoulder as I turned so I could maintain eye contact with her. Not that she could tell.

She shouted, "Face forward!"

I turned my head back toward the front and faced the direction of the silent cop car with the two dead cops inside. My eyes washed over their bodies again, closely. I got a better view of the damage. There were bullet holes all over the place —the front hood, the backseat, the rear windshield, and even through the headrests.

The policewoman walked up behind me, slow and steady, with her boots scuffling in the dirt. She stopped directly behind me, but outside of my reach, which was a smart move on her part. She had sized me up like a veteran law enforcement officer would. She determined it best to stay clear of my long reach in case I spun around and snatched the Glock from her hands, which I could've done.

She said, "Place your hands behind your back! Do it slow!"

I did as she asked. Knowing what she was going to do, I jetted my thumbs out. A half-second later, she grabbed my wrist and locked it in a handcuff. She followed with the other wrist and cuff. I heard the *clicks* from the handcuffs. The cold metal chilled my skin as it coiled over my wrists. I glanced back at her from over my shoulder. Not fast and not slow, just a steady glance. I kept my expression friendly. I had been arrested many times before, and by female officers before. I knew the drill.

In my experience, officers in arresting situations are hopped up on adrenaline and training, which told them to be aggressive, to make their voices sound full of authority and strength. They were trained to sound like they meant business. When an officer tells you to freeze, what they are really saying is *freeze or I'll shoot you.* And ninety-nine point nine percent of the time, they *will* shoot you.

I didn't know this woman from Eve. So far, she seemed professional, level-headed, and competent, but I wasn't a hundred percent sure she wasn't a bad apple. Lots of police departments have them. Bad apples would be just as quick to shoot you and sort it out later, instead of following procedure. Especially out in the middle of nowhere. No witnesses. And two dead cops as probable cause. So I gave her no provocation to shoot me.

I kept my voice friendly, but more toward the side of neutrality than familiarity. I said, "You're making a mistake. I didn't do this. I just found them."

She said, "Right. Now, turn around. Slow. Let me see your face."

I turned around, dawdling, and gazed down at her. She squinted her eyes, but not in the way that said she couldn't see me. It was more like she couldn't believe her eyes, like something amazed her, like she recognized me. She took one hand off the Glock and covered her mouth with it. She stayed like that for a long second and held the gun one-handed, pointing at my center mass. Then, she reached down and grabbed a small flashlight from her police belt, quickly, like she had rehearsed it many, many times.

She lifted it up and clicked the light on in one fluid motion. The beam was bright, white like a surgeon's light. The beam spotlighted straight at my chest and then moved up to my face. She stopped it, held it on my face. The flashlight beamed a powerful light on me. It blinded me.

I couldn't make out her features behind the beam.

The police officer suddenly broke protocol and stepped forward, closer to me than she should have. She stared at me for another long second. Suddenly, she did something completely unexpected. She lowered the Glock, a fraction of the way down. But she kept it pointed at me and kept her finger inside the trigger guard, in case she had to draw it up fast and put a bullet in me.

I could make out her face, but not enough to pick her out of a lineup. I saw just enough to know she was probably about forty, not much older than I was.

She looked at me strangely—strange for this situation. Strange for any situation where an officer is pointing a Glock at you one second, and the next, she's greeting you with the eyes of someone from the past.

The officer lowered the flashlight enough for me to see better. I saw her face. She had pale blue eyes and fair skin. I believe the tone was called porcelain. I imagined it wasn't a natural look in New Mexico, where there is plenty of sunlight. Maybe she only worked the night shift. And she had been doing so for a long time, judging by how pale her skin was.

She was about five-four, not short for an average woman, but an entire foot shorter than I was. She wore a bulletproof vest over her uniform. It looked bulky around her chest, like her breasts stretched the vest more than the design was meant for. Bulletproof vests are traditionally designed with men in mind. Men make up most of the vocational forces that utilize bulletproof vests. There are some companies out there with more form-fitting designs in their catalogue. Apparently, whatever department she belonged to in New Mexico didn't offer those.

Her uniform shirt had long sleeves. I could see a hint of a tattoo cropping out of her sleeve, over her wrist. It rode up the back of her gun hand. There was another tail of it poking out of the collar of her shirt. It came up her neck about a third of the way. I imagined it was all one enormous piece. I had a lot of tattoos myself. So I knew two things about it. First, the procedure was long and painful, which told me she had patience, and probably a high threshold for pain. And two, it was expensive. Big tattoos like that could cost thousands of dollars and take weeks or months to complete.

All of this told me she was tough and patient. She probably had thick skin, with a radar for bullshit. Most female cops like her do. There's an extra layer of bullshit for women to go through in male-dominated industries. Law enforcement was no different. It's far from a perfect world.

I glanced at her name patch. It was just a flick of the eyes. Her name patch was sewn above her right breast on the bullet-proof vest. It read: *Voss*.

I took a second glance, with another flick of the eyes to see her badge. It glimmered faintly from the moonlight. It was a small, gold star-shaped badge, engraved with symbols, representing New Mexico Law Enforcement. And there was a badge number. The symbol was probably the crest for the local city she worked out of, and not the county, because the side of her car read: *Angel Rock: Police* and not *Angel Rock: Sheriff*. She was a part of a police force and not a sheriff's office, which meant that she was on the force for a township or city, and not for a county, because sheriffs policed the counties of America, and police worked the municipalities.

Her flashlight flicked back up to my face. The light was bright in my eyes. I recoiled from looking at her badge. She lowered the beam, so it was no longer blinding me.

I returned my eyes up to her face. Her expression had completely changed from one of strangeness, to one of perplexity. *But why?*

She looked at me like she had seen a ghost, someone from years ago that she had thought was dead by now. And then, I knew why, because she spoke.

She said, "Widow? Jack Widow?"

# CHAPTER 2

The cop named Voss stared at me like she'd seen a ghost, a reincarnation of a memory she wanted to forget. I saw it in her eyes. There was something there—a recognition, more than a hint, but less than familiarity. She knew me. Obviously. She had said my name. The Glock trembled in her hand. It was subtle, but it was there. An untrained person wouldn't notice it, but I did. She became distant for a moment. Her mind had gone somewhere else, to a far-off past. Her eyes glassed over like condensation on a mirror.

There was pain there. It was in her eyes, like she knew me from an unwanted memory. It was something she ran from, something she fought hard to block out of her mind. I had no idea what it was. Whatever it was, it distracted her, only for a moment, but it had been there, and I had seen it.

If I had been the killer, it would've been bad for her. Her life could've ended right there. Because I could've head-butted her and knocked her out or killed her, but I didn't. She didn't strike me as a cop who'd make such a stupid mistake. I doubted she'd ever let a suspect overpower her, or give them the chance. Not even a slight one. But she had given me that one moment of opportunity.

She recognized me from somewhere and from the look in her eyes, it wasn't a fond memory, which was unlucky for me because she had me at gunpoint. And I couldn't remember her, which was unusual for me because I had a pretty good memory. But right then, I was drawing a blank.

I said, "That's my name. Do I know you?"

She looked confused, a bit disappointed, and then, visibly angry, like I should remember her. It was like she wanted to say: *You don't remember me? How dare you forget?*

I saw it in her eyes. But the anger quickly subsided. And she came back to reality. A glimmer of mistrust appeared back in her eyes, like she realized she made a mistake and let her guard down in front of a murder suspect, and a cop killer, at that. The Glock went back up all the way and she stepped back enough to keep out of my reach.

My opportunity to swipe the gun out of her hand and turn it against her was gone. I repeated, "Do I know you?"

She didn't answer, just repeated my name, like now she was unsure it was me. Like her eyes deceived her. Like her brain was playing tricks on her. She repeated my name. "Widow?"

Voss let the flashlight beam wash over my features, up and down like a prison-yard spotlight. She broke the same protocol once again, gave me a second chance to overpower her. She stepped closer again, closer than before, keeping the gun tight in her hand and her arm loose, so she could quickly flick the Glock upward, and shoot me. If she needed to. Voss said, "You look the same. Only more scruffy, older, like you're a man now."

*I've always been a man*, I thought.

Voss paused a beat, and said, "Lieutenant Widow."

I stared back at her, trying to find her face in my memory. It was strange, because she was unforgettable as she was now, but I couldn't find her. Not anywhere in my memory. I said, "I used to be a Lieutenant. That was a long, long time ago."

Voss said nothing.

Somewhat cretinous, I asked, "Do I know you?"

She didn't answer that. She just nodded in complete recognition like she had known me my whole life, like I was someone she'd never forget. She said, "Amazing. You look just as I remember you. Like out of a dream."

Silence.

Voss asked, "You don't remember me?"

"Sorry. I don't. But I can't hardly see you. Can you lower the flashlight?"

She paused a beat and breathed in heavily, like it was an act that was a complete betrayal of years of cop training. She said, "Sorry." And she lowered her hand. The flashlight beam fell off my face, but she held it so that it stayed on my torso.

I glanced back down at her name patch to make sure I read her name right the first time. Once again, it read: *Voss*. And nothing else. No first name. No first or middle initial. No indication of married or single. Nothing. It meant nothing to me.

Just in case, I searched my memories again. Still, I couldn't locate the name. I couldn't remember her name or her face.

Physically, I saw her height. I saw she was possibly less than a hundred and twenty pounds, without the heavy police vest and equipment. She was less than forty years in age. Maybe she was younger than me, but not much. We were close in age. Her hair was cut short, a couple of inches long and not a fraction more. There was no product in it. At least none of that stiff-hold nonsense. Her hair blew on top her head like short grass in the open breeze.

She had no wedding ring, but had a look about her that said she was married, or once married. It was that kind of mature *I've seen a thing or two* look married people had registered in their faces. I had seen it before, and I would see it again. No doubt.

Disappointedly, Voss said, "I guess I'm not surprised you forgot me."

I shrugged and stayed quiet.

She paused a beat. The air was crisp and continued to be a little windy, carrying with it a sense that it was only going to blow harder as the night progressed. It blew between us. Smells of the hilly terrain entered my nose—grassy plains smelled like far-off grazing animals and the night predators who hunted them.

Coyotes howled far away somewhere at the sky. At first, it was only from the north, but soon we could hear them from the south and the east. They sounded quite distant, but still the howls stirred the proper emotions in us. The kinds of emotions they were supposed to stir up in people. My alertness rose and so did Voss's, but neither of us acknowledged it. I didn't because it didn't scare me. Hardly anything ever did. Voss didn't acknowledge it because she was used to it, or she was fearless, or both. Nothing about her would've surprised me because she carried herself as a woman who had been through it all, and seen it all, and had come out of it standing tall—a hardened cop.

Voss broke the silence, and said, "I'm a cop now, out of Angel Rock."

"Angel Rock? Are we in that jurisdiction?"

She nodded, and said, "That's right. Just to the east of here."

"I passed through a ghost town to the west. What's that?"

I peeked back over my shoulder to the west, pointing with my chin. On my way into the boundaries of Angel Rock, after getting abandoned way out here, I had passed through the remnants of a ghost town. There were hollowed-out buildings, rundown houses, completely forgotten roads, and a town abandoned and eroded away by time. It looked like the town that time forgot. I remembered seeing an old two-story police station with an old police car parked out front. The tires had rotted away decades ago. Someone had probably stripped the engine out for parts years ago because there was nothing left but a shell. Rust had eaten away the paint.

We heard the howls again, fainter this time. The sound of coyotes in the distance seemed to quiet down like the end of a nightly chorus. The blades on the wind turbine still *whooshed* above.

Voss said, "It's a town called El Demonio. Well, what's left of it. There used to be a metal refinery there. The whole town was built up around it. When that shut down, the townsfolk abandoned everything. And now, we got these wind farms."

"El Demonio?"

"Yeah. That's right."

I asked, "Angel Rock and El Demonio? Angels and Demons? Is that for real?"

"It is. Believe me. We've heard it all."

Silence.

Voss's facial expression turned slightly warm, slightly friendly. She asked, "You really don't remember me?"

"I'm sorry. I don't. But I wish I did."

I was telling the truth. She was a good-looking woman—tough, tattooed, smart, commanding, and she had a firearm. That was pretty much my kind of woman to a T. I'd remember her if we'd met. No doubt about it.

I took a chance, and asked, "Since you know me, do you mind un-cuffing me?"

Her expression faded, like the cop side of her was giving her pause. She deliberated my request for a long moment. Finally, she looked at the lifeless police cruiser. She stared at the dark husks of two dead cops. Then she looked back at me. She asked, "Did you kill these guys?"

"Of course not."

"Did you have anything to do with it?"

"No! I literally found them a few minutes ago. Then you pulled up. Other than that, I know nothing."

"You're not hiding anything?"

"No," I said. "I promise. I just found them like this."

Voss looked at me. Suspicion lingered in her eyes. She stared into my eyes, like she was searching for the truth. Which was something she had probably done a thousand times before with various suspects throughout her years as a cop. Cop senses are an occupational hazard, but one that could save your life. Hers were as good as anyone's. She had survived this long. She trusted her instincts.

"Okay. I believe you. But Widow, if you're lying to me, you try anything stupid, I'll shoot you. No questions asked. Got it?"

I nodded. At first, I couldn't believe it. She believed me. If she hadn't known me, she probably wouldn't have taken the cuffs off me. I had to remember how she knew me. I tried again to summon a memory of her, but I couldn't. It just wasn't there.

Voss holstered her gun, but left the strap unsnapped. She approached me, put a hand on my bicep, and spun me around and unlocked my cuffs, just like that.

*She must've known me enough to trust me*, I thought. But that was my only clue, other than she wasn't a past lover. I knew that. I was a man, and we can be pretty dumb, but I wasn't a Neanderthal. I would remember her. No way would I forget a woman like her if we had been intimate. She knew me from something else. All I knew for sure was it was from my Navy days, because she had called me *Lieutenant*. Which also told me something. She knew me a long time ago. Twenty years ago was my guess because that's about when I was a Lieutenant, both junior and an O3. It was somewhere in that range.

I turned back around, slowly, and rubbed my wrists, really out of habit, not pain. Habit because I had gotten arrested a lot since I left the NCIS. More often than I preferred. I was getting used to being in handcuffs. I had been arrested so many times over the last six years, it was becoming a regular ritual. These days it seemed like whenever I walked into a new town, immediately the local law enforcement arrested me and locked me up in jail.

Suddenly, I thought of *Rambo*. He was just a former soldier, turned drifter, who walked into a town in Oregon, looking for a hot meal. And the first thing to happen to him was he got arrested for nothing. That was the first movie. The sequels, I couldn't speak of. I never saw them. They looked like cartoon action movies. I remember I saw the cover of one of the DVDs once, probably in the commissary on some foreign Navy base. John Rambo was on the cover, shirtless, sweaty, and firing a chain gun. The old eighties Hollywood male fantasy of a soldier's life. Ridiculous.

This was the first time that I had been freed directly after being placed in handcuffs. Maybe my luck was changing. Maybe not.

Voss reached her hand out, offered it up for me to shake, reluctantly, and said, "Lieutenant Widow, it's nice to meet you, again. Since you forgot me, I'm Lacy Voss."

I took her hand in mine gently, and shook it gently, and said, "Call me, Widow. No one calls me by military rank. Not anymore. Besides, I've not been a Lieutenant in over a decade."

"Has it been that long?"

"It has."

She stared up at me and shook her head in disappointment. She repeated, "Still have no clue who I am?"

"I'm sorry. I don't remember you."

"Forget it. It was a long time ago. I guess you're not in the Navy anymore? There's no water around here."

"No. I've been out for several years."

"So, what do you do now? What're you doing way out here?"

"I'm doing nothing. Just moving around."

"What's that mean?" she asked.

"I just live my life. I do nothing in particular."

"So you're a homeless drifter?"

"Home is where the heart is."

"How did you get out here?"

I said, "My ride left me."

"That's it? They left you out here?"

"Yes. I'm here looking for alien stuff. I was on my way to Roswell, when my ride ditched me on the side of the road."

I could see her hand inching toward her gun as her mind comprehended my story. It seemed like her hand and the lizard part of her brain were in tune. She was a good cop.

She didn't grab her gun. She simply nodded and looked past me and back at the dead cops. She asked, "What happened to them?"

I looked back at the two dead cops, the unmarked police car, and the holes left by the bullets that had shredded through the entire car. I said, "They got shot."

She glanced at me, and said, "I see that."

"It was by an amateur."

"You looked it over?"

"I did. Briefly."

"Widow…" she protested.

"Don't worry. I touched nothing. I stepped around the casings and the killer's footprints. I used to be a cop, you know?"

"Really? I didn't know that. I thought you were a SEAL?"

"That too."

"At the same time?"

I didn't answer that. Most people didn't know about Unit Ten, the secret undercover operation in the basement of an NCIS building in Quantico.

Voss said, "I didn't know you from the Navy, anyway. I was a civilian when we met."

I paused briefly, and then I asked, "In what capacity did I meet you?"

"No. You're not getting any more from me. You'll remember on your own. I'm sure."

Silence. I paused like I was thinking it over, and then I asked, "Were we lovers?"

She glanced at me sideways, and said, "If we were lovers, you'd remember it. No question. You'd never forget."

I had nothing to comment back to that. A look came over her face like she was struggling with some kind of big decision. Like she was conflicted on what to do next. Finally, she said, "I'd better call this in. I think it best if you take off. Better not even be involved. How am I supposed to explain that I found you here, and didn't arrest you? Two dead cops and a drifter lurking around them. You know. It doesn't look good. You're low-hanging fruit. They'll throw you in a cell till this is sorted out. And that could take days or weeks or months. Which means the real killer might get completely overlooked."

I looked at her in surprise. I asked, "You're letting me go?"

"I can't explain why you aren't under arrest, now can I? What am I going to say? I knew you for one life-changing moment years ago, and now, you can't remember me, but I completely trust you?"

I stayed quiet.

She said, "Widow, I find you over two dead cops. How am I not supposed to either shoot you or arrest you?"

"You could say the truth. I told you I didn't do it and you believe me because you know me. You know my character."

"That won't fly. All that will do is cause confusion and convolute the scene. In a case like this, the first twenty-four hours are crucial. I need to be focused on this and not trying to convince my guys you're not involved."

I shrugged, and said, "Guess you're right."

"I don't do this often. In fact, I've never done it before. You understand? But this is an unusual situation. I know you didn't kill these guys. But your being here is gonna stall whatever investigation will take place. Cops hate cop killers. And they will see you and assume you had something to do with it. You understand?"

I nodded. I got it the first time. She was right. I'm a nobody, with a crazy story about alien hunting and being abandoned on the side of the road. And I was here right when she pulled up to find two dead cops? Any other cop would lock me up and throw away the key before they even listened to my story.

She said, "I'm going to call this in. You go. Head toward Angel Rock. If you see another police cruiser headed this way, duck off the road and let it pass."

"Really?"

"These two are state cops. They're not locals. I got no idea if there's more of them headed this way. They might already know their guys are dead. They've got dispatch, radio checks, GPS tracking in the car, and more. State cops are gung-ho. They'll slap cuffs on you just for being here. And I'll never see you again. You're a drifter, out here in the middle of nowhere. That suspicion alone is all the evidence they need."

I nodded, and said, "I can help them. I may have seen nothing, but I can help them find who did this."

"Save it. I can't explain why you're here to the state police. They'll never believe me. You'd better let me handle this."

I shrugged. She was right. And I'm not a cop anymore. It's not my business.

Voss said, "Meet me at the diner in town in the morning. We'll talk more."

"Okay. Which diner?"

She smiled, and said, "There's only one. It's a small town."

I nodded, looked into her beautiful eyes, and looked away. I turned and walked east, down the old, bygone road, toward Angel Rock.

# CHAPTER 3

I walked the center of the forgotten road, thinking—like average people did on their daily commutes, only I was doing it at ten o'clock at night. The open road is a place of reflection for me. I supposed everyone gets that feeling when on long, quiet drives or long walks. Husbands and wives drove long stretches of road to and from work daily, and let their minds wander aimlessly. Truck drivers crisscrossed the American interstate system in stages of half-alertness, half-daydreaming. The open road was the modern place for meditation. What else was there to do but think? Or not. Whatever the case may be.

Some days, I walked for hours without a single memorable thought or care or worry. Other days, I had something on my mind, like tonight. Tonight, there was no quiet, reflective meditation. Not in my head. My mind thought about the crime scene. Two dead state police officers. The lovely Officer Voss. The amateur shooter. The bullet holes riddled through the dead cops, and the ones that missed and passed through the seats, the headrests, and into the backseat, possibly crashing into the trunk.

The primate part of my brain waited for the oncoming head-lights and the flashing light bars of one or two or three of Angel Rock's finest to back up Officer Voss. I expected cruisers to flood the night and the darkness and the empty road with their blue lights. No way was she going to stay alone back there, but so far, no other police car drove by. Not a sign of blue flashing lights. Not a noise or sound of a car engine or tires barreling toward me from the distance.

The only prominent sounds I heard were the howling of an ever-changing wind across the grassy plains and rolling hills. I heard the night breeze as it picked up dust and particles and swept the land. I heard more howls of far-off coyotes. The howls died down to low echoes like it was their dying breaths. Once it all died away, the road went silent. Except the giant wind turbines. They were spread far apart from each other, and they were five hundred feet in the sky, but the blades were so big, and the wind was strong enough, that I could hear their rotations like riding in a Black Hawk. Otherwise, the night was quiet.

I walked the quiet highway until it livened up and I saw city lights growing closer. Eventually, the road led me right to the edge of a town. I stopped walking, right there with the town in my sights.

I worried. My civilized brain suspected, asked questions. *Why was there no backup coming to help Voss investigate and secure the area? Where the hell were they? Why did she let me go so easily? Did she really know me?*

I stared at Angel Rock's lights in front of me. No car lights. No police cruisers sped out of town and toward the crime scene to back up their fellow officer. I saw none of those things. Just Angel Rock's town lights.

The town looked awake and active. I saw lights from various businesses all throughout the small municipality, scattered across the horizon like a far-off aircraft carrier floating on a dark ocean. The lights guided my way and beckoned me toward them. Voss had asked me to wait for her at the town diner. She had known me somehow. We could sit and have a conversation, where she could clear it up for me. However, right then, I was concerned about the quiet, noiseless night that lay behind me, where I had left her. *Why was it so silent?* Perhaps the shooter had returned. Perhaps he had been hiding out on the plains. Perhaps he had lain low out there in the darkness, where he watched and listened to our conversation. Maybe he knew that his perfect chance to kill another cop was coming. Maybe he waited and watched me leave. I wasn't a cop. Not to him. I wasn't in uniform. And I hadn't been a cop in six-plus years. He let me go. I wasn't his target. Maybe he was setting up an ambush for as many cops as he could. Perhaps I was wrong about him. Perhaps he wasn't an amateur after all. Perhaps he was a crazed cop killer hell-bent on ambushing law enforcement. Perhaps he was on a nightly rampage.

I turned and gazed back at the way I had come. I had left Voss far back there in the darkness. I had walked about three miles. About thirty minutes had passed. A lot can happen in thirty minutes—a lot.

I started the walk back to her at a faster pace than I had walked to town. I didn't run. I didn't want to get there and find that she needed help, and I was out of breath. So I fast-walked. Back to the scene of the crime.

# CHAPTER 4

The two-lane road was mostly straight, but not completely. I crossed over a point where the old blacktop became bumpier, worn-out pavement, like I had traversed a border between two townships, one with a good budget for roads and one without. It was the towns of Angel Rock and El Demonio. One thriving, the other run-down and abandoned.

I walked, stretching my legs out as far as I could, taking huge strides, not elegant but efficient. I covered ground faster this way.

Up ahead, I had expected to find Voss in some sort of trouble. Maybe the bad guy had returned to add her to his kill list. But when I arrived, she was alone. No backup. No sign of anyone else.

She hadn't called for backup. She had called no one.

Voss stood over the dead cops, same as I had before. She didn't know I was behind her, walking up the track. That wasn't because she had no situational awareness. It wasn't because she was bad at her job. It was because I was better.

My situational awareness was better than most people's. I was stealthier than most people. I had better be. The U.S. Navy spent $500,000 training me to be better, to be stealthier.

Voss stared at the state police cruiser, like she was studying the whole scene, trying to figure it out. She moved this way and that, tilting right, bending left, until she stopped and gazed at the bullet holes in the windshield. She investigated without backup, without a detective present. She was going it alone. It was unusual for a patrolwoman to be investigating a crime scene.

I asked myself: *why?* A thought struck me. The same thought that would strike anyone. Maybe she was more involved than just a patrolwoman who was passing by.

Then I looked at her car and knew exactly why. She was more involved, but not in a devious way. My ability to sneak up on someone might've been top-notch, but my ability to see obvious details was out of practice, which made me feel a little dumb.

Her black-and-white patrol car didn't read: *Angel Rock: Police*, as I had originally thought. I misread it. It read: *Angel Rock: Chief of Police*.

Her title wasn't Patrolwoman Voss; she was the chief of the Angel Rock Police Department.

*Why was she not calling for backup?* I thought. Being police chief meant she didn't have to. Although she should. It was the right thing to do. She could take her time at a crime scene if she wanted to. Still, nearly an hour without calling for backup seemed excessive, out of place.

It made little sense to me. It was time to ask her.

I didn't want to startle her, so I started making noise. I stomped my feet on the beaten dirt and walked up behind

Chief Voss's police cruiser. At the trunk, I stopped, and called out, "Voss. I'm back."

She did a one-hundred-eighty-degree turn while in a crouch and drew her Glock, fast, as if it had been done in practice countless times. She pointed it right at me. The weapon was ready to go before she made the full turn. A slow slipstream of dust and dirt drifted up behind her and whirled in the other direction like a tiny cyclone. I watched it circle and twist and die away into the night behind her.

I froze. My hands went up to the surrender position, as they had fifty minutes ago to the same woman, the same gun. I honestly wasn't sure that she wouldn't shoot first. The look in her eyes said that she was pre-programmed to fire, which no one would question. Two dead cops in the middle of nowhere at night was enough of a reason for any startled cop to shoot any stranger that snuck up from behind. No jury, judge, courtroom, or police officer would've even questioned the logic in her shooting me dead where I stood. And dead I would be. I knew it too. She wasn't the kind of cop to miss. She wasn't the kind of cop to wound.

Luckily, Voss didn't shoot me. Not yet.

I said, "It's me. Widow."

She kept her Glock aimed at me. She asked, "Why're you back? I told you to meet me in Angel Rock in the morning."

"I worried about you."

"How so?"

"You said that you'd call backup. I walked away to town like you said, but I saw no one. No flashing lights or speeding reinforcements. I worried that maybe the bad guy had returned after I left you. Maybe he'd done to you what he did to them."

"So what? You come back to rescue me? You think this guy could get the drop on me?"

I said, "I guess not. You're pretty fast with that piece. Guess I was wrong to worry. I should've worried about the killer more. I can be wrong, you know. Wrong as the next guy. I'm only human."

She said nothing to that. She stood from her crouch, and holstered her firearm.

I approached her slowly. I kept my hands up, but at shoulder height. I didn't want to see her Glock pointed at me again. Twice in one night was enough for me.

She said, "Put your hands down."

I put them down.

She said, "You should've kept going. Should've gotten a room for the night, and then met me at the diner, like I asked you. Now is not a good time to talk."

"Why did you stay out here alone? Why did you send me away?"

She didn't answer.

I asked, "Why all this time? Where's backup?"

Silence.

I said, "I saw Angel Rock. It's pretty small. Are there no other cops available right now?"

I waited for her to answer, but she just looked away, off into the distance.

A long moment passed between us, and finally she said, "They didn't come because I didn't call them."

"Why?"

"I'm the police chief. I don't need their help," Voss said. She looked around again like she was searching for the answers. "I don't have to tell you anything. You're lucky I let you go."

"Okay. Do it alone. I get that. I like that. But these are two dead cops. Don't you think that all your guys should be out here? Probably call the FBI as well. You need forensic teams and manpower out here scouring for evidence."

"It wouldn't matter. This guy is long gone. Believe me."

"Then call the U.S. Marshals. If he fled, he could be across state lines by now. You're gonna need to do a manhunt."

"It wouldn't make any difference," she said. I felt like she was hiding something.

"How do you know that?"

"No one kills two cops, and hangs around."

"You're wrong. Maybe he headed toward Angel Rock."

Voss said, "No way. The tracks head off in the other direction. Plus, I would've seen him."

"Maybe he turned around down the road. Maybe he ran that direction because he was scared, and then turned around somewhere. You can't track tire tracks on blacktop. Too many other tracks to account for, even on that empty road."

Voss nodded, and said, "It's not your concern, anyway. I think you should turn around and wait for me at the diner like I asked."

"I can't do that. If you won't call for backup, then I can't leave you out here alone. It wouldn't be right."

"Why not? Because I'm a woman?"

"No. It's just not my style to leave a man behind. Or a woman. Besides, my mother wouldn't approve of that."

She asked, "Are you close to your mother?"

"She's dead. Killed in the line of duty. She was a small-town sheriff, not a police chief like you. But everyone called her Chief. If she knew I left you out here alone, she'd curse me from the grave."

Voss dropped her shoulders a bit and cracked a smile.

I asked, "Besides, you aren't telling me something. So what is it? What're you not telling me? Did you know these guys? They weren't your cops. I know that because they're state police. So what's going on?"

Voss said nothing.

I asked, "You didn't just let me walk away because you knew me? Did you?"

"No. That wasn't the only reason. But I know you. Obviously."

I stepped closer to her, and stopped. I asked, "Who are these guys? They aren't ordinary state cops, are they?"

"What makes you say that?" Voss said, and looked at me with her pale blue eyes. They mesmerized me in the moonlit night. She seemed too well-lit to not be on a movie set. But sometimes, nature was like that.

I said, "These two guys are definitely some kind of detectives or higher-ranking cops. More so than just the kind that I'd find in your department. Yet, they're sitting out here. Alone. No backup. And they're parked pretty far off-road. They're not parked right on the shoulder. They were out here for something. Some reason. And it wasn't a stakeout. Not out here. There's nothing to stake out. Not unless they were investigating the grazing buffalo or the wind turbines. No. They were here waiting to meet someone, or they already met someone. Someone who didn't like what they had to say. Someone who killed them for it."

Voss said nothing.

I said, "That's it. They were here meeting someone, and that someone shot the hell out of them. And you know something. Don't you?"

"What? You think I met them and shot them?"

I stayed quiet.

She said, "You think I lured them out here, and murdered them in cold blood?"

"No. I don't. This was an act of passion. Heat-of-the-moment sort of thing. The shooter is amateur. No question. He probably never even fired a gun before in his life. You're a professional, a trained police officer, and a chief. I bet you're quite the marksman, too. No, this wasn't premeditated at all. This is completely sloppy."

"Because of the bullet patterns?"

"Not patterns. But the lack of. There is no pattern to it. The bullet holes are everywhere. The hood. The seats. Their torsos. The rear bench. This guy didn't do any aiming at all. Probably even had his eyes closed and jerked the trigger like a novice, the way he had seen in the movies. Hell, I wouldn't be surprised if he screamed while firing like he stole it right out of a damn Rambo movie."

*Got John Rambo on the brain*, I thought.

Voss asked, "What's the other part?"

"What other part?"

"That look on your face. There's a second part nagging at you. What is it?"

"The big thing is motive."

"You know the motive? How?"

I nodded, and said, "In a second. First, let's talk about the other reason that I know you had nothing to do with this."

"What reason?"

"Clean-up."

She said nothing.

"Right now, you're calm and collected. You're a professional. That makes you smart. You'd have killed them in a place where they could've been disposed of with little fuss. Out in a desert somewhere. New Mexico has got desert land. Right? Or you'd dump them in El Demonio, the abandoned town. No one would find them. But you wouldn't have killed them here, in the open like this, near a road. This is a desolate road, but any car could've come cruising along, or a nighttime pedestrian. A couple out on the road trying to get some privacy. A group of teenagers out here looking to drink a case of beer and not get caught, hoping to escape the sheer day-to-day boredom of small-town life," I said, and paused a beat. Then I said, "Hell, even one of your deputies could've come out here, trying to take a nap for an hour. You couldn't have predicted that. You could've guessed, sure, but not with one hundred percent accuracy. You wouldn't have taken a chance."

Voss nodded and said nothing.

I said, "So no, I don't believe you're the killer. You'd have picked a better spot. If you were going to do something like this in the first place, you wouldn't even have considered this place. It's too open. Too uncertain. Too great a risk. And they came out in a cop car. You know they have GPS. It's hard to hide a cop car. Plus, I'm here. If you had killed them, then I'd be dead and buried along with them. No question. Because you would've had to kill me too."

Voss said nothing.

I said, "Now, the shooter's motive. That's clear. Look at the circumstances. The shooting itself. The act. It looks like rage. Right?"

She nodded.

I shifted my weight and looked back down at the well-preserved foot tracks, and said, "It was done out of anger. Heat of the moment. Perhaps these guys gave him some bad news. This is clearly a meeting place. A rendezvous. Maybe even a drop-off point. My guess is that they were meeting with some lone individual and they said or did something that didn't hold up to their end of the bargain. This set the shooter off and he went into a rage. After they got back into their car, he started firing his gun at them and they didn't expect it.

"And I don't think that *he* even expected it.

"I think that this guy's demeanor or background or whatever showed that he was such a pushover, a novice, that the two dead cops never would've expected that he was capable of such a thing. They never even stopped to think that this guy would turn on them. It wasn't even in the cards for them.

"This was the act of a desperate man, a guy pushed beyond his limit."

Voss said, "Like the shooter reacted out of pure desperation?"

"In the world of dogma, you become free the day you decide to go to hell."

Voss twisted from the waist and stared up at me with a look that I haven't gotten in a while. It was a look that said to me *freak*. People had inadvertently given me this look many, many times and usually it was out of reflex more than anything. I never took it personally.

She said, "What?"

"It's from Aniekee Tochukwu."

"Who?"

I said, "He's a psychologist, wrote a book I read once."

"You can read?"

I smirked, and said, "It doesn't matter. I just think it applies here."

"Why?"

"Because our shooter acted out of desperation. That's clear. Therefore, he's a desperate man."

Voss said nothing.

I said, "These cops trusted the shooter's inexperience or his weak demeanor or his brittleness or all of it. See, they thought he was delicate, a gentle guy, a meek guy. They didn't think he was the type of guy who stands up for himself. Ever. He probably never had before.

"I'd guess that if you can identify these cops, then you can easily look through their computer's search histories or cell phone histories and find that they probably had files on this guy. Maybe even psychological reports. They assumed he was predictable and a weakling. Someone they could manipulate. I'd bet this wasn't the first time. Probably not even close. That is the other mistake they made. They got complacent, overly confident. They misjudged him. They overestimated their abilities and underestimated his capabilities. My guess is that they must've either had something on him, something that controlled him so he would do their every bidding, or they were completely stupid.

"But then again, it could've been a little of both. They're dead and he's not. So they were stupid to underestimate him, but I think they had something on him, and it was something strong enough that they figured no man would risk never getting it back. Probably some kind of evidence. Maybe state's evidence. Whatever it was, it was serious."

Voss asked, "So you think they were blackmailing this guy?"

"Maybe, or maybe he was an informant. But what's the difference? Isn't that what cops do to informants? They blackmail them with jail time for leads, for information, right?"

Voss stayed quiet.

I said, "Whatever the real circumstances, they picked the wrong guy. That's for damn sure. You bully a man long enough and you're gonna get punched in the nose."

Voss gave me that sideways look again. She asked, "Any guesses what their means of blackmail was, Sherlock?"

"Lurid pictures to hide from a rich man's wife. Or a politician trying to keep something from going public. Maybe it was information that'd get him sent to prison. Proof of a crime that he committed or just old-fashioned embarrassment. Who knows? Cops are privy to a lot of sensitive information about the public."

Voss looked back at the dead cops, at the unmarked cop car, and thought for a moment. I could see the wheels were turning in her mind. It was written on her face. She turned back to me, and asked, "How do you know all of that?"

"Just look around. Isn't it obvious? Look here," I said, and led her away from where she had been searching. She followed me over to the front of her police car's halogen lights. I pointed at the ground, tried to keep my boots pulled back away from the tracks. I asked, "See the footprints?"

She shone her flashlight's beam across the dirt and followed the tracks of two men that led from the unmarked Ford police car, with the two dead cops in it, back to where we stood. She asked, "Is that the cops' footprints?"

I nodded, pointed, and said, "Now look there."

Voss looked at where I pointed, and said, "Only three sets of footprints. I can see that. There's also a set of tire tracks over there, but how do you know that there wasn't another guy in the shooter's car? Or three? Or four?"

"Because look at how they were standing."

I pointed at the three sets of footprints, to a spot where they converged together in a cluster. I said, "This is a meeting place. The cops were waiting for a third person. A third man. A single man. Not two or three or four. They wouldn't have met with a guy who brought along company. At least, not without their guns drawn. They would've been suspicious if the guy had come with someone else in his car. Look here. They waited in their car for the shooter to show up. Once they saw him pull up in his car, they got out to meet him."

I looked down at the tracks, traced them backwards with my eyes. I imagined where the car must've been parked, and where it had driven up from the road, and then, I saw it turn off onto the beaten dirt.

I pointed at the place where the shooter's car had been parked, and said, "He parked his car there and got out. He walked to meet them right here. The cops made him stand out in front of their headlights, and waited right here in the middle, between both cars. Right out in the open. Only then, after they could get a good look at him, did they get out and walk over to him."

Voss said, "They visibly checked him to make sure he wasn't carrying a firearm too large to conceal."

I nodded, and said, "Maybe that's part of it. But this was an act of intimidation, too. I suppose they wanted him to stand there and feel humiliated—useless, powerless. They wanted him to feel at their mercy. They put him on display to show him they had the power."

"That's a little sadistic. Not what we're trained to do."

I nodded, and said, "Definitely, and that tells us something else."

"Like what?"

"One more second. Let's follow their actions first," I said, and I led her around the scene. We stepped lightly, avoiding the footprints and tire tracks. "They stopped here and talked. No struggle. At least no physical one. Maybe they exchanged harsh words, but these cops weren't afraid of him. Maybe they patted him down and found no weapons on him. They let their guard down. Then they gave him some kind of bad news, something that he was fearing. Maybe his biggest fear. Whatever they told him was enough to set him off."

I moved along the sets of tracks, and said, "The cops turned here and went back to their car. The shooter waited for them to get back in their car. He stayed where he was. He stood there for a long moment, deliberating what to do. He became enraged. He was probably stuck, frozen in place, because he didn't know what to do. The rage overtook him. Maybe he became temporarily insane. He didn't know how to react. The shooter became a hard-edged man. He went from a meek informant to a stone-cold killer."

Voss asked, "Like Jekyll and Hyde?"

"A man with nothing to lose. The rules didn't apply to him anymore. He had nothing left. He snapped."

She asked, "How on earth do you know that?"

I moved over to the kill point, and said, "This is where he stood when he opened fire on them." I mimicked the shooter. I held an imaginary gun out one-handed, like an amateur would. I mocked pulling the trigger, not squeezing it. Then I ejected a magazine, and inserted a new one, and continued firing. I pointed at the empty magazine on the ground. Voss saw it and nodded.

I moved my pointed finger away from the empty magazine and toward the shooter's tracks in the dirt, and said, "The killer's tracks go from where they met back to his car. He didn't run. He walked casually. On the front seat of his car, there must've been a gun waiting. Look here," I said, and pointed at the ground. "There are no tracks from him running back to the spot where he shot them. He sauntered to the car, grabbed a gun, and casually walked up to the front of their car like a man possessed. I bet they saw him and didn't even believe what they were seeing."

Voss nodded as if she understood. She said, "So they pushed him too far."

"Maybe they bullied him. Rode him too hard. Or whatever."

"So he'd had enough, and he literally snapped?"

I said, "They met with him before. Maybe a few times. They trusted the fact that he was weak. Probably believed that he'd never be so ballsy. Never. And maybe ninety-nine times out of a hundred, they'd be right, but this time they were wrong. They underestimated him. So he went back to his car, grabbed a gun, probably a Glock 23, and he shot them."

She asked, "How do you know the gun? Did you find it?"

"No. Of course not. I would've told you that first off. I'm guessing make and model. There are twenty-six bullet holes and twenty-six casings on the ground."

"Maybe he didn't fire all his bullets?"

"Rage like this, he did. He emptied the magazine, and he did it twice. There's an empty magazine over there," I said, and pointed back at the empty magazine on the ground. "And the second would still be in the gun. I didn't touch it, and I couldn't make out the markings in the dark, but I bet they both hold thirteen bullets each, pairing them with a gun from a short list."

Voss studied the magazine on the ground. She said, "And the Glock 23 is on that list. But it isn't the only gun that has a thirteen-round magazine. What about a Heckler and Koch USP? It holds that many."

"Right, but it's a Glock magazine. Glock is the gun they both have in their holsters and it's the one that you're carrying."

"What's that mean? You're back at thinking I killed them? You just got finished telling me you didn't believe that."

"I don't. But you aren't the only cop who is issued a Glock. These guys could've been killed by another cop. Maybe. Is that why you're not calling backup? Were you already investigating someone?"

Voss didn't answer that question directly. She said, "You just convinced me this guy is an amateur. How would a cop be an amateur? And a cop who has never fired his gun before? That's unbelievable. He'd at least have fired it in training and practice. Firearm practice is required, you know. At least, in my department it is. I can't speak for the SEAL team you were a part of."

"True. But I like to have an alternate theory. You never know when you might be wrong, and I'm wrong just as much as the next guy."

She frowned at me, and said, "Guess now you're going to give me another lesson. Show me up."

"I'm not trying to do that. It's not my intention. I'm just trying to help."

"I'm sorry. Of course, I'm glad for your help. I guess you weren't lying about being in the NCIS. What else do you see?"

I said, "In our second theory, this guy might be a cop."

"Explain?"

"The meeting itself. Sure, it could've been an informant meeting them out here. That's the most plausible theory. But it signals that these two cops were corrupt. I mean, meeting an informant way the hell out here? In the dark? Seems shady all the way around. So it could be they squabbled over money or blackmail or whatever."

Voss asked, "But your second theory, the cop one?"

"It makes more sense that it was a cop or someone in law enforcement who met them out here. Look around. This is a good meeting place for cops who want to talk about something sensitive. Or something they wanna talk about with some discretion."

"Or could've been something off the books, or illegal, like the exchange of money for a bribe. Or something," Voss added. "But what about the amateur angle? You said the shooter was an amateur."

"Amateur doesn't mean inexperienced. Amateur means slap-dash, unskillful, substandard, or unprofessional, which in my experience some cops are. No offense."

"None taken."

I said, "Four cops fit this category, and they're found in every police department in every corner of the world. They aren't as common as most, but they're out there."

"And who's that?"

"Rookies or retirees or desk guys or volunteer deputies. How many states employ volunteer deputies who ride along with real cops?"

She nodded. She understood. It was a possibility.

I asked, "Does New Mexico have volunteer deputies?"

She nodded again, and said, "Some counties do. They're called reserve police. But this county doesn't. The reserve police are mostly used in urban areas like Albuquerque. But these two are state cops, not volunteer deputies."

"The dead cops were, but that doesn't mean the shooter wasn't."

Voss said, "True. Maybe he could be a rookie volunteer. They're novice by definition. Inexperienced."

"Sure, they practice and practice, but fieldwork differs from training. All the training in the world can never truly prepare a person for real-world experiences. It can be helpful, but sometimes a guy who is not prepared will fall through the cracks. A guy who isn't ready for this line of work and may never be. Do you have any rookies in your department?"

Voss shook her head, and said, "No."

"Retirees?"

Her eyes opened, and she nodded. She said, "We got some old flunkies from El Demonio. They used to be cops. Before the town went belly up. I know of one guy who lives in Angel Rock. We get complaints about him from time to time. He's a real bastard. Keeps to himself mostly, though. I couldn't imagine him having business with state cops."

"Sounds like he could be worth looking at."

She said, "Yeah. Maybe. We'll have to keep them on the list."

# CHAPTER 5

Voss stepped around the front of her police cruiser. The lights from the halogen bulbs washed across her uniform pants like floodlights over an ocean at night. She turned and faced south and leaned back against the cruiser's wheel well, like she needed a moment to think.

She stared at the black, far-flung horizon and sighed. The night moon watched over us like a hulking mass of reflecting light and darkness. The stars were out and bright. Sparse clouds hovered aimlessly in the sky. Coyotes howled again in the distance like passing trains. The wind whooshed and gusted across the hills and plains, causing the massive turbines to spin and crank. Voss breathed slowly and deeply like she was lost in thought.

I said, "You still haven't answered my question."

"What question?"

"Where's the backup? Why didn't you call any of your people out here?"

Voss ignored me and closed her eyes. She breathed in and out, like seeing me had stirred up something. Something bigger than the two dead cops. Something monumental, pivotal to the woman she was now. She pushed off the back of the cruiser and stepped away, and paced back to the road. Her mind went off somewhere, deep in thought, like she couldn't help it. She was in a trance of thought. Some of it was thinking about the crime scene. Some of it was a memory that invaded her mind. A memory she just couldn't shake. *Was it a memory of me?*

I turned and followed her, keeping some distance to give her space. We hopped and skipped over tire tracks and footprints and shell casings. We walked back down the track and down to the two-lane highway. Voss stopped and stood dead center of the lonely old road. I stopped walking and stood with her, in front of her and to the side, not blocking her view.

First, she turned her head and stared off toward Angel Rock, looking at the faint lights from the small town. They were faint and narrowly visible. Not sure if it was the distance or because the town was so small. It emitted little light. But you could see the lights.

Voss stopped and turned her head back straight. She craned it up to look at me, and said, "I was following them. That's why I'm here."

"You were following them? The dead cops? Why?"

She paused a beat, like she was weighing the choice of trusting me or not. She said, "Because I didn't like them. The sight of them. The look of them. There's something…off about them. *Was* something off about them."

"What was off about them?"

"Something was wrong with them. Something odd. Something dark. Like a bad aura. They gave me a bad feeling. You know what I mean?" she asked, and paused. "I've seen them before. Several times. They came through my town every couple of weeks like clockwork. They did it for months. At first, I assumed it was part of their route, even though I never saw state cops patrolling my town before. And not state detectives. At first, they came every couple of weeks. But this last month, they've been coming every week. Last week. The week before. This week, they came every day."

I shifted my weight to one side, and leaned on my left foot, faced north for a moment, opposite her. I looked down at her, and said, "Sounds like they were interested in something going on here?"

"There's nothing going on here. Angel Rock is a quiet town. Always has been."

"Something must be going on here. They're dead."

"These guys were up to something, Widow. I know it. I don't think it was handed down to them like orders. I get the feeling it was something else. Something they shouldn't be doing. Truthfully, I knew it the first time I saw them."

I stayed quiet as she laid it out for me.

Voss said, "They rarely stopped in Angel Rock—at first. Except to catch lunch at the diner. Which isn't suspicious in itself. But it's the way they did it. The way they carried themselves. My officers saw them. We've all made note of them. No one complained. None of my citizens filed complaints. Not formal ones. But there've been rumors—whispers."

"Whispers? Like what?"

"The local females, especially the young ones, they've said things. Not directly to me. Not most of them. But I hear things. They didn't like the way these two cops spoke to them or looked at them or behaved with them. This one girl—she works at the diner—she said these two guys came in, sat in her section, and looked her up and down. They would lock their eyes on her chest. They stared at her. She said one of them would lick his lips every time he got the check. He made it real obvious to her."

I said, "That makes them sound like creeps, but staring isn't a crime. We had guys like that in the Navy and the Marine Corps. Of course, they're usually young guys, not quite corrected yet. We cut them slack at first. Most of them were just boys a month before going off to boot camp. The military knocks that sort of behavior out of a boy real fast. Turns us into gentlemen."

*Well, most of us,* I thought.

"Widow, this isn't a couple of over-hormoned boy-men. These were cops, grown men. And that waitress is only sixteen years old. They knew it too. Had to have known it. It's so obvious."

I paused a beat, and said, "That's worth calling their commander over. Did you?"

Voss didn't answer. She said, "It put them on my radar. That's not the only thing. The other is they kept passing through my town, but they never checked in with us."

"Are they required to?"

"No, but have you ever heard of that before? You mentioned your mother was a sheriff of a town. The FBI. The Marshals. The ATF. Even the State Police? Did they ever come through her town without telling her they were there?"

I shook my head. I couldn't think of that ever happening to me, or my mom, or any other cop I knew. Not in my experience. Never. I said, "In the NCIS, we always informed the ranking officers—base or platoon or unit commanders—that we were paying their region a visit, unless it was covert. Even then, someone high up the chain of command was notified—

standard operating procedure. I guess if they were just passing through, why would they? Sounds like that's not the case."

"It's a simple professional courtesy. At least stop by my station. Make your presence known. Not these guys. They just ran through, acting like we were invisible. Like they were some kind of VIPs. They behaved like they were above reproach. So I got interested. I got curious back when they first showed up. And even more when they started coming every week."

"Did you call their C.O.?" I asked again.

Voss nodded, and said, "I called their switchboard and got the runaround. I called them over and over. Finally, I got a desk sergeant. He told me they were on official business. And referred me to an obscure statute and department policy, which said I wasn't in their chain of command. In other words…"

"He brushed you off."

"He was telling me to butt out without telling me to butt out."

"But you didn't?"

"No. I followed them—five more times after that. It was always in the dead of night. I tried to stay out of sight, but the last two times they lost me. I had to pull off the road."

"What road? This one?" I asked.

Voss nodded, and said, "This stretch of highway is pretty straight and flat. They'd see my headlights coming up on them easily. It makes it hard to keep up and stay out of sight all at the same time. It made little sense though."

"Why?"

"Look around. There's nothing out here but wind turbines and grass."

I stayed quiet.

Voss said, "It's weird, but I kept losing them in the same spot. Like they knew I was following them. They kept shaking me loose at the old windmill."

I looked at her, and then, above her head at another wind turbine. It was Brobdingnagian and forlorn, out farther than the closest one, like it was an outcast. I asked, "Old windmill?"

Voss looked at me and glanced at the wind turbine I stared at. She said, "Not like one of those. It's an old relic windmill from like two hundred years ago. It used to be a tourist attraction thirty years ago. There was a family that lived around it. Those houses are all gone now. A bad twister blew through here and wrecked it all, but the windmill still stands."

"They lost you there?"

"Yes. But I'm not sure where they went. They would be on the road, and then, gone. Like that," Voss said, and she snapped her fingers.

"Did you ever see them meet with anyone? Could be a clue to the killer."

"No."

"So what made you come flying out here with your lights flashing?"

"This is the first time they came this way. Usually, they went to the windmill, in the other direction, on the other side of Angel Rock. I was confused at first. I hoped maybe they were leaving. But they weren't. I kept a good distance away from them, more than usual. I thought maybe they made me.

Maybe they were luring me out to the wrong direction to confront me with questions or belittle me or something. I backed off to keep from getting seen. I drove about twenty minutes until I couldn't see them anymore. So I stopped and got out. I stood on the hood of my car and scanned the landscape. I didn't see them. They gave me the shake. I wasn't sure if it was on purpose or not."

I stayed quiet.

Voss said, "When I doubled back, I knew I lost them. At first, I figured they were having fun with me. You know? They saw me and led me out here as a gag, maybe to show me they were smarter than me. Like they were better than some local cop from the sticks. So I returned to Angel Rock and went to the station. I didn't tell my guys. I was embarrassed and pissed off. I felt like they were mocking me. I sent my guys out in other directions and told them not to return without hitting their nightly quotas in traffic tickets. I just wanted them out of my hair. They know my tone. They know not to question me. I even told the night desk guy to go out for a long dinner break. I told him I wanted to be alone."

I asked, "When was this?"

Voss looked at her watch. I noticed it. The watch looked familiar, more familiar than she did to me. And it was familiar because I had seen a lot of SEALs wear it. It was a Casio G-Shock DW-6600. It was a man's watch. It looked big on her wrist. She wore the band notched up as tight as it would go. She wore it upside down on her left wrist. So when she checked the time, she had to flip her wrist palm-up to read the time. This version of the G-Shock was old. The watch first appeared in the SEALs team in 1994, before my time. I had seen older guys wear this version, way back when I started. Nowadays, guys wore the newer versions or other comparable watches.

Voss said, "Close to three hours ago now."

"What drew you out here?"

"I got a call at the station. Some motorist said he heard gunshots out this way. He said that they were quick in succession. He thought they might've been from an assault rifle, which is illegal to fire within twenty miles of the city. So I called the desk guy back in, and sped out here. I saw the lights from the road and found you—a guy I've not seen in years."

I asked, "Did you get the cops' names?"

"Yes. After I lost them earlier tonight, I checked them out with their direct unit commander."

"Unit?"

"Yeah, they're a part of a special task unit."

"That's interesting. What kind of unit?"

"I don't know. It could be drugs or smuggling or something. I went online. That's how I got their unit commander's name. His name is Crocket. I called him up. He's working tonight. Know what he told me?"

I asked, "Crockett? Like Davey?"

Voss cracked a half smile, and said, "I didn't ask, but I'm sure he gets that one a lot."

I stayed quiet.

She said, "And Sonny too."

I shrugged.

She asked, "You know? Sonny Crockett?"

I shrugged again, looked at her blankly.

"From Miami Vice?"

Nothing from me. No response.

She said, "Anyway he told me that one of them was on suspension and under investigation. He recently shot a suspect. Crocket told me it was all routine. It was a justified shooting, according to him. And the other one was nowhere near my town. He said the other one was out on patrol and was supposed to be way off in the northern part of the state somewhere."

"That's curious."

"I know. Then he said he'd check on him for me. He kept me on the line, put me on speaker so that I could hear. He radioed the guy. I listened, and the guy answered, sure enough. Crocket asked him where he was. He replied he was up near Farmington. Which is far north from here."

She paused a beat and stared at me.

I stared back. Her pale blue eyes peered into me like she could see my soul. At that moment, there was a glimpse of her in my memories, but it was just a glimpse. It faded away, like a single echo into the night. I couldn't put my finger on how she knew me.

Voss said, "I listened. I didn't dispute his claim, but he was definitely not where he said he was. I saw him here with his partner all day."

"They're both here now."

Voss glanced back at the corpses. She said, "The one in the passenger seat is the guy that was supposed to be on suspension. I got their photos off their file jackets. I pulled that too. His name was Colin Aragon."

"For real?"

"Yep."

"Like from *The Lord of the Rings*?" I asked. I expected Voss to have no idea what I was talking about, other than recognizing the title of the movie. But I was wrong.

She said, "No. That's Aragorn, not Aragon. It's spelled different and pronounced different."

"You know Tolkien?"

Voss paused a quick beat. A partial smile cracked over her lips, which might surprise the uninitiated, the public who've never served in law enforcement, but not me. I was initiated. A dark sense of humor and dark perspective was a vital tool in any good cop's arsenal. Voss said, "Aragorn. Elfstone. Strider. Eagle of the Star."

I smiled, and said, "One ring to rule them all."

Voss's half smile faded away. She said, "The driver's name isn't much better. It's Bobby Broome."

"Bobby Broome?"

"That's his name."

"So I looked them up, learned about them, and followed them every time they were here. And I still have no idea what they were doing."

I said, "Sounds like these guys were dirty?"

"That's what I think. Why else would they be out here? Makes no sense."

She looked at me one more time and turned her head slowly toward the dead cops. She said, "I need to find out why they were here. I know you said this already, but the killer *could* still be in town. And the reason these two were here could be his motive."

"Are you going to call in your guys now?"

"Soon. Not just yet. If these guys are crooked and out here doing something illegal, then maybe I got a bent cop in my department. I need to know."

"Can you keep this quiet? I'm not a lawyer, but eventually this will be in front of a courtroom. The shooter's defense might pick apart the time it took you to report this to the FBI."

Voss said, "I can't keep it quiet forever. But I'm the chief. It's officially under investigation now. Nobody's going to fire me for not informing the FBI or my own guys right off the bat. Only the mayor can fire me, anyway. But even he needs a lot of cause for it. And the DA won't object as long as it's in a *timely* manner. But timely can be stretched. I won't sit on it for two days or anything. But until I know more, it's okay."

Voss paused, like a thought occurred to her. She said, "What if they were meeting an FBI agent here?"

"With that terrible shooting? I doubt it."

"They got support agents who aren't required to keep up with their shooting. Support agents aren't in the field very much. Could be something like that?"

I said, "It could've been the local ice cream man. We got no idea who it is. You can't do this alone. You need help."

"I need to know who it is before I involve my guys," Voss said. Then she paused a beat and looked at me. She said, "I'm not alone. I've got you. You can help me."

I stayed quiet, like I was pondering it, but I already knew I would help.

She said, "You owe me. In a way."

"I owe you? For what?"

"First, I could arrest you just for being here. No one around. Two dead cops. It could be you. And two, you owe me from before."

"What before?"

"And three, you owe me for forgetting me. Remember me and you'll think of the reason you owe me."

I stayed quiet. I could've gotten out of getting involved in this if I had just kept going when she let me go two hours ago. But I was involved now. Voss seemed like a good cop, but she could be in over her head. It could be dangerous for her to go at it alone. I could help her for now. I could always walk away first chance I got. So I agreed. I said, "Okay."

She said, "We need to find the shooter and do it before the sun comes up. This road is barely used anymore. Drivers tend not to take this route at night because it's dimly lit. There's no need for improved lights since most people don't use it as a thoroughfare. It's more like the scenic route. The daylight can be a different story. Drivers will cut through this way sometimes. If someone drives this way after sunup, there'll be no hiding an unmarked police car with two dead cops in it. Someone's bound to get curious."

"Plus that guy," I said, and pointed at the driver. "Bobby Broome only has a few hours left on his shift. His C.O. will wonder why he's not calling in. I'd guess that after they don't hear from him, they'll radio him. They may have radio checks in place already. When he doesn't answer, they'll start finding other ways of locating him."

"Right, like the GPS system. All of their cars have them."

"We won't be able to keep this investigation secret for long."

Voss said, "Plus Crocket will realize that I called him at night for information on the two of them. And when he can't locate them, he'll start calling me here. I shouldn't be lying to him. That's why I say we've got till sunup."

"We'd better get to it."

"What now?"

I said, "Let's take a closer look at the crime scene."

# CHAPTER 6

As the New Mexico night surrounded us, a cold front blew in from the east, and nature's musical notes rolled off of the low, rolling hills. Voss stood beside me. We scanned the crime scene together. From the road, our silhouettes must've looked like a normal woman being towered over by a giant monster. A horror movie creature standing with his victim, close together like they were friends.

Voss looked at everything with me. There was impatience in her eyes, which was natural, I supposed, since we had been staring at the crime scene for another thirty minutes without speaking. I had already put the pieces together, but I didn't want to lay out what I saw too freely. She was the cop here. I didn't want to overstep my bounds. And she saw right through me. She said, "We've looked over this already. So now what?"

I stayed quiet and circled the unmarked state police car, kept looking. I remained careful not to touch anything. I watched every step I made, not wanting to disrupt any forensic evidence such as footprints or tire tracks. All like before. Together, we looked carefully around the car one last time. I counted the bullet holes again. Double-checked my math. Then I pictured the bullet trajectory.

Impatient, Voss said, "Tell me what you see."

"The shooter stood here," I said, pointing to a spot in front of the driver's side windshield. "He stood ten feet from the grille. He was right-handed. Judging by shoe size and depth of his footprint, I'd guess he was five-ten, maybe five-eleven."

"You can tell that by looking a shoe print?"

"Sure. It's easy. Any average deer hunter can tell the same. They go for big bucks. When tracking animals, that's what they look for, not fawn or doe."

Voss half rolled her eyes but said nothing. She already knew that.

I asked, "Is there a dashcam? Maybe it recorded something?"

"No. This vehicle isn't equipped with it. These two weren't doing traffic stops. It's supposed to be more invisible on the street. We couldn't access it, anyway. Not right now. It'd be back at their HQ. Crocket would have access to it. If there was one."

"Okay," I said. I imagined the sequence of events in my head. "Here's how I picture it. The shooter met with Aragon and Broome out here in front of the car. Probably in the headlights. They stopped and talked in a trinity circle at a distance of about twenty feet. The headlights were off on the police car when I arrived, but on during the meeting. So either the killer shut them off, or the cops did when they got back into the car. The evidence suggests the shooter was an amateur, and that meant he wouldn't have thought to turn off the lights. Most likely. I figured the lights were already off. The cops got back into their car and switched them off."

"Why would they do that? They'd lose visibility of him."

"Maybe they shut them off as another intimidation tactic."

Voss asked, "Intimidation?"

"Yeah. Like they argued with the guy here," I said, pointing at the circle of footprints in the dirt. "Then to tell the guy it was over, to tell him he missed the deadline and the deal was off, they returned to their cruiser and shut off the lights. It was like the final word."

Voss looked at me sideways. She had her flashlight on and arched it up towards the sky, so I could see her facial expression.

I asked, "What?"

"Intimidation?"

"Sure, that could fit."

"That's the dumbest explanation I've ever heard. I met these guys. They weren't rocket scientists, but they were state detectives. They weren't that childish."

"I admit it's dumb. But it could be true. It's no dumber than alpha wolves peeing at each other's feet to mark dominance."

Voss snarked, "I don't know. Maybe you shouldn't think so hard."

She twisted the flashlight beam back down. We were about fifteen feet apart. I put my hand out in the light beam and beckoned her closer. She saw it and closed the gap between us. I pointed at the ground. She traversed the light and studied the footprints again.

I said, "Look for a flashlight then."

"I got one."

"Look for their flashlight."

She asked, "You think they used one?"

"The headlights were off. If they hadn't switched them on, then they must've used a flashlight. It's gotta be here somewhere. Maybe it's in their car?" I said, and turned to the car with the dead cops in it.

"It's not," she said. "I searched it already. I didn't see a flashlight. Although, they should have had one. Maybe the shooter took it?"

"Maybe. But we should look anyway. There could be prints on it."

She said, "We'd have to send the flashlight out to a forensics lab."

"Can you do that?"

"Sure. It's in Roswell. They won't be open until tomorrow," Voss said. Then she stopped and turned, walked back to her own cruiser.

"Where're you going?" I called out.

She muttered something I didn't hear. She went back to her own car and popped the trunk. She dipped down inside it and came back out with something in her hand. She closed the trunk and walked back over to me. There was a small stack of evidence bags stuffed under her arm. They were ziplocked and marked *Property of Angel Rock Police* on the sides. She held out a pair of blue surgical gloves.

She said, "Put these on so we contaminate nothing."

I took the gloves and started to pull them over my hands. They were snug, but they would fit. I said, "They're pretty tight."

She put hers on with ease. There was still plenty of room in hers. She could've squeezed in another hand equal to her own size in each glove. She said, "They're extra-large."

I shrugged and struggled to get the gloves on both hands. The left one tore from my knuckles down to the band. But they held as they were meant to.

Voss pointed her flashlight beam back to the ground, and we searched for a dropped flashlight. We searched for fifteen minutes. We combed over the terrain. We searched a nearby ditch. We searched all around where it was clear the killer's vehicle had been parked. Voss scoured her flashlight beam over the low hills and into the dips and through the scattered bushes and rocks, but she found nothing.

I said, "Okay. I know you searched the police car once, but let's look again."

She stopped her search for the flashlight and joined me by the dead cops' police car. She stayed there and watched as I walked away carefully and followed the foot tracks again. I stopped at the meeting place and looked back at the car, then I traced the footprints again with my eyes, slowly. I came to the same conclusions all over again. The same scene was reenacted in my head. The two cops met with someone. The motive was probably money, blackmail, or some variation of the two. They told him something that he didn't want to hear. The two cops returned to their car, probably laughing at him, mocking him. The shooter stood here for a moment, and then he went back to his car. He grabbed a gun off the front seat, came back at them, and shot them both dead, then reloaded and emptied the second magazine into them. He walked the whole way. Probably held the weapon out in front of him at arm's length like a hot potato he couldn't get rid of.

Voss said, "See anything?"

"Nope. Same as before. Maybe the motive is money."

"Could be. It usually is."

"It's gotta be something of value. The shooter met with them here and they told him something that angered him, something that made him snap. He went back to his car, slow. He ducked inside and grabbed his gun, and the extra magazine, which was probably on the seat. He must've known that they wouldn't have checked him for weapons. And he was confident they wouldn't check his car. He got his gun, came at them, stopped there, fired until he was out of bullets, reloaded, and did it again."

I pointed to the ground where his tracks had stopped, and back at the two dead cops. I held out my right hand, cupped it with my left, and made a gun gesture. My index finger pointed straight out, and I mimicked squeezing an invisible trigger. I pretended to fire thirteen rounds at the two dead cops. I looked down my index finger from my thumb like it was the stock sights on a Glock and aimed and fired. Each time I jerked back in a quick and soft recoil like the Glock has. I could picture each bullet firing through the bullet holes in the car, windshield, and through the dead cops. But I was an experienced shooter. This guy wasn't. He probably fired with his eyes closed. Bullets sprayed everywhere. That's why he hit all over the car. He was lucky to even kill both cops. It's a case of numbers. He fired thirteen shots and many of them hit their targets. But most of them didn't. They were wild shots.

Voss watched and stayed silent for a moment. She said, "This could've been some kind of payoff, maybe. Where money exchanged hands or was supposed to. Maybe he didn't bring it? And an argument broke out."

"Or maybe they didn't bring it and that's what set him off. And he shot them."

Voss asked, "We know they gave him some sort of bad news. But what? Did they tell him they didn't have his money? Or he told them he didn't have their money? Also, why not just shoot him? Were they giving him a second chance?"

"Maybe they just wanted to toy with him," I said. We moved back to the dead cops' car. I examined it once more, double-checking the mental list of everything inside the car that I had already accounted for. There were two dead cops, two department-issued Glocks, holstered and unfired. There was one Remington Model 870 neatly perched. The stock end rested in a cradle. The barrel and the muzzle pointed upward at the cab's ceiling. It was locked in place and untouched. In the backseat, there was nothing but bullet holes in the upholstery, and a spray of cloth and stuffing from the seats strewn about. They had been blown out at the time of impact and had long since settled on the seat.

I stared at the corpses up and down. I reached out and popped the driver's side door open. Voss didn't object. The door swiveled open, and broken glass from the windshield shifted and made low cracking and tinkling sounds.

The door swung all the way open. I bent down and stared into the interior. I knelt on one knee, planting it on a hard patch of dirt, and I studied the inside closer. I looked back at Voss, and asked, "Can I borrow your light?"

She nodded and handed me her flashlight, butt first. I took it and turned the light to the inside of the police car. I traced the beam across the faces of the dead cops, down their chests, and across their torsos. The light washed over them and across the bullet holes and over seeping blood stains.

Voss asked, "See anything interesting?"

"They're dead. That's for sure."

I kept looking. I scanned the carpets, under the seats, and the foot wells. I scanned the pedals and the cup holders and the undercarriage of the dash. I found nothing of interest.

I reached down and grabbed the lever to release the trunk. I jerked it in one quick motion and heard the lid *snick*, and the trunk opened up. I retreated away from the cabin of the cruiser, slumped my weight back down on my heel and rested on my knee for a second. I looked back at Voss, and said, "Let's have a look in the trunk."

She nodded and waited for me to stand up, then followed me back to the rear of the car. I left the driver's side door open and walked past the backseat and around the bumper. I stepped over a dip by the back tire. The wind picked up and blew the cold night air down from the low mountains way off in the distance. I felt it brush over my head and across my face. I looked back at Voss and watched it ruffle her hair and then let it settle back into its default position.

Voss and I stopped in front of the trunk lid. I reached out and jerked the lid all the way open in one quick motion like the contents might've been a trunk full of rattlesnakes. But there were no snakes. The contents were standard for a police car. There was a bullhorn, a first aid kit, two pairs of dirty mud boots, three road flares, two orange cones, one roll of yellow police tape, two raincoats, a spare tire—fully aired up—a black and yellow carjack, an unopened pack of Duracell DD tactical batteries, two grime-covered shovels, an opened box of crime scene gloves, a box of evidence bags, and a bright yellow fire extinguisher fastened just above the rear right tire well.

I shone the flashlight beam across the objects, but nothing of particular interest jumped out at me. They were pretty standard, a little dirty and used, but standard. I twisted downward and scanned the interior of the trunk. I looked closely at the edges and the lining and then at the metal roof of the trunk.

The black rubber lining around the lid had been compromised, but not in a subtle, time-altered erosion or cracked kind of way. This was a disturbed way, as if something or someone had tried to claw out of the trunk from the inside.

"Look at this," I said, and washed her flashlight beam over the inside of the trunk lid.

Voss came closer to me, put her left hand on my back, and leaned in, next to me, over the bottom trunk lip. Her body pressed up against mine. Her scent wafted into my nose. I smelled her. I couldn't help it. She smelled nice, like orange blossom and tangerine and magnolia and orchids and Osmanthus. It was a delight of wildflowers. It wasn't perfume. It smelled more like some kind of body wash.

I tried to ignore her body as it pressed up against my back, which was no easy task.

I pointed the flashlight beam at the rubber seal.

Voss tilted her head and stared at it. She made a sound indicating she saw exactly what I saw. She said, "What did that?"

"An animal? Maybe they had a dog in here?"

"It's against regulation to lock a dog or any other living animal in the trunk of our cars. Same rules apply to the state police. Not to mention, it's horrible."

"These guys are far off the regulation game already. Nothing about them tells me they gave a shit about the rules and regulations. Like you said, they were up to something. Maybe they locked a person in here?"

"Why would they do that? They can lock a person in the back of the car," she said, and then, she fell silent, like she was considering the possibility, imagining it. She stayed still for a moment.

I couldn't move because she was leaning against me. I waited for her to either say something or to stand back upright. She spoke first. She asked, "What if they did lock a person in here?"

We fell silent again while we both contemplated this scenario.

The wind slowed for a moment like it was deep in thought with us, and then picked up again. A cold, violent wind gusted across the land, through the scattered rocks, the grass, the low hills, and over the roof of the car. I felt it brush through my hair like a raging river.

I stared at Voss, which wasn't hard to do. She was easy to look at.

Abruptly, the radio from her police cruiser *crackled* and broke the silence. We heard the kind of chatter noise that transmitter radios made when someone on the other end held the *talk* button down.

The radio *crackled* again, followed by a pause of nothingness, and then, a male voice came over the waves. He said, "Chief? Come in."

Voss pulled away from me and stepped off from the crime scene, avoiding the footprints and the tire tracks in the dirt. She walked back to her own car in a curved arc. She walked a radius that kept her far out and away from the two dead cops like she was walking around invisible police tape.

She made her way to her police cruiser, leaned against the door, and reached in through the open window and grabbed a radio off the dash. She pulled it out through the window, and stood up, stretching the curled cord out. She pulled the radio up to her mouth and clicked the *talk* button and spoke into it. She said, "Sean. I'm here. What's up?"

The wind carried their conversation far and out like it was being transmitted over loudspeakers.

Sean must've been the desk guy she mentioned, I figured. The guy on the other side of the connection said, "What's your twenty?"

Voss responded, "Whaddya need?"

The guy named Sean said, "There's a 10-56A at the motel on Baker Street."

I stepped back and away from the trunk and the dead cops' car. I walked over to Voss, following the same curved trajectory she had in order to avoid contaminating evidence. I reached her and saw her eyes widen, and she buried her head into her forearm, like in an *Oh, great!* kind of way. Then she lifted her head back up and squeezed the *talk* button on the radio. She asked, "10-56? With an A?"

I searched my memory for police radio codes and recalled that a 10-56 stood for suicide, but a 10-56A? I wasn't sure what the *A* stood for.

Sean said, "Yes. Some guy tried to off himself."

Momentary static emitted over the radio and another *crackle* sounded. Sean came back on, and said, "In the motel."

Voss asked, "10-72?"

Silence.

Sean said, "Ah. Er. Not sure what that is."

Voss sighed like she was used to underwhelming performances from the desk guy named Sean. She asked, "Is there a gun involved?"

Silence fell across the radio again, and I imagined Sean as an average cop in uniform. I saw the guy sitting back at the station, in a metal chair, hovering over the radio. His eyes double-checked his notes, so he got the information right before he blurted it out to Voss. Sean said, "Affirmative."

Voss said, "Get Howard over there ASAP! And call the paramedics!"

Sean said, "Howard's already here. He was nearby. He called the ambulance too. That's why I asked your twenty. Because they might beat you there."

Voss said, "Okay. Good. What's the guy's condition?"

Sean said, "Bad. I'm not sure to what extent. That's all I got."

Voss said, "Have the ambulance take him to the hospital. Make sure that they restrain him just in case. Tell Howard to stay with him and I'll meet him at the hospital."

Voss clicked off the radio. She looked at me, and said, "I gotta go to this. You should come."

"I could stay here and look around some more. Make sure no one stumbles across it. Messes with anything."

"No. I'm taking you. I've trusted you more than I should already. I can't leave you behind."

I asked, "You don't trust me?"

"I trust you enough, but I'm not leaving you here. No matter whether I knew you from before. No arguing. Get in the car. Let's go."

I shrugged and stepped close to Voss and passed her. I went around to the passenger side of her cruiser and stopped. I pulled the gloves off. Not sure what to do with them, I shoved them into my pocket. I opened the door and dumped myself down in the seat, and shut the door behind me. The seat was tight, my knees were in the glovebox. I reached down between my legs, felt for a seat bar, and racked the seat all the way back.

Voss ripped off her gloves and shoved them into her pocket. She got in on the driver's side and stared at me as I fumbled with the seat belt before shutting her own door. The steering wheel was low and pulled close to her. The seat was racked all the way forward in a way that would've been completely impossible for me, but she had a small frame. It was perfect for her. She put the transmission lever in reverse, backed up, turned, and slowly drove away. She didn't want to kick up rocks and dirt behind the car, blowing it all over the crime scene. She waited until we were out of the dirt and back onto the two-lane highway, then she stomped on the gas.

The police light bar stayed on. Once we were fifty yards away from the two dead cops, Voss switched on the sirens. They blasted to life, echoing over the landscape. The echo died away as the sound carried farther away from us.

# CHAPTER 7

Voss's police cruiser roared through the small town of Angel Rock. She turned left and then right, running a stop sign, ignoring two red lights.

Voss turned the wheel and maneuvered us through one street and onto the next. She only slowed to hug tight corners. We dodged potholes and slowed just before a huge bump with no clearly marked sign warning us of an approaching bump in the road. She already knew it was there. She had all the streets memorized and could probably have driven with the headlights off and blindfolded.

Angel Rock was on the smaller side of being a small town. It might've been smaller than the one I grew up in. But it was bigger than others I had seen over the years. Angel Rock fit neatly in the American small-town category.

We drove on, weaving in and out of lanes and hugging corners and running traffic lights and stop signs, until we rounded one last corner. Voss pumped the brakes but didn't slam them like in the movies with howling tires and furious smoke. We slid to a stop in front of a medical campus with a hospital and medical office park. There was a neat grassy lawn out front. It was cut short.

Green hedges lined the front of the buildings. Tiny, black sprinklers jetted up from the ground, spraying water at the hedges and over the grass. The sprinklers circled and sprayed and cycled back to their starting positions to start the process all over again.

The largest building, made of dark tan concrete and brick, had the words *Angel Rock* and *General Hospital* painted in red-and-white letters stacked low on the bottom of the third floor at the top of the building. Bright exterior lights shone down on the lawn and parking lot like spotlights on an empty stage.

Voss put the car in park, switched off the ignition, and pulled out the keys. She didn't look at me. She just popped open her door and used one hand on the steering wheel to heave herself out of the seat.

I asked, "This is the hospital?"

She leaned back down and peered into the cab at me. She said, "They don't do heart transplants or anything. It's part of a larger chain of medical centers. They bought the old hospital. They're all over the county."

"Better than no hospital," I said, taking off my seatbelt. I grabbed the outside of the door pillar and hauled myself up and out of the car. Voss shut her door, and I shut mine. I followed her up a thin cement walkway over the grass and to the side of the dark tan building. She led the way through an emergency room entrance and glanced at a security guard behind a desk like they knew each other—which they did.

I ducked under the rim of a pair of automatic doors and followed her. The doors sucked shut behind us. I glanced over at the security guard. He wore an official hospital badge and black nameplate. The nameplate read: *Gene*.

Gene jumped to his feet when he saw Voss as if he was in the military and she was a superior officer. I half-expected him to salute like an Army private seeing the base commander. But he didn't.

He didn't say *hello* or *hi* or any other normal, official greeting. He simply nodded at her, and said, "Chief."

He reached down to the top corner of his desk, pressed a button, and buzzed us through a pair of closed glass security doors.

Gene looked me up and down, from my boots up to my face. He made no indication of an impression. I returned in kind, only I didn't look him up and down. Voss moved through the security doors the second they opened up in a wide enough gap for her to squeeze through. I had to wait two seconds longer than she did, until they were nearly all the way open, so I could follow through.

Voss led me into a short corridor, to a pair of double brown doors with three-foot square windows in the center of each. Through the glass, I could see three or four nurses shuffling around, frantic, and one doctor.

Voss pushed through the doors, and I followed her. The room was big. It was oval-shaped with dozens of offshoots. They weren't really private rooms, more like nooks. Some were covered by closed curtains. Others were exposed and empty. We were in the ER.

No one stopped to look at us or even acknowledge that we were in the room. The staff was all preoccupied.

One of the nurses was in blue scrubs, while the others wore green. I wasn't sure if there was some kind of symbolic difference between the different colors or if it just meant that the nurse in blue scrubs had laundry to do and the only pair she had left were the blue ones.

They all seemed to be working on one patient in particular, because the doctor was standing over him and the nurses were scrambling to help.

Voss and I stopped in the center of the room and listened.

The nurse in blue said, "Bullet wound to the head."

A nurse in green said, "I'm paging Dr. Garcia."

The ER doctor said, "Nurse, don't page him! Run upstairs and get him! Stat!"

Dr. Garcia must've been the only other doctor in the building who could help in this situation. He was probably making his rounds upstairs and having a quiet night that was about to be interrupted by the guy who had a bullet wound to the head.

Voss turned and pushed me back—out of the way of the nurse in green who was headed out the double doors to search for Dr. Garcia. We stepped back against one wall and tried to stay out of the way of the commotion.

Over at the other end of the big room, I saw her deputy, the guy called Howard. His eyes were on the ER doctor and the nurses as they worked to stabilize their gunshot patient. I suspected the patient was our attempted suicide—the 10-56A.

Blood soaked into Howard's uniform shirt. There was a lot of blood. It was spread across his chest and stomach and his right forearm, including a standard black watch with a black rubber band. A dark red stain of blood smeared across the faceplate, obscuring his ability to see the time.

Voss nodded in his direction and grabbed my forearm. Her hand barely covered half of it. She jerked and pulled me behind her and led me over to her deputy. We stopped near him. There was shock on his face, like he never saw something as horrific as a gunshot wound to a man's head before.

Without skipping a beat, with no introductions, I looked the deputy up and down, fast. I pointed at his shirt, and asked, "From the guy?"

I said it as if we were old friends and I was a member of the team. It happened naturally, organically. I wanted to avoid the long, drawn-out introductions and explanations about who I was and what my interest was and what my qualifications were and the like. I preferred to skip right to the part where I asked a question and got a direct answer. So I acted like an established member of the team. I was a man deputized by the police chief herself. It was a tactic used by federal agents every day, all over the country.

An FBI agent from a local field office is assigned to a new case to investigate a homicide in a small town with small-town cops with small-town minds, who don't like the federal government, or federal government agents coming in and pissing all over their jurisdiction, showing them who's really in charge. This caused friction for the FBI agent. It meant wasted time and wasted energy and wasted words. It meant meeting deputies and shaking hands and going through the rudimentary hazing from the local boys. So what do the FBI agents do? They present themselves as members of the team right away. Make that known. Make it accepted beyond any doubt. Don't give the natives time to think, time to question, time for their insecurities to kick in.

The FBI agent says: *Hey, man. I'm one of you. I'm just a guy with a job to do. I didn't come here to interfere with your case. I didn't come here to walk all over your toes, to tell you how to do your job. I came with better resources. So let's work together and burn up some of Uncle Sam's money to solve this crime. What do you say?*

This tactic worked for the FBI, so why not for me? But I didn't have to employ it, apparently, because Officer Howard didn't need convincing that I was a part of the team. One look from

Voss and he knew better than to ask questions. If I was with her, then I was spoken for and verified and vetted to the full extent of her power, and that was good enough for him.

Officer Howard looked up at me. He asked, "What?"

Voss said, "This is Widow. He's consulting with me on something else."

The deputy looked me up and down but said nothing, no comment, no opinion on his face at all. Voss didn't explain my presence any further than that.

I said, "The blood on your clothes. Is it from this guy?"

Howard looked down at his shirt as if it were the first time he realized he was covered in blood. He nodded and looked back at Voss.

She asked, "Who is he?"

Howard said, "His license says his name is Ryan Saunt."

Voss asked, "How bad is it?"

Howard said, "Bad. I don't really know. He bled. A lot. But I don't think that his brain was hit. Looked like the guy didn't even stick the muzzle in the right spot."

I asked, "What's the right spot?"

Howard sneered at me for a short second and held his breath and then exhaled with a kind of question implied in the gesture, like *who are you again?* The question faded and he half-shrugged, rolling his shoulders up and dropping them in the same second. He said, "I mean he didn't fire it into his temple or his mouth like a man who really wanted to die would do."

Voss asked, "So why'd he do it?"

Howard shrugged, and said, "Attention, I guess. I don't know."

Voss asked, "Any witnesses?"

Howard said, "No."

Voss asked, "Was there a note? Anything?"

Howard said, "No note. No witnesses."

I said, "Describe it for us."

Voss looked at me, and Howard didn't. He kept his focus on Voss but acted like a question from me was a direct question from her, and he answered it. Howard said, "It looked like he fired it into the top of his head. Possibly at the eleven o'clock position."

Howard stopped there. He added nothing else. He trembled a bit. And I realized they saw little violent crime in a community this small. Maybe Howard had never even seen a guy shot before.

Voss said, "Howard? What else?"

Before Howard acknowledged Voss, I reached a hand out, gently, and grabbed her wrist. I squeezed it just to get her attention. She glanced at me. I said, "We should talk to the doctor."

Voss seemed to pick up on what I was saying, and she nodded back. She looked back at Howard, and asked, "Howard, where's the gun?"

Howard said, "Back at the motel. I left it. What was I supposed to do? The guy was bleeding everywhere. I couldn't just leave him there while I bagged and tagged the weapon."

Voss said, "It's okay. That was the right thing to do. Did you lock up the room?"

Howard said, "Yeah, I locked the door behind me. I gave Clark the key. He should be sitting in the parking lot with the key, waiting for you."

Voss said, "Okay."

I asked, "Who's Clark?"

Voss said, "The motel's night clerk."

I paused a beat and thought, *Clark the clerk.* I asked, "What about the doctor?"

"Let's check," Voss said, and she looked at Howard, gave him an order. "You stand outside Saunt's cubicle. Keep watch."

Howard didn't question. He didn't argue. He stumbled over to Saunt's cubicle and stood out front, but stayed out of the path of the nurses and doctor who scrambled to save Saunt's life.

Voss and I passed Howard and stepped to one side of the chaos around Saunt. Two nurses, one of the ones in green and the one in blue, stood near the ER doctor as two male orderlies walked back and forth, gathering different supplies.

I stayed close to Voss, smelled her scent again, which was just as subtle as earlier but got to me. She stopped at the curtain. We didn't go in. She grabbed one of the orderlies by the arm. She said, "I need to speak to the doctor."

The orderly was a short and stocky black guy, not much older than me, who looked like he knew how to handle himself. He looked like had he'd been a boxer in a past life. His ears had proliferated like a fighter who neglected ear protection, a common side effect on a boxer's face. His ears were puffed up into themselves like small, bloated mushrooms glued to the sides of his head. He didn't seem embarrassed about it, like he was used to everyone staring at them. He kept his head shaved like he was proud of them. The orderly said, "That could be awhile, ma'am."

Voss asked, "How bad is the guy?"

The orderly turned and glanced back into the cubicle at Saunt and at the doctor, and then he looked back at us. He said, "The guy shot himself in the head. Looks bad. Excuse me."

The orderly pulled away from us and went back into the room to help the doctor and the nurses.

Voss turned to me, and said, "I've got to handle this. Let's go take a quick look and grab the gun from his motel room. Then we can get back to our main problem."

I nodded and waited for her.

Voss took one last look at the doctor and the nurses and the orderlies. She turned to lead the way back outside to the parking lot and her cruiser. Before we exited back through the ER doors, she stopped in front of Howard. She said, "As soon as the doctor is free, call me and give him your phone. I want to talk to him."

Howard said, "Okay, Chief."

Voss turned and walked out, and I followed.

# CHAPTER 8

We drove to the motel so we could grab the weapon, stick it into an evidence bag, and get back to the two dead cops. Voss drove the same way as when she went to the hospital. She weaved in and out of passing cars and ran stop signs and traffic lights. She was a good driver—faster than a school bus driver but slower than a Formula One racer. The light bar on the roof flashed blue lights which bounced off closed storefront windows and vacant spaces and *closed for the day* office buildings.

Before we left the hospital parking lot, she keyed the attempted suicide guy's name into a police computer mounted on the dashboard, over the center console. The computer clicked and hummed. It pulled up the guy's driver's license on the screen. I could barely see the screen from my angle. But I figured the guy's license was issued in New Mexico, or one of the neighbor states, because it came up on her screen fast, like it was in the first database searched.

Voss paused and stared at the screen. She read a bunch of common pedigree information off it. I imagined there were things like home ownership, medical records, and other public and nonpublic information. She browsed over everything and listed off the highlights to me as we drove.

The guy who shot himself was named Ryan Miles Saunt. Voss admitted she never heard of him before. According to her, Saunt was new in town, probably a tourist, and definitely not a local. From his photo ID on his license, she remembered seeing him for the first—and only—time in the diner, one day the week before. She said she paid him no attention. He was just a guy eating in a diner, something she had seen many times every day for years. There was nothing special about him, and no reason to think twice about him. People came and people went. Angel Rock wasn't a *sit around and see the sights* kind of town. It was a slow-growing, slow-moving, quiet place. Although, she admitted they got their fair share of alien-UFO enthusiasts who came through with questions and conspiracies on their minds. But mostly, alien tourists stuck to Roswell with questions about a UFO crash from over sixty years ago.

Voss and I pulled up to the motel in her police cruiser. She stopped past the front office but didn't park. She glanced around and saw that the motel clerk was no longer sitting in the parking lot, like he was when Officer Howard left. We needed the key to open the guy's room.

Voss was about to get out and head inside to the front desk, but the motel clerk named Clark peeked out a huge window and waved at us. Voss signaled for him to come outside. He stepped out of the front office and onto the gravel parking lot.

Voss reversed the cruiser and stopped directly alongside Clark. He walked over and leaned down and looked in through my window. He didn't pay me much attention, just a quick glance at my eyes, and then, straight at Voss.

He said, "Hi, Chief Voss."

Voss looked across me at Clark, and said, "Clark."

Clark asked, "You're here about that guy, right?"

Voss said, "Of course. What room is it?"

Clark stepped back away from my window and made a big show about crossing around the hood of the police car, around to Voss's side. He leaned down and peered in. He looked at her, looked across at me, and hesitated, looking fearful. He looked confused. At first, I thought it was just because he didn't know who I was. But then he fidgeted like he was more nervous to see me. I realized he was confused, not because he didn't know me, but because I wasn't sitting in the backseat with handcuffs on.

Voss saw Clark's fidgeting and nervousness too. She said, "He's with me. A consultant. Which room?"

Clark stuck his hands in his pockets and shuffled around for the key. After a serious fishing expedition, he pulled out a key and held it up for us to see. He said, "Room twenty-one. Down the left side."

He didn't point the way. He just said it.

Voss didn't wait for anything more from him. She grabbed the key out of his hand and tapped the gas with her foot on the brake. The car revved up, and Clark got the hint and backed away. Voss accelerated, and we were off down the gravel lot. She drove the length of the parking lot. People were scattered everywhere. Apparently, the sound of a gunshot, the sirens from Howard's car, and the ambulance had mustered them out of their rooms, and they never went back inside.

After seeing Voss's car, many of them moved closer to the edges of the parked cars, staying just behind the rear bumpers. The crowd was mostly women and children. The adults seemed to all be over fifty.

I said, "A lot of people in this motel tonight. Does Angel Rock usually have such a big occupancy?"

"The motels are full off and on. There's no real rhythm or reason for any of it. People veer off the freeway, drive a little, get lost or stop for gas, and they stay the night."

"Is this the only motel?"

"No, there are two others. Here we are," she said, and stopped the car in a space in front of room twenty-one. She threw the gear into park. She left the light bar flashing. No sirens, just the blue lights spinning and flooding across the faces of people standing around the parking lot.

Before she got out, Voss popped the trunk. Then she stepped out and left the engine running. She closed the door behind her. I stayed in my seat and waited. First, Voss stopped at the trunk, opened it, and ducked down inside. She came out with more gloves and a couple of evidence bags. She shut the trunk lid, stepped around the passenger side of the car, and gestured for me to follow. I got out of the car and slammed my door. I felt a crick in my neck that hadn't been there before. I cracked my neck to one side, and then, to the other— left and right. It *cracked*. The sound was audible.

Voss glanced at me with curiosity in her eyes.

I asked, "What?"

Voss said nothing and turned and walked up to the door to room twenty-one. I followed, glancing back once at the sea of faces of the motel's other occupants. The other officers hadn't arrived yet. There were no cops holding the crowd back. They were just standing around, being orderly on their own accord. No hassle. No fuss. They all seemed to know what had happened and what was going on.

There was no police tape in front of the door. Voss stopped in front of the door for a long second and frowned, like she was disappointed. Howard had put no tape up. Then again, what was he supposed to do? Dump the dying Mr. Saunt down in the dirt and then put up police tape?

Voss made no comment about it. Instead, she handed me another pair of gloves to put on. I put them on, and she did the same. She used the key that Clark had handed her and tried it in the door's lock. I stayed back and scanned the crowd of people behind us again. They remained a good distance back, keeping to themselves, but staying curious. No one came up to ask questions or volunteer information. It was all quiet.

I said, "We should ask around and see if anyone knows the guy."

"My officers will handle it when they get here," Voss said, and turned the key in the door. The lock clicked and the door to room twenty-one swung open.

The light was still on in the room. It shone in a dim, almost seedy sort of way, where everything wasn't lit up brightly, and all the bulbs in the room were a yellowish hue, as if the white had been blocked by months of dust covering the bulbs.

The first thing to hit us was a smell. There was a hint of blood, but there was also something else. It smelled like musk, like someone had been living in the room for weeks.

Room twenty-one was as typical as any plain motel room I'd ever seen before. The ceilings were low. Dull brown carpet covered the floor. There was a haphazardly-made bed with two nightstands, one on each side. There was a round, wooden table with a pair of hardwood chairs near a corner.

There was a laptop on the table. It was open but password protected.

The room's seedy lighting came from two table lamps posted on each side of the bed on the nightstands. The walls were wood paneling, trapped in time from three decades previous. There was a bathroom. The door was wide open, and the light was on. Ugly green tiles covered the floor and continued up the shower wall. The curtain was three-quarters drawn. There was a toilet and a sink and a mirror. Everything was generic and old and unremarkable.

We entered and looked around the room. We started to the right and moved left, corner to corner. The first thing to jump out at both of us was the gun that the guy used in his attempt to blow out his own brains.

Voss immediately went for it. It rested on the bed in a pool of blood. The blood was still wet. There was more blood splattered on the back wall, above the headboard. It was more than expected, because the guy was still alive. The blood loss alone was incredible. It looked like more than the human head could spare.

I scanned the room as Voss moved to the weapon. On the table, by the bathroom door, there was an open suitcase. The guy's clothes were scattered everywhere. They looked clean, but most of them were unfolded and slapdashed about, like the guy grabbed them and tossed them out of the case, one after the other, like he was desperately searching for something. It was chaotic and frantic, not at all like a man casually unpacking.

Voss said, "Here's the gun. I got what we need. Let's go."

But I didn't react. I didn't move because I saw something peeking out from under a half-folded brown shirt. I knelt on one knee and reached into the suitcase and picked it up. It was a Sony digital camera. It was black and metallic looking, but had a hard plastic case. There was a small screen on the back of the camera for viewing the pictures.

Underneath the camera, there was a white envelope. It had creases and folds, like it had travelled through a lot of hands to get here. It was open and had never been sealed. There was a bloodstain on it. I picked it up and looked at it. The blood-stain was a single fingerprint. I pulled back the flap with one finger and peeked inside. There was a small plastic object inside.

I put the envelope down and inspected the camera first. It looked new, not as if it had come right out of the box but like it hadn't been used much, like a recent Father's Day gift or something. It was appreciated but not used as an everyday item.

The screen was on. A low-battery light blinked across a paused image. I got a better grip on the camera's shell and scooped it up out of the suitcase. I stared at the screen and the image. Slowly, I rose to my feet, camera in hand, eyes locked on the screen. I kept my back turned to Voss.

I stayed quiet for a long moment, frozen by what I saw on the camera's screen.

Voss said, "Widow. Guess what kind of gun he shot himself with?"

I stayed facing away from her, and said, "A Glock 23."

Voss asked, "How did you guess that? You recognized the gun from the doorway?"

I shook my head involuntarily and rose to my feet. I turned around to face her.

She looked up at me and saw the horror on my face. She asked, "What?"

Silence.

Voss asked, "Widow, what is it?"

I showed her the digital camera. I held it out to her, like an offering to a guest, my arm fully extended. The camera lay in the palm of my open hand. The screen faced her. Voss stopped and stared. Her face instantly mirrored the horror on my face. She froze and said nothing.

I said, "Because it's the same gun Saunt used to murder Broome and Aragon."

On the screen of the camera was a still image of the two cops in the distance, alive and standing in front of their police cruiser. It was the same patch of dirt where I found them dead in their car. The timestamp on the corner said it was from hours ago.

# CHAPTER 9

crossed the room and moved closer to Voss. She stood there underwhelmed and unimpressed by the image on the camera. But she couldn't take her eyes off it. She reached up and took the camera in the palm of her gloved hand.

I didn't tell her about the envelope, not yet. I said, "You look disappointed."

"I guess I am. I can't believe we caught the guy this easy. He just fell into our laps."

"That happens sometimes."

"I thought there would be more to it. I was thinking two crooked cops, there's probably something deeper here."

"You found the killer. That's justice. Pretty simple."

"Alleged killer. And yeah. I know. I just thought they were up to something more. It was in my gut."

"There still might be more. We might just be looking at the surface. We still don't know motive."

Voss stayed quiet.

I said, "Better bag the Glock and tag it as a murder weapon now."

Voss dug one of the evidence bags out of her pocket and handed it to me. She said, "Do it for me, please?"

I nodded and walked over to the weapon, shoved the envelope into my pocket. I opened the evidence bag and pincered the Glock by the grip with my index finger and thumb. I held it up into the dim light and studied it like I was inspecting a live mouse I had caught by the tail. Voss stared at the little screen on the back of the camera for a long moment. I slipped the gun into the bag and sealed it. Then I placed it on the bed. I moved and scanned the rest of the room for anything else of interest. I started at the bed, where Voss had found the Glock 23. I looked down at the floor beneath it and got down on one knee and checked under the bed. There was nothing.

Voss set the camera down on the table near the open bathroom door. She returned to the bed and scooped up the bagged gun and took it out of the room and walked back to her police cruiser. She left the door to the motel room open. I watched her through the open door. She used one hand to open the car door. She plonked herself down on the seat, leaving her legs outside the car. Voss leaned over and across the middle console, past the computer terminal. She snapped open the glove box and placed the bagged Glock 23 inside. She sat back upright and picked up the radio and radioed the guy at the desk. She told him to get Howard and another deputy back to the motel and set up a perimeter.

I watched her through the open door until I noticed something. Behind the door, on the floor, tucked up close underneath a dresser, I saw a pair of dark green boots. I walked over to them and lightly kicked them over. The left boot toppled over. I nudged it again and tilted my head and stared down at the bottom. I could see under a tremendous amount of dried dirt the number zero. I nudged the heel of the shoe and a lump of dirt crumbled off. I could see the size clearly printed on the sole. It was a pair of size 10 boots. More dried dirt was stuck up in cracks between the treads.

I turned and walked back across the room to the bathroom and looked inside. I glanced over the sink and saw nothing out of the ordinary. There was a small closet behind the wall with a shelf inside for towels and toiletries. Everything in the bathroom was pretty standard and seemed normal. But the shower curtain was closed. I entered the bathroom and pulled back the curtain.

The tub was full of dirty water, like the guy had drawn the water, taken a bath, and left the water in the tub, before putting the Glock to his head and pulling the trigger. Then I noticed a broken disposable razor on the edge of the tub. The blade had been torn out. It rested on the edge of the tub. There were traces of blood on the blade, like a wrist-cutting starter kit. The guy had thought about more than one way to kill himself, changed his mind and went for the gun. Probably because it was faster. No chance of changing his mind, once the trigger was pulled.

I closed my eyes and pictured Saunt contemplating it. He shot Aragon and Broome in their cruiser. He emptied two of the Glock's magazines back at the crime scene, ejected the first one, and left it. Maybe he had a spare magazine here in the hotel. Maybe he forgot about it and was going to try the razor to the wrist first. I pivoted on my foot and craned back to see the open suitcase. I saw nothing but clothes. Nothing else of interest.

So I turned back to the tub. After Saunt killed the cops, he probably drove straight back to this motel room. Nothing in the room was knocked over or disturbed by a man in a rush, except for the suitcase. Therefore, he wasn't in a rush. Which told me he didn't come back and start planning his escape, like a guy who just brazenly shot and killed two cops would do. He wasn't scared. He wasn't panicked. He didn't rush back here and frantically pack up his belongings and plan his escape from police. He came back to this room with a different plan of escape. He returned to this room intending to kill himself.

He made a makeshift plan. First, he ran a bath, got in, and thought about doing it with the razor. But then he did it with the murder weapon. Maybe he remembered he had an extra magazine in the suitcase and that's why it was the only thing in the room in disarray. He sifted through it for his extra magazine.

I opened my eyes and walked out of the bathroom. I stopped and looked back into the motel room from a different perspective than before. Before, I had scanned the room from the front doorway in. Now, it was from the bathroom out, but there was nothing new to see—almost nothing.

On the floor, right against the wall above the bed, snug so tight to the lip of the carpet that I had almost missed it, was a black rectangular object like a remote control to a TV. Only the room had no television set. At first, I thought it must've been the guy's cell phone or a missing camera attachment, but it wasn't.

I bent down and looked at it. I didn't pick it up. It wasn't a remote control or a piece of the camera or the guy's cell phone. It wasn't any of those things. It was an empty magazine from the Glock 23. After he dug through the suitcase looking for the one in the gun, he ejected this one, and left it on the floor.

Voss slammed her car door and reentered the room. She asked, "Got anything else?"

I said, "The second empty magazine."

"From the Glock?"

I looked at the bullet count and confirmed it. I said, "It holds thirteen bullets."

"Have any idea what went down here?"

I recounted to Voss everything Saunt did, the way I saw it—the attempted suicide, the boots, the empty magazine, the new magazine, the bathtub, the razor blades, all of it. It was all desperation and remorse.

In the end, Voss said, "Okay, the Glock, the empty magazine, plus the camera with the picture. That's enough evidence to satisfy me. Saunt is our cop killer."

"If we can figure out which car is his, tire tracks will put him at the murder scene. Anyone could've taken the photo of Broome and Aragon with the camera."

"We can get that from Clark. Motel patrons are supposed to register their license plates, make and model of their vehicles. It's probably parked out in the lot," Voss said, and walked over behind me. I stood back up straight. I hadn't touched the empty magazine.

Voss said, "You can hand me the magazine."

I nodded and knelt again and scooped up the empty magazine for her. She whipped out a new evidence bag from her left pocket and held it open for me. I dropped the magazine into it. She sealed the bag, making sure each side was evenly sealed, and then, she held it in one hand down by her side.

I said, "Let's have a look at the camera. We should check out the rest of the pictures. There could be one of him at the scene."

Voss nodded and rotated counterclockwise and walked back toward the bathroom. She stopped in front of the table and picked up the camera. She waited for me to circle around her, which I did. I stopped behind her and looked over her shoulder at the camera's view screen. Voss began looking through the other images. She swiped the pictures to the left, starting at the one we had already seen.

There were pictures of the state police from a distance, at night, and still alive. The quality was low, like amateur private investigator stuff. There were pictures of Aragon and Broome in the daytime. I glanced down at the buttons on the camera. There were no words, only icons, some of which I knew and a bunch I didn't. I knew the little lightning bolt button was to adjust the flash on the camera. I knew the little magnifying glass icon indicated a zoom in and out feature. Plus, it doubled as the zoom function on the lens.

What I wasn't sure was what the little book icon did. I'd hoped that it stood for the date and time. I said, "Hold on."

Voss stopped sifting through the photos. Carefully, I reached around her. My hands came close to her forearms, almost brushing against her. I pressed the book icon button and put my hand back at my side. The camera's viewing screen flashed quickly, and a date and timestamp appeared over the image.

Voss said, "This picture is from two weeks ago."

"Keep going. Let's see how far back it goes."

She swiped again to the left. The next picture was of a green rucksack and the next was a picture of it unzipped. My jaw fell open at what was inside the bag. I couldn't see Voss's face, not dead on, but I imagined her jaw fell open as well.

Cash money filled the rucksack. A lot of it. There were hundred-dollar bills rubberbanded together in an undiscernible amount. It looked like thousands of dollars.

I grabbed Voss's wrist gently, instinctually, and said, "Motive."

"So this is about crooked cops?"

"Not necessarily. But maybe."

Voss stepped forward and turned to face me head on. She handed me the camera like she was tired of looking through it. She said, "You look through the rest. I need a second to think."

I nodded and took the camera from her. She was right. It was a lot for any chief to deal with, small department or not. Voss felt a little out of her depth. In one night, she had found two dead—potentially corrupt—cops, and the killer, who had shot himself in the head, and a camera with pictures of a bag filled with money, and me—an unknown quantity from her past— and I couldn't remember her.

Voss stepped away. She faced away from me and scanned the room for new evidence. I continued to sift through the camera's digital memory. It was just more of the same.

I pulled the envelope out of my pocket and stared at it. The bloody fingerprint. *What does it mean?*

I pulled the flap back again and stared inside. I reached in with two fingers and pinched the plastic object and pulled it out. It was a small memory card, which was for digital cameras. I knew that much.

I ejected the old memory card out of the camera and inserted the one from the envelope. The camera accepted the card. The screen showed an hourglass icon like it was updating. Finally, the new card's contents came on the screen. There was one folder. It was labeled: *Saunt*. I clicked on it and opened the pictures inside. The first came up on-screen like a camera roll. This picture differed from the previous ones on the other memory card. This photo made the hair on my arms stand up. It sent chills down my spine.

There must've been an expression on my face to register it because Voss stopped in the middle of the room. She stared right at me. She asked, "What?"

"There was this envelope under the camera," I said, and held up the envelope so she could see it. "There's a bloodstain on it. It's a fingerprint."

Voss approached slowly.

I said, "There was a second memory card inside the envelope. I just swapped it out for the one in Saunt's camera. And…"

"And what?"

"It gets worse."

Voss came back over to me, grabbed the camera from me, and looked at the viewscreen. She locked in on it with a dead stare at the photo on the display. The glow from the backlight display was bright in the dim light of the motel room. It sprayed across her face and highlighted her features. Her jaw dropped.

"Oh, Jesus!" Voss said, and her hands went up and covered her mouth in both horror and shock. She might've been overwhelmed seconds ago, but now she wasn't just out of her depth. She was in shark-infested waters without a lifejacket.

I stayed quiet.

The picture on the screen was of a teenage girl. She was probably fifteen or sixteen or seventeen. Her clothing was torn and ripped and destroyed. Dirt and grime covered her face. She looked terrified and disheveled. Her face was shrink-wrapped in dried tears, but only on the right side because her left eye was swollen shut from a black eye. Purple blood vessels webbed over her eyelid. The skin was black as night. It puffed out like a tiny, black volcano, about to erupt at any moment. It looked so bad; it would surprise me if she ever saw out of it again. The skin around the black volcano looked rotten. At some point, it had been covered in blood and pus.

The fist of my free hand clenched tight out of anger at seeing it. My fist was so tight, I could've hammered a nail with it.

Voss winced. Her face turned a deep shade of red. She whispered, "Widow, is this real?"

I stayed quiet and reached over her and flicked the screen to the next picture. It was worse than the first one.

Voss gasped. She clutched at my arm and looked away. Her eyes stared down at the floor.

I stared at the new image and wished I had swiped no farther. I wished I hadn't turned around a couple of hours ago. I should've just kept on walking. I should've kept going straight through Angel Rock and onward to Roswell. Aliens would've been much better than what I got.

The next picture was of a different teenage girl. She was completely nude. No torn clothes. She was similar in age to the previous one, only she wasn't the previous one. This one was a brunette with a rounder face and a piercing above her right eye. What was once a piece of silver eyebrow jewelry was now caked in dried blood. Makeup and dried mascara ran down her face days before the photo was taken. This girl didn't have a black eye like the previous one, but she was obviously dead. Voss gasped again. It was an angry, audible sound like a loud exhale of air.

I stayed quiet and stared at the screen in rage and horror.

The next picture showed the dead girl's whole body. She was handcuffed to a bed in what looked like a basement. It was dark and dank. The floors and walls were part concrete and part dirt. There were pipes on the wall and ceiling. There was a huge dirt-covered farm sink, off to one side of the bed. There were dim lights with extension cords dangling from them. There were disheveled, bloodstained sheets on the bed.

She had died in agony. It was all right there, big, and obvious, like a message.

The girl's breasts had been cut off. Not sliced off halfway, but completely removed as if they were scooped out with a shovel. I could see them. They were gory and slopped onto the concrete part of the floor—two bloody mounds of meat and veins and fat and tissue.

Blood was everywhere. It covered her chest and midsection. Huge, dark pools of blood soaked the sheets beneath her. Her throat had been cut—sliced from ear to ear.

Voss breathed heavily like she was angry, angrier than me.

I looked at the picture a little longer. It turned my stomach. But there was one more detail. A figure stood between the dead teenager and the camera. His back turned. Half his body off camera. He reached out a gloved hand and held her head up by a tuft of hair. He held her face forward for the camera to get a clear picture of her.

If an image was worth a thousand words, this one wasn't. It wasn't worth a thousand words. It wasn't worth five hundred words. It wasn't worth one hundred words. It wasn't even worth ten words. It was only worth three, and Voss said them.

She said, "Someone's gonna pay."

# CHAPTER 10

We stood there in silence for a long moment. Voss broke the silence first. She asked, "What is this?"

I stepped back, took my eyes off the camera's screen, and pulled out one of the hardwood chairs from the table. I sat in it and stared at the wall across from us. I moved my eyes across the wood paneling, and then I peered through the open doorway out at Voss's police cruiser. I looked at the light bar and watched the blue lights spin around and around. I stayed quiet for a second. Then I looked down the side of the police car and at the emblem on the side again. It read: *To Protect* across the top and *To Serve* across the bottom of the Angel Rock police ensign etched on the door.

I thought, *To Protect*.

Voss said, "Widow? What is this?"

"It looks real."

"I know. But *what* is it?"

I pinched the envelope between two fingers, reached it out, and showed it to her. I said, "The envelope. There's a bloody fingerprint on it."

"What's it mean?"

"It's proof of life."

"Why?"

I stood up from the chair and stepped back over to her.

She repeated, "Why?"

I put my hands on her arms and stared down into her pale blue eyes. I said, "It could be for a ransom. The first girl. The one who's still alive. She must mean something to Saunt."

"We've got to ask Saunt about this."

"We can't. Not yet. He's probably in surgery. Not to mention, he might not even wake up again, at all."

Voss paused a long, solemn beat, like she was reevaluating her entire life. She said, "This is the worst thing I've ever seen."

I removed my hands from her arms and reached one out and clamped it over hers and the camera. I squeezed it gently, and said, "I know. Me too."

She whispered, "It's horrible."

I pulled the camera away from her, like that could take it all back. She didn't fight me. I looked at the viewer screen again and the dead teenager. I swiped my finger across the screen and scanned back to the picture of the first girl. I stared at it. Nothing in the shot gave away clues where she was except that it was some place dark, probably a basement, but nothing definitive. She might not have even been in the same spot as the dead girl. The background was slightly different, and yet similar. Plus, the first girl wasn't dead. There was a bed and similar piping and lighting, but the sheets were clean. There was no blood. The photo was pointed at a different angle, which didn't allow me to see if the farmer's sink was in the other corner or not. It could've been the same basement, but there was no way to tell for sure.

Voss pulled closer to me and looked as well. She wiped a single tear off her cheek, and asked, "Do you think the first one is still alive?"

I didn't answer.

She said, "If this is the only picture of her on here and she's alive in it, then she might still be alive now."

"That's the assumption we should work on. Until we know otherwise, this girl is alive."

"Okay. So how do we find her?"

I said, "I think she's near Angel Rock. Somewhere. They'd want her to be nearby. She's the motive."

"Saunt killed Aragon and Broome over this girl. So did they tell him she was dead?"

"They could've lied to him. Maybe he didn't have the full ransom. Maybe they wanted to motivate him. Or hurt him. Make him suffer a bit. She could be alive. In fact, I bet she is alive."

"How do you know?"

"Because why tell him she's dead and then let him walk away? They'd kill him too. Sure as anything. No sense letting him live unless it was a trick."

Voss nodded along but said nothing.

I asked, "What do we know about Saunt?"

"He tried to kill himself."

"What else?"

Voss stared down at the floor as if she were counting the threads in the carpet. She said, "The obvious questions are: why did he try to kill himself and why is the girl motive?"

"We saw the money. We have the fingerprint and the memory card with the photos. They must be proofs of life. The obvious answer is: it was ransom money because they have this girl. At the crime scene, they told him she was dead, maybe."

Voss nodded and looked back at the camera. She looked at the viewer and saw the living girl's face again. She asked, "Who is she?"

"If you look closer into Saunt's background, I bet you'll find he has a teenage daughter or niece or something like that."

"The daughter angle makes sense."

"I think so too."

Voss said, "If his daughter is missing, there might be a report or an Amber alert."

"That's *if* it was reported to begin with."

"I just can't believe that two state detectives would do something so horrible. Even if Aragon and Broome were assholes. Still, kidnapping for ransom?"

I said, "I know, it's evil. But it adds up. The murder scene. The meetup. The way he snapped. That Aragon and Broome underestimated Saunt. They probably staked him out for months and thought he was a good candidate."

Voss asked, "What if they've done this before?"

"We know they have. The dead girl is probably real. Probably from the same evil racket. They've probably been doing this for years. If we research, we probably could uncover a host of dead or missing children and their fathers."

Voss's face changed back to the hardened cop. She said, "We should confirm the girl is Saunt's teenage daughter."

"I agree. Can you find out?"

Voss nodded, and asked, "You really think she's still alive?"

"We should alert the FBI. Kidnapping is their thing."

"That could endanger her."

"How so?"

"Not saying we can't trust the FBI, but if we tell them, someone else who might be involved in their department might get wind of it. Aragon and Broome are cops. If they're committing these horrible crimes, there could be a third man."

I said, "We should tread carefully."

# CHAPTER 11

Voss and I returned to her police car after she bagged the laptop—which we couldn't access without Saunt's password—the empty magazine, a shell casing we found on the floor from Saunt's suicide bullet, Saunt's boots, the bloodstained envelope, the extra memory card, and the camera, which had a dying battery. I squeezed the clothing spillage from Saunt's suitcase together and closed it and carried it out first. Then I went back in for a power cord I presumed was for the camera. It had a tiny, flat end which looked like it could fit into the camera someplace. I wasn't sure if it was the right cord or not, but I had seen no other loose power cords in the room and, as far as we could tell, there was no cell phone. Saunt's cell phone was maybe in his vehicle, but more likely in a pocket of his jacket or his pants, which were at the hospital.

Voss also took the motel room key off one of the nightstands. The key was clearly marked by a round metal badge that had the motel's name and room number written on it in small letters and numbers. Next to the motel room key, underneath a lamp, she also found a set of vehicle keys.

At her police car, Voss popped the trunk and tossed in the bagged evidence. I watched as she shifted them around to make sure they were stationary and not in danger of being tossed about in the car while we drove. She kept the key set out and in her palm. She slammed the trunk shut without giving me time to toss the power cord in.

I stuffed the cord into one of my pockets.

Voss took her gloves off and stuffed them into her pants pocket. I did the same. She jingled the set of keys in her hand, Saunt's keys. She asked, "Can you drive Saunt's truck?"

"Sure. But I don't have a license."

"If you don't tell, then I won't," she said, and tossed me the keys underhanded.

I caught them and held them with my pinkie finger going through the key ring. It was a tight fit. The keys were attached to a fob with buttons on it. I asked, "Which truck is his?"

"It's the Silverado," Voss said, and pointed at a maroon-colored Chevy Silverado with New Mexico plates.

"How do you know?"

"Click the alarm button."

I looked at the fob. There were two buttons: one marked with an icon of a lock and one with a red button. I pressed the red button and a vehicle in the lot screeched and the lights flashed. I looked up.

I looked down at the key and reversed it. On the back, there was a Chevy emblem. I pressed the red button again, and the alarm stopped. Then I pressed the lock button and the truck's dome lights lit up, slowly and laggardly. The door locks clicked as they unlocked and fog lights on the front of the truck lit up the pavement in front of the tires.

I looked around the parking lot. There were two other Chevys in the lot, a Malibu and a blue Camaro. I asked, "How did you know his was the Silverado? Why not the other two Chevys?"

Voss smiled, and said, "I'm smarter than you think."

"Was it because the key has no open trunk button, and the Silverado is the only Chevy without a trunk?"

She moved around to the driver's door of the police cruiser. She said, "Damn. I didn't think of that. I knew it was his because of the color. It's maroon."

"So?"

"When a man picks a maroon truck, it means nothing on its own. But did you see his clothes? Did you check out his socks next to his boots?"

I shook my head.

She said, "Saunt is colorblind. His clothes didn't match. His jacket and his shirt were both gray.

"How do you know? They look like they match to me. They're both gray. Ugly, but gray."

"Colorblind people often wear gray because they don't know it's gray. They think it's different colors.

"Okay."

Voss said, "His socks are two different shades of white and from two completely different pairs of cotton socks. It's probable that he's colorblind. My dad was like that. He always picked out maroon or dark red or gray-colored vehicles. He thought they were blue. My first car was gray. He thought it was black. I never had the heart to tell him."

I nodded again, but I wasn't sure if I bought the colorblind thing or not. She mentioned her dad. I thought back, tried to think if a colorblind guy with a beautiful daughter meant anything to me. It didn't. I still wasn't sure how she knew me.

Voss said, "Follow me. We're going to the station."

"Lead the way."

She got into her cruiser and shut the door.

I got into the cab of the truck and felt around under the front seat for the bar to set it back, but I couldn't find it. Then I switched my hunt to the door, with no luck. I looked over at the console in the middle and found it, nice and neat next to the seat adjustment controls for the passenger seat. The interior of the truck had a lot of aftermarket stuff. Maybe that's why the seat adjustment was there? It had to be moved to accommodate something else that was added. I wasn't sure. I was no mechanic.

I hit the little lever all the way back and my seat started moving slowly, automatically. It stopped when it went as far back as it would go. I released the lever and sat upright. It was comfortable. I had plenty of leg room and enough room between my lap and the steering wheel. I reached out and grabbed the door handle and pulled it shut. I jammed the key into the ignition and turned on the engine. I gave it some gas. The engine roared to life.

The radio blasted a country music station. Music *boomed* over the truck's speakers. I didn't recognize the song, but it was a male's voice, and it was on a chorus. I listened to the words. The song was about his wife leaving him, which seemed to be just about every country song that's ever been played anywhere. Today's country music was a lot about sorrow and lost loves, like the new blues. I looked for a knob to turn it off, but there wasn't one. Instead, there was a touch screen that lit up the center of the dash. I looked at it. There was a menu which led me along a string of choices such as map, connect Bluetooth to phone, radio, and status. I ignored all the choices except radio and pressed it with my index finger. The screen flashed and changed quickly over to a choice of preset stations and scanning and volume controls.

I didn't see an *off* button, so I pressed the volume control and held my finger there until the volume was all the way down and the country singer's whiny chords faded into silence.

Voss reversed her cruiser and straightened it out and got in front of me. I pulled out of the space and stopped behind her. She led me to the end of the lot, where she stopped and exchanged a couple of words with Clark through the open window of her car. Then she headed out to the road, turned right, and slowed to allow me to stay close.

I followed about a car-length away. Heavy clouds overtook the sky overhead, and the moon vanished behind them. We drove, staying at a speed comparable to the speed limits in small towns all over America. Although I never saw a speed limit sign posted.

I followed her through another turn to the right. At a stoplight with no other cars, she shrieked her sirens to warn oncoming drivers that we were passing through and not stopping. We barreled through the light as it changed to red. We drove on for another three blocks, and then, she flipped on her right turn signal and pulled into a parking lot.

The parking lot was shared among four different departments, all shared in one government building. One was the Angel Rock Police, which was clearly marked at the top of a sign near the road. The government building also housed the local district attorney, the city clerk, and a public library. They all shared the same building and the same parking lot. The police department took up the lion's share of the building. It had the entire first two floors and the district attorney's office was on the third. The library shared the top floor with the city clerk's office.

Public libraries were one of my favorite places to visit because the books were free. Unfortunately, you needed a library card to check them out. I hadn't had a library card in decades.

I pulled into the parking lot behind Voss. She parked her cruiser up front, near the entrance to the building, which, ten to one, was her own designated parking spot. I kept on driving through the lot and parked the truck far away from the line of police cruisers. I didn't want to block parking spaces designated for official vehicles.

After killing the Silverado's engine, I hopped out and shut the door and clicked the lock button. The alarm *beeped,* and the lights went off.

Voss waited for me behind the trunk of her cruiser. She popped it open and began taking out the bagged evidence. She handed me the heavy stuff, including the suitcase and the boots, which were too large for her evidence bags. She also handed me the bag with the camera in it. She scooped up the rest and closed the cruiser's trunk. She headed into the police station, and I followed.

The first-floor lobby was occupied at the entrance by a night guard seated next to a metal detector. He wore a brown uniform, freshly shined boots, and a polished badge on his left breast pocket. He had a clean shave, a jarhead haircut, and a military look in his demeanor and face. He was even more militarist and steadfast to his station than Gene, the guard from the hospital.

The guard stood straight up as Voss entered, like she was his commanding officer in a military unit. He did everything but salute.

Voss said, "Franklin, this is Widow."

He nodded and gave me a half smile that said he was required to be polite. It also was a warning that he had his eye on me. This was his domain, and I was the newbie. Any seasoned centurion will tell you that the newest faces are the first ones you automatically suspect as possible threats to the peace.

"Hi, Franklin," I said.

He said, "Pleasure. Walk on through, please."

Voss didn't wait for his permission; she walked through the metal detector, and it sounded. I went through after her, and it sounded again.

Franklin gazed at me, but said nothing about it. He didn't know if I was carrying a weapon or not, but I wasn't. The camera in the evidence bag or the Silverado keys in my pocket or something in the suitcase had set off the metal detector.

There was no loose change in my pockets and no belt buckle or belt. I got lucky with this set of gas station clothes. The pants fit snug on my hips. The only metal on me were the keys and the camera, the prongs on the plug to the camera, and the small button on my pants, which was too small to set off the detector anyway.

I ignored Franklin's suspicion and followed Voss down a short hall and past an empty counter, where the daytime secretary probably sat, as well as the night desk guy Voss had sent off to a long dinner. He wasn't there, must've stepped out for a moment.

We walked past the empty counter and through a swinging half-door.

The station was a basic bullpen setup with two offices at the far back of the wall. The first office had a frost-glass window on the door, which read: *Chief Voss*. The other office was empty and had nothing written on the window in the door.

Voss opened her door, which wasn't locked, and walked in and set the evidence bags on her desk.

"Put the suitcase down over there," she said, and pointed at the corner of the room. I did as instructed. Then she said, "And the camera here." She pointed at the desk.

I set the camera, still inside the evidence bag, down on the desk and reached into my pocket and dug out the charging cable and the plug. I set them down as well, and I said, "We should plug the camera in. The battery is low."

"Go ahead. There's an outlet behind that chair," Voss said, and pointed at a gray leather lounge chair that looked like it belonged in a man cave and not in the chief's office. I stepped over to it and pulled it away from the wall and saw the outlet. I picked up the evidence bag with the camera in it and unzipped it.

Voss said, "Use gloves."

I said, "I won't touch it."

I didn't use gloves. I reversed the plastic in the bag and held the camera with it, pinched it tight in one hand and held the power cord in the other hand. I slid the charger end into a port on the bottom of the camera. Then I shoved the plug into the wall outlet. The screen came to life and showed a glimpse of the last image we had seen. The dead girl and the gloved hand reached out toward her. The camera screen shifted to a large battery icon. It flashed green, showing that the camera was charging.

I turned and dumped myself down in the lounge chair and left the camera half in the bag and lying on the chair's arm.

Voss took a deep breath, sighed, and said, "I gotta call the FBI. We can't sit on this anymore."

"I agree. If we don't call them now, they might find out. And that's bad for you. Bad for the case. Bad for the girl. The FBI will know what to do and how to get her back. Hopefully."

"If we can get her back."

I nodded.

Voss sat straight in a black swivel desk chair with no arms and a low back and small wheels on the bottom.

The office wasn't big, but it wasn't small. It was the same chief's office that was in thousands of police stations in thousands of small towns with budget constraints across the country. This one was better than many. Voss was lucky to have an office, I supposed, but not lucky enough to have a window with a view, or a window at all. Instead, there was a wall with exposed brick. It was old and painted white. Not sure if it was a design choice, or if they built the floor over something else, like an old industrial factory. There was a lot of fine detail. Each individual crack and line was etched out to showcase the architecture. On the other wall, the one that separated the two offices, there were multiple hanging photographs and framed achievements—all Voss's, I suspected.

I got up out of the lounge chair, turned my back, and stepped over to the wall. I looked at the rows of Voss's achievements. It looked to be something that took over a decade to accomplish. She had done some impressive things. The first thing I saw was a bachelor's degree in criminology from the University of Arizona. Next to that she had a letter from a *Wilson Marks, PhD* with his personal signature. Under his signature was his printed name and underneath that was his job title: *Chair of the Criminal Justice Department at U.A.*

The letter congratulated Voss for the promotion to chief of police. Next to the framed letter was an award with the state seal smack dab at the bottom righthand corner of the page. The award was some kind of certificate of appreciation, given to Voss by the *Office of the Governor of New Mexico.* It said so right on the award. The governor's name was a name I didn't recognize. The date on the certificate was from four years earlier, which probably meant the current governor of New Mexico wasn't the same guy who signed and awarded the certificate.

Voss called to me. She said, "I'm going to call the FBI first."

I swiveled from the waist, looked back at her, smiled, and said, "Okay."

I turned back to the wall of achievements and moved on to the rest of the photographs, which took up the bulk of the wall. The first several photographs were happy times with, I assumed, coworkers. There were photos of barbeques, softball games, snowboarding in the mountains, and one large group of people surrounded by tents at night and a roaring camp-fire. The photographs were filled with people and smiles and cheers and good times. Good memories.

In every picture, I noticed something about Voss. All of her coworkers and friends seemed to be paired next to someone. The pattern continued in most of the photos. Each person posed next to the same person in the next photograph, but not Voss. She always stood alone. The others seemed to pose with their spouses and partners.

In every photo, nowhere did she appear to be *with* anyone. Even though she was surrounded by people, she was alone. I moved farther down the line.

Behind me, I heard Voss sigh like she was on hold or going through the local FBI office's automated phone menus, until finally she got to a pause after a question. She said, "I need an agent."

Nowadays, living-breathing operators are harder and harder to come by. I made few calls to the FBI, but I imagined it's the same as the rest of government, which moved to using automated menus but kept all the useless bureaucracy. The automation probably made it all more useless. To become more efficient, they've become less so.

Reminds me of the term *red tape*, which originated during the Civil War, when Union soldiers had to travel all the way to Washington D.C. to repeal certain orders, to collect unpaid wages, to refute wrongful terminations, or to accomplish other things. When the soldiers arrived in D.C., often their papers and documents were bound by red tape.

There was an entire row of photographs of a boy. First, he was young, then he grew. I followed along them like it was a time-line of a child growing to a man, until finally, he reached the age of eighteen. The second to last photo was of him in a cap and gown. It appeared to be his high school graduation. The last photo was him standing in front of the University of New Mexico, which I imagined was in Albuquerque.

In all the photos, there was Voss. She aged alongside the boy. In the first photo, she looked very different than she did now. She was youthful, vibrant, and joyful. But there was a naivety to her, like a lot of young people. There was a look of hopeful-ness on her face. Something that you can lose as you get older, more acquainted with the real world. I think it happens to those of us who are unfortunate enough to be touched by tragedy, like crime or war.

As the photos of the boy and Voss progressed, I watched her change physically too. They both grew. Over the years, the boy turned to a young man, but his mom became harder. In the beginning, she was soft. It was in her eyes. It was in her body, her demeanor. By the end, she was muscular, tougher, more like a hardened cop, and not like a new mother. More than a hardened cop, she became a hardened woman.

I saw the progression of her tattoos. She began with none. Not by the end. At the end, like me, in the last photo, she had sleeve tattoos covering her arms.

Something else in the photographs. There was no father. No husband. No partner. But Voss wore a wedding ring in some of the early ones. I went back to them and checked. There was a ring. I turned around and looked back at her at her desk. She talked on the phone to the FBI. I glanced at her hand. No wedding ring now. I inspected the rest of the photos on another row, and in the next several pictures, she appeared younger. They were from farther in the past. I was examining her life in reverse.

There were more good times. More accomplishments. More police stuff. There were some photos of her winning different physical competitions. Some looked to me to be what they call CrossFit. Others were long biking races. Others were those mud obstacle courses with names like *Spartan Race* or *Dirt Warriors.*

Off to the right, beyond the rest of the photographs and accolades and memories, there was a single frame hanging on the wall. There was a glass case. Inside, there was a folded flag. There was no inscription on the case. No indication of who the flag was supposed to represent. No indication that the flag was even for Voss. I didn't see any signs that she had been in the military. Sometimes veterans will keep a flag from a foreign base as a keepsake. Sometimes they'll get one and give it away to someone special as a gift. I wasn't sure about this one. A folded flag on display doesn't mean military. Not necessarily. Police departments give out flags. So do the Boy Scouts.

Suddenly, I realized it might be for her husband. Maybe he had been a cop before her. Perhaps he was killed in the line of duty and the department gave her the flag. Maybe she didn't put up a plaque or inscription with his name on it because she didn't need it. Maybe she didn't want it. Maybe she wanted to know what the flag meant and keep it to herself. Or perhaps, the inscription plaque was being replaced. There were dozens of explanations for a missing inscription.

Voss went quiet behind me. I turned back to look at her. She was waiting on hold.

I walked back closer to her and stopped a few feet from her desk. I stared at her, and asked, "How do you know me?"

Voss stared at me for a second. Her eyes shifted up and to the left like she was searching for the proper response. She moved the phone away from her mouth, and said, "I won't tell you. Not yet. I want you to remember. You're a good guy, Widow. It'll come to you. I have faith."

"Give me a hint?"

"If you don't remember before this is all over, I'll tell you. Maybe."

"Can I ask questions?"

"You can do whatever you want."

"Will you answer my questions?"

She shrugged, and said, "Try me."

"Okay. Are you married?"

Voss paused a beat, and said, "No."

"I saw you have a son."

"Yes. Simon. He's a good kid."

"He's in school now?"

She said, "Yes. He's going to be a lawyer. Unless he changes his major again."

"I didn't see a husband. Were you married?"

Voss paused a solemn beat, and said, "I was. Once upon a time."

"Is that how I know you?"

Voss went quiet. She didn't answer because, right then, someone came on the other end of the line, and her conversation resumed.

# CHAPTER 12

V oss put the phone's receiver back to her mouth and talked with someone on the other end of the line.

I stayed quiet, but I thought about her. I tried to remember where she knew me from. There were no photos of her ex-husband on the wall, or there were, and I just didn't know which man he could be. Maybe he was in them as part of the group, but not next to her as a partner. Either way, it was useless. I didn't recognize anyone from any photos. I guessed that wasn't how I knew her.

If she knew me from my Navy days, that's a sixteen-year span of time. Plus, I've been out for six-plus years by this point. That means it's possible I knew her twenty-two years ago. A thought occurred to me. I went back to the wall and the photos and stared at her son. He was tall. Over six feet. He looked pretty fit. He had a thick head of fair hair. He needed a haircut, but that's how boys his age wear their hair —messy and unkempt. He was a good-looking kid. But I saw no resemblance to myself. Still, he looked to be younger than twenty-two, in the most recent photo.

So far, Voss informed me she was married once. Maybe that was my only clue, for now.

"Uh, huh. Yes. I need to speak to an agent from New Mexico," Voss said, and went silent like she was waiting. She slumped down in her chair like she was tired of the rollercoaster of their phone system.

After a long pause, she said, "I'm calling from Angel Rock. We've got two dead cops here. And possibly a kidnapped teenager."

There was another long pause as Voss listened to someone on the other end. Whoever was on the other line must've said something shocking because Voss suddenly stood straight up, knocking back her desk chair to the ground. She squeezed the phone, and said, "Are you kidding?"

I stared at her intently and studied her facial expressions. Her anger emoted on her face like a flashing street sign. She turned a shade of red as if the person on the other end of the line had just told her some majorly surprising news, something dramatic, like New Mexico had just been annexed and was no longer under the jurisdiction of the FBI, and now, Voss was on her own.

She raised her voice, and said, "Yes! Connect me!"

Suddenly, Voss ripped the phone away from her ear.

I asked, "What?"

She looked at me and shook her head, but said nothing. Then she put the phone back to her ear, and asked, "Why wasn't I consulted?"

She paused and listened, and then she said, "I'm the police chief in Angel Rock!"

The person on the other end must've started talking again because she went quiet and listened hard. I saw it on her face.

After several more minutes of her nodding and saying *right* over and over, she got off the phone. She didn't slam it down, like I expected, but she left her hand on top of it while it sat in the cradle for a long minute before she moved on.

She turned away from the room and stared at the opposite wall, the brick one. She looked at the brick.

I waited, and finally, I asked, "What did they say?"

Voss spun around to face me. She said, "There's an FBI agent named Oliver."

I stayed quiet.

She said, "He's already here! In Angel Rock! He's been in and out of here for a week. There's an investigation. I guess they didn't want to include me in it. Is nobody supposed to stop in and include my department?"

"They kept you in the dark. Why?"

"I don't know."

# CHAPTER 13

Voss turned around and picked up her fallen chair and set it back on its wheels. She pushed it under the desk. She asked, "What the hell is going on?"

I shrugged, and asked, "Did they tell you?"

"No."

"I like coincidence as much as the next guy, but two dead cops, who could be crooked," I said, and paused a beat. "They weren't supposed to be here in the first place, a potential missing girl, Saunt trying to blow his own brains out, and now an FBI agent secretly in town. That's a lot of coincidence. Too much."

"He's gotta be here because of the two cops. Maybe he's here investigating them?"

"Maybe. It makes some kind of sense. Maybe they got wind of them somehow. But there could be more going on."

Voss said, "Come on. Let's go find him."

"Don't forget about the girl. Whatever is going on with the FBI might help us, but we can't let her get lost in the shuffle. It's likely this FBI guy's goal differs from our own."

She nodded.

I said, "Let's leave the camera to charge, but what about the Glock?"

Voss said, "We'll lock my door. Don't worry. The stuff in here isn't going anywhere."

"What about the crime scene? There're shell casings, the magazine, and the dead cops."

"With Howard at the hospital, I'm too short-staffed to worry about that now."

"What about the desk guy? He can go sit on it?"

She half chuckled, and said, "No way. He's not doing that. He's best here. Besides, I gotta have someone here. We left the crime scene alone this long. It'll be fine."

I nodded and thought about asking her about her former husband. *Where was he now? Did he die in the line of duty? What happened to him?* But I didn't. I took one last look at Voss's wall of memories and the flag and turned and stepped out of the office.

Voss followed. She stopped behind me and locked her door. We walked through the deserted bullpen, past the empty counter, and back to the entrance.

We passed Franklin, who stood up again and acted like he was going to salute Voss, but he only nodded and did the same to me. Voss took the lead and led us out of the building and to the parking lot. She stopped near a handicap ramp.

I asked, "Want me to take the truck?"

She glanced at Saunt's Chevy and then at me. She asked, "Why?"

"Two vehicles are better than one."

"Yeah. Actually, maybe you shouldn't even come. I don't know this FBI guy. I've never met him before. So there's no personal or professional relationship built up. It'll look bad having you there. What am I supposed to tell him? *Hi. This is a guy I met years ago who doesn't remember me? Oh, and by the way, he was standing over the two dead cops. Oh and he is now helping me with the investigation.*"

"You could tell him the truth. If you wanted to. You don't have to tell him all of it. Just tell him I used to be an NCIS agent. And I'm helping with the investigation. You could say we're old friends and I was in town, visiting you."

She shook her head, and said, "It's weird. If he's here because of Aragon and Broome, he might've been investigating them. He might already have me listed as a potential crooked cop, who was in on something with them. He will find it strange that I let you tag along."

"It's a risk."

"Yeah. It won't look right. He may not believe it. I don't want to get rid of you. Let me feel him out. Just wait for me. I'll contact you after."

I shrugged and stayed quiet.

She asked, "Do you like coffee?"

A smile crept across my face, and I said, "Coffee is life."

"Take the truck and head over to the diner. It's on Heston Street. You'll like it. It's good. They've got good coffee. Tell Gerry that I sent you."

"Is he the owner?"

"Gerry is short for Geraldine. She's a waitress. Usually works all night."

Voss said nothing else. She walked away and got in her cruiser and fired up the engine. I waited until she pulled out before I walked over to the Silverado. I pulled Saunt's keys out of my pocket and clicked the unlock button. I opened the door and climbed in and slid into the seat. I glanced in the rearview mirror and watched Voss's taillights fade away into the gloom.

I started the truck and stared at the touch-screen electronics in the dash, like an ape staring at fire for the first time. I wasn't dumb. Obviously, I knew how to work complicated machines, but I go long stretches without using complex, thinking, manmade devices. That knowledge fades back into brain storage sometimes. It takes me a second to switch from being a primate to being an intelligent person.

I knew that getting directions on a built-in map and control-ling the radio were the main features of the instrument. *But did these things come with internet browsing?*

I swiped my hand across the screen and watched as the main menu lit up. I studied the different buttons. Voss wanted me to go to the diner and wait, but what she really wanted was for me to butt out while she did solo work. All that stuff about the FBI agent, and how was she going to explain my involvement to him was true, but she could've sent me to do some research or to check something out. I could go sit on the crime scene for her. I could be put to use. I wouldn't sit around and do nothing.

I could've listened to her, but I kept thinking about that girl in the photo, the one who could still be alive.

Waiting was something I was good at. I'm a patient guy by nature, but patience wouldn't save the girl in the photo's life. If she was still alive, that is. Right now, she needed my help.

I sifted through the buttons and saw that the last button was a down button, which showed there were more off-screen buttons. I pressed it and found nothing that reminded me of an internet browser button. No search button. No internet browser icon. No *Google* icon or any other icon for an internet search feature.

Except that they were all digital, the buttons performed the same basic features that could be found in any regular Silverado, except for a map function. Everything else was the same standard set of buttons that have been in every other car for years—air conditioning controls, heating controls, pop hood, and radio controls. Nothing new.

I thought about how some things stayed the same, but then I thought, *if it ain't broke then why fix it?*

The American automobile has undergone a plethora of cosmetic changes since the sixties. There were some models of cars that were so popular from that era that they returned to the market decades later to become popular again, like the Ford Bronco or the Chevy Camaro or the Dodge Challenger. Hollywood wasn't the only industry that liked to regurgitate its past hits; the automobile industry was just as guilty of remakes and reboots. Same old wine, new bottle.

I couldn't just go to the diner and sit still and wait around for Voss to get through with her conversation with this FBI guy. I wasn't even sure that she would come back and get me after. *What if this FBI guy was a boy scout? What if he suspected me? What if he had the Angel Rock mayor recuse her from this whole investigation? What if he got the governor to do it?*

He wasn't going to just let me tag along. To him, I was a civilian. Even if he looked me up and *could* access my files, which I doubted because they're classified beyond classified, he'd still figure I was out of cop work. I was a nobody. A has-been. He'd view me as a person of interest.

Conceivably, Voss had thought of this too, and that's why she sent me away. I couldn't blame her. It was her career and her job and her reputation. I wasn't about to endanger that. The murder mystery surrounding the two dead cops could be left up to her. It wasn't my job to solve it. It wasn't even my prerogative. If they were as guilty as it seemed, then they got what they deserved, as far as I was concerned. But the girl in the photo might be alive and might run out of time. I needed to find out what her connection to Saunt was. Since he was incapacitated, the only thing I could think to do was search online. However, I didn't have internet or access to a device to search on.

Still, I wasn't dead in the water. I just needed to come up with a plan. I needed to do a little research. I could help without being around Voss.

*Don't run to your death* is one of many SEAL mottos. Before I know what else I'm getting myself into, I better do some recon. And what goes hand-in-hand with research? Coffee.

# CHAPTER 14

People always say stuff like *everything in moderation,* or *too much of anything is bad.* That's not true about one thing. One thing is good in excess and is never enough. Coffee is that thing. Coffee is key to everything. I drink a lot of coffee.

I sat at a corner booth in the diner Voss sent me to. A menu was face down in front of me. I was near a window. I wanted to see people approaching and passing by in case Voss came this way.

The diner was a newly renovated place. The building was old, with brown brick and a single large streetlight rooted out at the edge of the parking lot. The light was shared between the main street and most of the diner's front parking lot.

The diner was slapped in the middle of a parking lot, surrounded by a midwestern-style shopping plaza, like a strip mall. There were all kinds of stores and small businesses in each of the spots. The strip mall's owners were doing okay because everything looked rented.

The waitress named Gerry was a white woman in her mid-forties. She was the youngest employee in the diner. There were two other waitresses working the same shift. They were older black ladies with big smiles and warm demeanors. Both had long, manicured fingernails. They stood side by side behind the counter and talked and giggled, like a couple of old gossiping birds.

Gerry greeted me with a smile when I walked in. She waited for me to sit in her section, which wasn't on purpose, but a happy accident because I was going to ask for her service anyway for two reasons—I needed a favor and Voss suggested her. I figured dropping Voss's name would get Gerry to help me out.

Gerry walked out from behind the counter and stopped at the corner's edge and grabbed silverware out of a gray plastic container. I heard it clanging together as she pulled out a fork, a knife, and a spoon. She clumped them together in one hand and grabbed a menu out of another cubby attached to the wall next to the counter.

She walked toward me, menu in one hand and silverware in another. Halfway to me, she noticed I already had a menu, and she dropped the one she had grabbed on an empty table.

Gerry stopped in front of me, and said, "Hi, hon. Do you need more time to look at the menu?"

She leaned across the tabletop, grabbed a napkin hanging out of napkin holder, and jerked it out. She laid it out on the surface of the table like a picnic blanket. Then she positioned the silverware out on top neatly in front of me.

I said, "Hi, Gerry. Voss sent me."

"Oh, good. Will she be joining you?"

"Maybe. But maybe not."

"Want to order something?"

"Coffee," I said.

"Any food?"

"Not now. Just coffee and I need a favor. It's a big one."

"What's that?"

"I need to borrow your cell phone. I promise to give it right back."

She said nothing.

I said, "I'll tip extra for it. Of course."

"Did you lose yours, sweetie?"

"I don't have one."

She paused and thought it over. People were funny about their cell phones, which I completely understood. Cell phones were full of all kinds of personal information including passwords and contacts and emails and debit and credit card numbers. Nowadays, a person's cell phone was like a diary, bank account, and private photo album all wrapped up in one. It's a personal vault of information that people voluntarily carried around with them. Which I didn't understand because phones are linked to the internet. These days, a bored fourteen-year-old can figure out how to hack someone's cell phone.

Giving it to a friend to borrow required a certain level of trust established. Giving it to a complete stranger was normally out of the question. You wouldn't give your diary to a stranger or your bank account information or your pin numbers. Some people had other private things to worry about. Some people had naked selfies to worry about.

I said, "Don't worry. I'll give it right back. I promise. You can hold my ID if you like."

Gerry smiled slowly, and said, "No, that won't be necessary. If Chief Voss sent you, then you're vouched for."

She reached into her pocket and pulled out an older generation iPhone, which I was sure was the iPhone 4 because it had that steel and glass look, which I remembered from that design and model. I had used them before.

I reached my hand out, open-palmed. Gerry dropped the phone into it like a set of car keys from a reluctant drunk passing off her keys to a designated driver.

I said, "Thank you. I'll give it right back."

"Just don't make any international calls. AT&T charges an arm and a leg for it."

"I only need the internet. I won't be making any out-of-country calls. I promise."

She smiled and turned and with her eyes peering over her shoulder, she said, "Be right back." And she walked away from the table.

I turned to the cell phone and realized I had forgotten to ask for her passcode, but then, I swiped the unlock button and saw it didn't have a passcode, which was a massive security failure on Gerry's part. Then again, we're not talking about a Pentagon staffer's mobile device.

The screen unlocked and went to the home screen. Her iPhone was rather empty compared to most I had seen in the past. There were your basic apps and nothing else, no excess and no folders and only the one page. There was no reason for an extra page because there were no spillover apps.

Her wallpaper was a photo of her and a young girl, maybe a daughter or a granddaughter. There was large age gap between them. The girl was young, maybe five or six. Given this, I presumed it was a granddaughter.

I pressed the *Safari* icon and the internet browser opened.

I clicked on the search box and typed my first question, which was where the FBI field office in New Mexico was. Albuquerque was the location that I assumed, but I was wrong. The nearest was in Denver. In fact, the Denver office served every county in New Mexico and Wyoming.

*What were the odds that an FBI agent from the field office in Denver would stop in Angel Rock at the same time Voss and I found two dead crooked cops?* The obvious answer was not good odds at all.

The logical conclusion was that FBI Agent Oliver was here for a reason, and that reason was related to the two dead cops. Had to be.

I clicked on the screen's back button and returned to the *Google* search page and typed in my next question, which was about Saunt.

I typed in *Ryan Miles Saunt,* and I got one exact hit and a bunch of generic ones. The first one was a Facebook page, but it wasn't for Saunt, it was for a business called Skylark Company.

I clicked the link and followed it to a Facebook page. It looked like some kind of computer business or online business or software company. The page had about two thousand likes and dozens of photos. I clicked on the photos and saw several pictures of Saunt, smiling and hugging different people. The guy seemed cheery and friendly and well-liked. There were several more pictures of Saunt shaking hands with other business-looking associates.

There were photos of company picnics and relay races and family days and baseball games. The company employees appeared to be a happy bunch, like one big corporate family. I ignored the rest of the photos and returned to the main page.

I clicked on the *about* page and read up on Skylark.

Skylark was a business owned by Ryan Miles Saunt and founded back in 1995. It started as a software development company and prospered through the internet bubble, and then had some rough patches in the 2000s, but remained open and stable.

I couldn't find any information on what exactly they had designed, but it must've been something lucrative, because Skylark had around a hundred employees.

The main headquarters was a building they moved into back in ninety-five, and where they remained today. It was in a city called Pablo, New Mexico. It was about two hundred miles southwest of Angel Rock. It wasn't as big as Albuquerque, but was an actual dot on a map, whereas Angel Rock was not.

I looked down the page and found a link to Skylark's main page. I clicked on it and waited for it to load. Just then, Gerry returned with a white mug on a white saucer, which was a little fancy for me. I didn't complain because the coffee was hot and black.

She set the saucer and coffee down on the table. The black liquid inside rippled around by the effect, but not a drop spilled out—a true professional. Gerry asked, "Do you still need my phone, hon?"

I smiled, and said, "Just a little longer, ma'am. I'm just looking up something. I appreciate it."

"Is it for like a school project? No offense, but you look a little old for school."

"No. Nothing like that. I'm helping Voss with a case."

"Okay. Take your time. Just call me if it rings. I'll come back in a bit to get it."

I nodded.

She remained where she was, and then she asked, "How about some food, hon?"

"Not for me, ma'am."

But then, as if on cue, a delicious smell wafted at me from the kitchen and my stomach growled. The smell was faint at first, but became luring, too luring to disregard. I realized I had eaten little since earlier in the day and I was starving. The smell of fresh French fries and greasy burgers on the grill in the back overwhelmed me. So I said, "On second thought, let me get something."

"Oh, great." Gerry said. She paused and dug a blue ink pen and a yellow receipt pad out of her apron, and she asked, "What're you having?"

"You got a cheeseburger plate?"

"The best around!"

"It got a side of fries?"

"This close to Texas? You better believe it."

I said, "Sounds good."

She wrote my order down along with the prices for each item. She asked, "What kind of cheese?"

"Cheddar."

"Want all the fixin's?"

"Yes, ma'am."

She nodded and scooped the menu up from the table and turned and walked back to the main counter.

I looked back down at Gerry's phone screen, expecting to see the website for Skylark. But there was no page. Instead, I stared at one of those broken-link page warnings. The page I searched for was closed.

I clicked the back button, and the screen refreshed back to the Facebook page for the business. I scrolled down the page to view the comments. The recent ones were all negative. Some followers were so mad they used a lot of colorful swear words in their commentary. I read the first couple and skimmed several others. They were all basically the same. Several were addressed to Saunt, personally, like they were left so angry they took it out on him.

The comments ranged from nasty remarks to straight questions, but they all wanted to know why Saunt had closed the company. Most of the commenters were disgruntled ex-employees. There was mention of bounced paychecks.

I cut and pasted the Skylark name into a new Google search page and clicked enter on the iPhone's tiny digital keypad. The results came back with some online news articles from a newspaper and from television news, both local to Pablo.

I clicked on the newspaper's link and skimmed the page. It was all about the sudden closing of Skylark, which had employed people and contributed to the local economy. The article only speculated about why Skylark's founder and CEO closed the doors so abruptly, but the rumor was that he had gone completely broke in the last two months. The reason was unknown.

Saunt stopped coming to work and withdrew all the money out of his accounts and the company's commercial accounts. Then he vanished. The news article said he had broken no laws by doing so and that there wasn't any known investigation into his disappearance. Still, it was unusual that Saunt drained his banks accounts and left his company and employees high and dry. Plus, he abandoned his house in Pablo. There was no public record of him selling either his business or his home. Currently, he still owned both.

I read a little farther and found he had no wife, no son, but there was a daughter. Her name was Janey Saunt. Age unknown. However, she must've been in high school because the article said the local school had no record of Saunt pulling her out of school.

*His daughter*, I thought.

I went back to Skylark's Facebook page and looked at the company pictures again. I scanned the family events, including the picnic and relay races, like I had done on Voss's memory wall in her office.

I didn't have to look too hard or too far to find a photo of Saunt and his daughter, Janey.

There she was, Janey Saunt, smiling, happy, and alive.

She was the same girl from the photo on the memory card in the envelope with the bloody fingerprint, the living one. She was the girl from the photo who looked terrified for her life. She was Saunt's teenage daughter—Janey.

# CHAPTER 15

**Q**uestions. My mind raced with them. They swarmed my brain like puzzle pieces.

*Was Janey abducted? Did the two dead cops do it? Were they holding her for ransom? Is that why Saunt murdered them? Did they tell him something he didn't want to hear? Had they already killed her?*

The puzzle pieces were all mixed up in a chaotic pile in my head, but they were there. Together, they would form a picture—an answer. But what?

Gerry returned with my cheeseburger and fries, which smelled just as good as they did when they were cooking back in the kitchen. Only now, it meant less, because I thought of Janey. The black eye. The basement. The farmer's sink. The bloody fingerprint.

*Don't run to your death—eat first.* A personal motto with a twist on a SEAL one.

Gerry set the plate down in front of me. Steam rose from the fries. She said, "Don't you like the coffee?"

She asked because I hadn't taken a sip yet, which was out of character for me.

"I'm sure it's good. Everything looks good. But I'm gonna need to ask for the check. I have to eat and run."

"Okay, hon," Gerry said, then turned and stepped away to add up the total charges. She returned to the counter, fished out her pen and pad again, and started calculating my order.

I stared at her phone and wondered if I should call Voss straight away with the information I found. I didn't have her cell number, but I could call the switchboard and wait until I was patched through to her. But then, I thought about the two dead cops and the FBI agent who had been here. The probability that he was here, and it wasn't related to Aragon and Broome seemed highly unlikely. It gave me pause. *Could we trust this Oliver?* I wasn't sure, so I kept it to myself for now. I didn't want to call Voss in front of him and give anything away, not till I could verify Oliver was one of the good guys. We had two very horrible cops so far. What's one FBI agent thrown into the mix?

I finished using Gerry's phone. So I set it down and pushed it across the tabletop, and left it near the edge for her to pick up.

I grabbed two larger fries and shoved them into my mouth. They were salted to perfection but piping hot. I had to do the leaving-my-mouth-open thing and blow air out at the same time. I grabbed the coffee and took a drink. It was good, not the best coffee ever, not as good as Voss had advertised, but it was far from the worst I ever had. It was lukewarm now because I had let it sit there too long, which was good because the fries were too hot. The lukewarm coffee counteracted the heat from the fries. And the caffeine from the coffee overrode everything else to me.

I scarfed the cheeseburger down and ate most of the fries, then drained the coffee. I did it all fast. In the service, you learn to eat fast enough to win the gold in the Olympic Food Eating Race—if there was such a thing. After, I took a wad of cash out of my pocket and paid the check. I left a five-dollar tip for the meal and service, and an extra twenty-dollar bill for the use of Gerry's phone.

I didn't wait for her to come by for change. I got up and headed out the door and back to the Silverado. I wanted to find Voss and check on her FBI contact. Also, to tell her about what I had found, but I didn't know where she was. So I went back to the scene of the crime to take another look. I wanted to see if we overlooked anything. Earlier, when we were searching, we didn't know about the missing girl. Maybe there was more at the crime scene.

I clicked the unlock button on the Silverado's key fob and got in and started up the engine. I backed out of the space, turned back to the road, and drove out to the main road and turned. I drove through the town, past a church, a few strip malls, and the hospital, where Saunt was fighting for his life.

I passed the police station. There was a police car in the parking lot. It could've been Voss. So I slowed and made a U-turn and looped back through the lot and stopped near the parked cruiser. I left the engine running and inspected the parked police cruiser. Instantly, I knew it wasn't Voss's. Her car read: *Chief of Police* on both doors. This one didn't. It only read: *Angel Rock Police Department*. Maybe it was Howard's car, which meant that there was news about Saunt. I figured the news wouldn't be good, not if he left his post at the hospital. It suggested that Saunt lost his battle and his life. I hoped not. But I needed to find out. So I left the truck parked near the front this time, switched it off, pocketed the keys, and entered the police station. I nodded at Franklin, who didn't question my returning or being alone, and this time I didn't set off the metal detectors because I passed the keys around the detector on a small tray.

Franklin let me go through without question. I made it to the police station part of the complex, but this time I didn't make it past the front desk because seated at the desk was a police officer I didn't know. He was a black guy, young, maybe thirty. He was built like a streetlight with a thick upper frame, and long skinny legs poking out from under the desk. He was seated, but appeared tall, even seated.

I walked up to the desk and nodded a friendly *hello* at him. He stayed seated. A pleasant, but suspicious smile stretched across his face. He said, "Hello. Can I help you?"

I said, "Yes. You can."

"What can I do for you?"

"Has Voss checked in with you?"

His eyes narrowed when I said *Voss*, which I imagined was a natural, chary reaction since he had no idea who I was, and Voss was his commanding officer. He said, "She hasn't been around for a while. What's this about?"

I didn't want to step on any toes, especially those belonging to an armed cop shaped like a streetlight. Didn't want to tell him I was helping her with her current investigation, not me, a nobody civilian he was seeing for the first time. So I said, "We're friends."

Which turned out to be the wrong word to use because his expression turned from friendly to one of utter disbelief and apprehension. He asked, "How's that?"

"It's not important. I just need to know if you've heard from her?"

The guy thought for a moment and half-shrugged, and said, "No. She could be anywhere. Need me to call her?"

"That's unnecessary. She's meeting with the FBI right now."

"How do you know that?"

"Like I said, we're friends."

The desk guy started to say something else, but I didn't want to waste any more time. So I said, "I need you to get a message to her. It's important."

"Not important enough to wait?"

To which, I didn't respond. Instead, I paused a beat, like I was thinking. I couldn't bring up the dead cops in the desert because I didn't know what he knew or how he'd react if I told him I knew. But I needed to relay the message to her. I figured the best course of action was to just leave a vague message and not explain it. I said, "Tell her that Widow was here."

He listened.

I said, "Tell her that the girl's name is Janey Saunt. Tell her she's Saunt's daughter. Tell Voss that I'm going back out there. And that she needs to meet me out there as soon as possible."

The guy said, "She has your phone number, right? Since you guys are such good friends."

"I don't have a phone. Or I would've called her myself. Don't you think?"

The guy said nothing to that. He just kind of sneered, and said, "I'll text her now. Let's see if she'll respond."

"Okay."

He slid his chair back and stood up slowly, like it was an act of congress to do so. There was something wobbly about him. He got all the way up on both feet and moved away from the chair. There was a slumpy dent in the leather, like he sat there all day, every day. The guy half limped away from his desk and came around to the front. He leaned back and sat on the top of the desk and dug a phone out of his front pocket. He stared at the screen and swiped and pressed buttons. After he got where he wanted to go, he turned the phone sideways and used his thumbs to type. He was pretty fast with it.

The guy read the text out loud as he typed, as if he was my secretary and I was dictating to him, with a hint of snarkiness. I understood why this guy was a desk guy and not out in the field. He made Officer Howard look like a rockstar cop. He said, "Chief. Guy here says he knows u? Widow."

He stopped and stared at the screen. I didn't know if he was waiting for a reply or not. Nothing came, and he started typing again, but then, he paused and read to himself. Then he read to me. He said, "I'll be damned. You're right. She says she's with the FBI now."

"Tell her the rest. Tell her the girl's name is Janey Saunt."

He typed again and read out loud again. He said, "Widow said: girl is Saunt's daughter—Janey." He stopped and waited and read her response to me. He said, "She replied with a question mark. Hold on. She's typing."

I stayed quiet and peered at the desk guy's nameplate. It read: *Kemp*.

Officer Kemp said, "She says *OK* in big capital letters, which means she's impressed with this information. I know. She texts me most of the time."

"Tell her to meet me out there. Tell her ASAP," I repeated.

The guy took to typing it out on his phone and dictating it all to me again. He said, "Widow says to meet him out there ASAP."

He paused and waited for a second, and then, his eyes shot open in disbelief like he had read the text wrong. He looked up at me, and said, "She says to give you a radio."

I stayed quiet for a long moment, like I was waiting for the radio, but really, I was thinking about something else. I said, "Ask her if I can have a gun. Maybe you could deputize me. Temporarily."

Kemp looked at me and his face resonated a resounding *NO WAY!* But he shrugged and typed my request. He said, "Widow wants gun."

No response. So we waited.

We waited over a minute, which was a little uncomfortable because Kemp had no idea who I was. He was operating on blind trust. And so was Voss really, but he didn't need to know that.

"She's typing," Kemp said.

I inched closer to him and glanced down at the screen and read it to myself. It was upside down, but her response was unmistakable. Voss typed: *no.* I glanced down at the screen and read it. She hadn't capitalized the negative response or used an exclamation mark at the end. It was an unsure negative. In the end, I accepted it. I understood she hadn't wanted to give me a weapon. A weapon would've indicated that she was accepting full responsibility for my actions, and, even though she trusted me, she didn't trust me that much. Not yet.

Kemp said, "No."

I stayed quiet, and we stood there in silence for a moment.

Kemp said, "She hasn't said anything else. Want me to ask her anything?"

"No," I said. I didn't want to involve him any more than I already had. Voss could tell him and her other guys if she chose to. It was her department, not mine.

"Alright," Kemp said, and slipped his phone back into his pocket. He slid off the desk and stood up straight. He was tall, nearly as tall as me. He turned and limped back toward the bullpen. The limp made me wonder if that's why he was the desk guy. He had a bad limp in his right knee.

He stopped, glanced back at me, and said, "Well, come on."

I followed him, and asked, "None of my business, but out of curiosity, why the limp?"

"It's usually not this bad. I was shot in the line of duty. It was years ago. I'm used to it now. The limp is worse on some days than others. I get arthritis from it."

I stayed quiet.

He said, "It really acts up when we get weather."

"Skies look pretty clear out there tonight."

Kemp kept walking. He led me past empty desks and past Voss's office, back to a gray door in the far back of the floor. He slipped a key out of the same pocket with the phone in it and into the doorknob and unlocked it. He pulled the door open. It slid open with no creaks or other sounds. Kemp leaned into the darkness and reached into the room and fumbled on the wall until he found a light switch. He flipped it. Tube lights on the ceiling above powered slowly like they were waking up.

The room was the police storage space. The inside was about ten-by-ten feet. On one wall was a cage that protruded out about two feet. It was locked with a padlock. Inside were police-issued SWAT gear and firearms. I saw four Heckler and Koch MP5s and five Glocks of different variants. Next to the MP5s were seven Remington Model 870s. The same shotgun that was still locked in place in the front of the dead cops' police car. It was a common shotgun among police units all over the country.

On the other wall, which was where Kemp led me, was a handful of police tactical vests and Kevlar vests, and flash-lights and radios stacked neatly in an electrical recharging tray.

Kemp reached over and snatched one of the radios out of the recharger and twisted the knob at the top until it switched on. Static kicked up over the air and we listened. He put his ear close and switched channels, until he came across the channel he was looking for.

"This one works good. Full battery," he said, and handed it to me. He added, "Keep it on this channel. It's the channel we use for unofficial department chatter. That's where she'll try to contact you. The next channel to the right is the depart-ment's standard channel in case you need it."

I nodded and thanked him.

Kemp said, "I'm not sure what's going on, but if Voss is giving you a radio, then it must be important. I'm no idiot. I'm thinking whatever it is, it must be the reason she sent me on that long dinner break."

I stayed quiet.

He said, "And now she's with the FBI. Must be hush-hush. You some kind of government consultant or secret agent or something?"

"I'm just a guy."

Kemp nodded and said nothing. He handed the radio to me. We both turned and walked out. I went first. Kemp stopped and switched off the light and closed and locked the door.

I didn't wait for him. I walked back through the bullpen and glanced over at her office on my way out. I saw the pictures on the wall through the window, the framed letters, the accolades, and the folded flag.

*How do you know me?* I thought again.

I left the police station, passed Franklin, nodded goodbye, and got into the Silverado and headed out of the parking lot.

# CHAPTER 16

The Silverado drove fine. It was a good truck, older model, but there was a lot of money spent in it and probably under the hood too. I took it out of town and down the long empty stretch of highway, until I reached the crime scene. I slowed the truck and pulled up close to the highway shoulder, looking for Voss's cruiser's tire tracks, which I found. I followed the tracks off the highway and down the track to the dead cops and the cruiser. I came as close as I dared and parked. It was pretty much exactly over the top of where Voss had parked earlier. I left the headlights on to provide light. No reason to shut the engine off. The gas tank was good, and it wasn't my dime, anyway. I clicked a lever on the steering wheel and the high beams shone across everything. I grabbed the radio out of the cup holder, jumped out of the truck, and shut the driver's door and walked out in front of the light beams.

I should've requested a flashlight, but I didn't.

I clipped the radio onto my front pocket and surveyed the headlights' reach. They illuminated the dead cops, their car, the tracks in front of the car, and little else, but that was all I would need to see. I walked over to the dead cops and surveyed everything again.

Nothing changed from earlier. I saw nothing new.

I closed my eyes and listened. Sometimes it was good to look at things with fresh eyes. I reimagined the whole scene again. Saunt. The cops. The meeting place. The circle. The bad news. Aragon and Broome demanded more money. Saunt had already paid them, probably several large sums. They still demanded more. He told them it was impossible. So they told him Janey was dead. Then they returned to their car, probably relishing their lie. Saunt stood there frozen for a moment. He was scared, infuriated, and then, filled with blinding rage. So he retreated to the Silverado, thinking it was over. He grabbed the Glock and the extra magazine and hopped out of his truck. He fast-walked back to Aragon and Broome. I pictured them watching him and laughing. He raised his gun, probably shut his eyes, and pulled, not squeezed, the trigger. Bullets sprayed erratically, but he was close enough to them that even a child could hit plenty with twenty-six shots.

I opened my eyes. And felt like I had a good image of the shooting. It didn't help me find Janey. It didn't tell me if she was alive or dead. But it gave me a good sense of what happened.

Suddenly, my radio crackled, and I heard Voss's voice, staticky, call me over the airwaves. She asked, "Widow?"

I snatched the radio off my pocket and pressed the *talk* button. I said, "It's me. Go ahead."

"Are you out on the plains?"

"Yeah. Are you alone?"

She said, "No. I'm with Oliver. You were right. Janey is fifteen years old. She's Saunt's daughter. Mother is dead. There's no stepmom or wife."

"I know. I looked him up on the internet."

"Then you know about Skylark, his business?"

"First Janey vanished. Teachers, the school, her friends, no one knows where she is."

"Right. Do you know what happened?"

I said, "Ryan Saunt withdrew large amounts of cash out of his personal accounts. After he ran through that, he took it out of his business accounts—retained earnings, tax accounts, payrolls, everything. Over the course of the last two months, his business went broke and closed its doors. His employees, friends, and family have no idea where he went or why."

"That's right. It's strange."

"It gets worse."

Voss asked, "Tell me."

"Are you alone?"

"It's okay. Go ahead."

"Aragon and Broome abducted Janey Saunt. Held her for ransom. Sent Saunt the photo of the dead girl. They told him that if he didn't want the same to happen to his daughter, then he better come to Angel Rock with a bag full of cash. Which he did. And then, it wasn't enough. So he had to get more and more. I'm sure if you check with his accountant or lawyer, you'll find he took everything out in clumps because they kept changing the amount. They wanted more and more."

Voss said, "That's what we're thinking as well. They kidnapped her."

"They kidnapped her. Beat her. Abused her. Sent him pictures of her and met him way out here. They wanted money. Simple. At least, on the surface."

"Janey went missing two months ago. They held her hostage for two months?"

"I don't think this was a normal, run-of-the-mill kidnapping."

The radio crackled, echoing through the darkness.

Voss said, "How's that?"

"I don't think they did a lot of research on him. I think he was targeted out of desperation," I said, and released the *talk* button.

Voss said nothing.

I squeezed it again, and said, "Here's what I see. Two state cops. Not brilliant guys, but dangerous. Sick. Twisted. We saw the other dead girl. So we can assume they've done this before. Maybe a few times. Maybe several times. But this time they didn't just want one ransom. They wanted installments. That's why they met him more than once. That's why it went on for several weeks. There's no money in their car and no money in his truck and no money in his motel room. Which suggests they met him before. Think about it. They asked for a ransom. He paid it. So they thought they could squeeze him for more. Why not? Maybe they were gonna squeeze him dry."

Voss said, "How much did they get?"

"I don't know. Depends on how much he had. We don't know how many payments he'd made. Which is why he brought the gun with him this time. Which is why they were so careless around him. They've met with him several times before. And this time they got lazy, complacent with him. They trusted him to be a pushover."

Voss said, "That makes sense."

I paused a beat—thought I heard a noise off in the distance. I looked and saw nothing. But I stayed still and watched. There was nothing.

"Widow?"

I came back on the radio, and said, "They asked for more money. And they kept pushing him for more after that. That's why he cleaned out his company. He was desperate. They kept on pushing him, threatening him. *We'll kill her*, they told him. They gave him another week, and then another, and so on. You said these guys had been coming through Angel Rock a lot. Therefore, all of their meetings were probably out here. It's secluded, isolated. It's perfect. Saunt got a room and stayed in Angel Rock, near their first two meetings. He got desperate. He brought his gun. At first, he thought he could reason with them. He told them he was out of money, and they told him she was as good as dead."

Voss said nothing.

I took a breath, and said, "Maybe he questioned she was even still alive. So they gave him the envelope with the bloody fingerprint. But that wasn't good enough for them. They wanted him to see. So they included the memory card with the dead girl and Janey. To remind him."

I heard the same noise again and clicked off the *talk* button. Something fast moved off in the distance. I couldn't tell what it was. I paused and listened for a long second, but it was gone. There was nothing.

I got back on the radio, and said, "He told them he was out of money. They showed him the camera with the dead girl and pictures of his daughter. They told him she had little time left. They told him the last girl's family didn't pay and look what happened to her. Like a threat. Only sadistic because they had the proof. They gave him one last chance to come up with the money. They didn't know he was completely broke. They'd gotten all of it. He kept it from them, which was smart on his part because they would've shot him dead right there. They wanted to give him the proper incentive, so they gave him the camera, but it was dying so they gave him the power cord."

Voss said, "You're right. Gotta be."

I asked, "Are you okay?"

"Yeah. Don't worry. We can trust him. Really."

I asked, "Can he get us more guys out here?"

"Not tonight. But first thing in the morning."

"Janey might not have till morning. We got no idea who else may be involved."

Voss said, "For now, we're on our own."

"Then you'd both better get over here. We gotta start searching for her."

"Do you think she's still alive?"

"We have to assume so."

"We're on our way. Just stay put," Voss said, and clicked off the radio. Static fell over it, and she was gone. I clipped the radio back to my pocket.

The night fell silent around me. I heard the noise again, but this time I knew why I couldn't figure out its origin. It was because there were two different noises, behaving in unison.

The first was a loud roll of thunder off in the distance, above the low hills and mountains. It rumbled soft and looming. There was no sign of rain or lightning. Not yet. But it was coming. Certainly.

The desk guy back at the station, Kemp, had said his bum leg always acted up whenever there was *weather*. So he would know. I doubted he was wrong too much about it.

The second noise came from behind me. I heard it again. It came from the police cruiser. I started walking back toward it. I stepped close enough to hear the faint sounds of a song. I thought it was the car radio, which was impossible because it would've been playing earlier when Voss and I were here. Then I realized it was a cell phone ringing, with a personalized ringtone. It played a familiar tune. It was an Aerosmith song: "Livin' on the Edge". Which was weird because they also had another song called "Janie's Got a Gun". And we were searching for Janey Saunt.

*Janey. What did her daddy do?* I thought.

The Aerosmith tune buzzed inside the cop car, inside one of the dead cop's jacket pockets.

# CHAPTER 17

angled myself down and around the driver's side door and opened it and leaned in. Using the leftover gloves Voss gave me, I reached into the dead cop's pocket and found his phone. I pulled it out slowly.

I stared at the phone's screen. It read: *Incoming Call.* The caller's name was in the phone's registry. Broome had him labeled as first name *Mister* and last name *Man.*

*Mister Man?* I thought. *Whatever.*

Just like Gerry's phone—the waitress—there was no unlock code on Broome's phone. Guess these cops had no reason to lock their phones, either. They probably left them locked up when they weren't *on duty.* Why would they lock them? They felt safe because they were armed with badges and guns.

I stared at the screen. It rang again. I swiped at the screen to answer the call. I tried my best to muffle my voice, which really wouldn't have mattered since I had no idea what these guys sounded like in life.

"Yeah?" I asked, quick, like a fast greeting from someone who was too busy to be answering the phone but had to take the call.

The voice on the other line said, "Broome? Where the hell are you? I've been calling you guys. Neither of you have answered. What's going on?"

I waited. I wanted to say as little as possible.

"Broome? I asked you a question," Mister Man repeated. He spoke with command, like he was a Master Chief, and I was a nobody sailor. He spoke like he outranked me, like he accepted nothing less than total obedience.

"Angel Rock," I said.

"Still? Do you have the money?"

"No."

Mister Man asked, "Why? Didn't he have it?"

I stayed quiet.

He said, "I told you he didn't have any more. I knew he was tapped out."

I stayed quiet.

He said, "Did you take care of it? What did you do with the bodies?"

"Not yet," I said muffled.

Silence. Mister Man said nothing for a moment, like he was trying to figure out if he was talking to someone else. He was becoming suspicious. He said, "I'm having a hard time hearing you."

I paused a beat. Then I said, "Bad reception."

"Okay. Well, listen. If he don't got it, kill him. And get the hell back here. The local cop woman is already suspicious. She called about the two of you. She's been snooping around the department servers online."

I said, "Don't worry."

But I got too callous, too stupid, or maybe I just didn't care anymore, because he had given me something he hadn't intended to.

Mister Man paused. He was suspicious. He asked, "Broome?"

"Yeah. I'm here."

Silence fell over the phone again. Another pause passed between us. Mister Man's voice came back on. I listened hard, tried to pick up any background noise, trying to hear anything else that might give me more information about him. But there was nothing.

"You're not Broome," he said.

"No. I'm not."

"Who are you?"

"I'm just a guy. A nobody."

"Who is this? Where are my guys?"

"Maybe I'm a cop."

"Bullshit. The cop in Angel Rock is a woman."

*He knew about Voss. He probably knew about the whole department.*

I said, "I'm the new guy."

"There is no new guy."

*He knew the Angel Rock Police Department's lineup enough to know I was lying.*

He asked, "Where is Broome?"

There was no sense in lying to him, I figured. Not anymore. I said, "Broome's dead."

Mister Man paused a long beat, and then, he asked, "What about Aragon? Is he dead too?"

"As a doornail."

Mister Man's voice dropped to a deeper pitch as if he was trying to make himself sound intimidating. He asked, "Did you kill them?"

"No. I didn't kill them."

"Did Saunt kill them?"

"I got no idea who that is," I lied.

"What happened?"

"Someone shot them to bits. It wasn't me. I just found them."

He asked, "Who are you?"

I stayed quiet.

"Who are you? Tell me!" he repeated.

"It doesn't matter who I am. All that matters is what I'm gonna do."

"What're you gonna do? Call the cops? I've got a surprise for you then."

"What's that?"

"Let's just say that they won't help you."

I said, "What makes you say that?"

He said nothing.

"Don't worry. I'm not gonna call the cops. Why would I do that? I'm going to take my newfound treasure and go to

Vegas. Have the time of my life," I lied.

Silence. Then Mister Man asked, "What treasure?"

I paused for dramatic effect, and said, "The bag full of cash."

He fell silent—and not for dramatic effect. It was real. He didn't know where the money was. *Broome and Aragon must've been stashing it somewhere and didn't tell him.*

Mister Man asked, "You got the money?"

"Yeah. Bag full of it. I don't know how much. You know? I just found it. I haven't had time to count it."

"Hold on," he said. Then he paused and repeated, "Hold on. We can cut a deal."

"I'm not interested in a deal. I got the money. Any deal you'll want to cut requires me to turn it over, right? And for what? A percentage? A finder's fee? Why take a slice when I can have it all?"

Silence. Mister Man was thinking.

I said, "Plus, I got two dead cops here. And they were up to no good. That's obvious. A blind man would see that. I don't know who you are, but I'm sure if I ever get caught, this information will be interesting to the FBI. So I think I'm better off holding on to it. You know? Like an insurance policy."

I stopped talking and looked around and listened. There was nothing but the night, the clouds, the moon, more buffalo roaming in the distance, and the silence. I listened closely to the phone line, still no clues as to his location. No bustling tables or clanking silverware telling me he was in a restaurant. No hissing air noise from an open car window. No breeze like he was standing outside. Nothing.

Above me, thunder rumbled and rolled over the plains. The wind turbine swung its giant blades, whooshing in circles. I listened for the thunder or the turbines to resonate on his end of the line in case he was nearby. But I heard nothing. No rumble. No echo. No sound at all. Which meant nothing. The guy could've been indoors.

I said, "Gotta go now. Thanks for the cash."

"Wait. Wait."

I hung up the phone, kept it in my hand, and settled my arm down to my side. I stepped away from the driver's side door and the phone started ringing again. I ignored it and shut the door and went to the rear of the car. I leaned against it and waited.

It stopped ringing, must've gone to voicemail. Several seconds later, it started ringing again. "Livin' on the Edge" rang out across the silence.

I clicked the *talk* button and answered it. I said, "Hello?"

Mister Man's voice came over the line, and he said, "Don't hang up. Please."

I stayed quiet.

He spoke like he was negotiating terms. He said, "Listen. I'm a powerful guy. Why don't you keep the money? Like a reward."

"I plan to."

"We can still make a deal. I can help you."

"I'm listening."

Mister Man said, "I don't even care about the money. I just need to know more details about what happened to my guys."

"Why should I tell you? What's in it for me?"

"There's more money."

"This is plenty of money."

"But we can give you more."

"I don't need more."

He said, "There're more cops involved in this situation. Cops that I can control. We could be strong allies for you. Perhaps we can help each other. There could be more money in it for you down the line. Think about it. What're you going to do with it? Spend it? You'll need more. There could be an endless stream of income in it for you."

I smiled, and said, "More? Keep talking."

"You got a criminal record?"

"I might."

"We can help you. We can make that disappear."

"I'm nobody. A drifter. I don't need your help. Ain't nobody going to find me unless I want them to."

He said, "Okay."

I waited, let him sweat a little, and then, I asked, "How much more money are we talking?"

"Double what's there."

"Double?"

I sensed Mister Man smiling. He thought I was on the hook. He said, "To start. We could do a long-term thing. Like a salary for a position in our organization. Only your job would be to keep what you know to yourself. Maybe you could do things for us, from time to time."

I stayed quiet, made it seem like I was considering his offer.

He spoke, trying to add to the pot. He said, "Double's a lot more than just what you got. Imagine what you can do with double. You could visit Vegas a lot more often."

"Okay. What do I have to do?"

"Tell me what's going on."

I smiled. He bought it. "I told you. I'm a passerby. And I was passing through the town when I discovered two dead cops out in the middle of nowhere."

He said, "Outside of Angel Rock?"

"That's right."

*He knew where. Broome and Aragon must've informed him beforehand.*

He asked, "What else? Give me details?"

"There's not much to tell. I found a couple of dead cops. A discreet location. And a bag full of money."

Mister Man said, "That's it?"

"Yep."

"There's not another guy?"

*He was asking about Saunt. Maybe he wants to know what Saunt knows.* I said, "Yeah. Sorry. There's a third guy. He's dead too, though. That's where I got the money from."

"Tell me. How did it go down?"

This was a smart move because he was asking me to give him a shot-by-shot play. Part of it could serve as a test to see if I was FBI or some other law enforcement agent. A federal agent would've known how it went down and been able to describe it with crime scene investigation vernacular. It would've been second nature, an unbreakable habit, an occupational hazard.

I'd experienced it before in the field when I used to go under-cover. Really good marks would test me. They'd casually bring up keywords, ask questions. They'd tried to see if I'd say something, use a term, that an untrained person wouldn't know. So I said, "Looks like a big shoot-out, but what do I know? I'm not a cop."

"So everyone's dead? They shot each other?"

"That's what I said. Looks like someone started shooting, and they all got each other. Just like that. There's blood and bullet shells everywhere. Even some of the cash was blowing around in the wind. I had a helluva time scooping it all up."

Silence fell over the phone again, and then, he asked, "What about cops? Any local ones on the scene?"

"If there were cops here, then I wouldn't be here with the cash. I woulda split already."

"Right."

I said, "There's a local police department here, but I doubt they know anything. If they did, they'd be here already instead of me, like I said. This is all off an abandoned high-way. I saw no flashing lights or heard any sirens. Not so far. I've not even seen a single car drive through."

"Right. Okay."

"How do I get the money? The *double* part, you promised?"

"You can come to us."

I said, "No way! I don't trust you. I was born in the middle of the night, but it wasn't last night."

"Clearly. I see you're smart. So what do you suggest?"

I paused and looked around. I thought for a moment. This location was too out in the open. They'd see me from a mile off. Maybe not in the dark, but they might have night vision technology for all I knew. I needed someplace less known to them, less out in the open. So I said, "You come to me."

Mister Man said, "Okay. We need to clean this up anyway, before the local cops get involved. Consider us on our way."

*Us. How many are there?*

Mister Man asked, "Where do you want to meet?"

I didn't answer that. Instead, I asked, "When will you get here?"

"Soon. Keep this phone on you. I'll call you when we get there."

"Okay."

"Where do we meet you?" he repeated.

"I'll tell you when you get here."

"Okay. What do I call you?"

"Call me Widow," I said. I didn't see any reason to give him a fake name. I wouldn't show up on any search he did. Nothing that I wanted to hide would show up, anyway. At worst, he'd confirm that I'm a drifter, like I claimed to be. That would just put him at ease.

I needed to find Janey; that was my top priority. I didn't know if this guy knew where she was, but he sounded like the head of the snake. No question. If he didn't know exactly where she was, he'd have an idea.

I asked, "What exactly went on here?"

"What do you mean?"

*Stupid, Widow*, I thought. Being too curious could give me away. I said, "Just curious. This looked like a drop, but the other dead guy, you gotta see him. He looks like some kind of accountant."

"Don't worry about it. I'll see you soon," he said, and clicked off the call. The line went dead. I played around with Broome's phone for a moment, trying to see if I could find any clues, but I discovered I was wrong about it being unlocked. It must've had a feature to let a person answer an incoming call without unlocking it. But that was it. All his folders were locked, and only unlocked by a passcode that I wouldn't get. Not off a dead man.

So I slipped the phone in my pocket, and pulled the gloves off, balled them up and put them in the same pocket. I figured it didn't really matter if I got my prints on the phone anymore.

I looked back at the scene one last time. More thunder rolled across the sky, echoing over the rolling plains and the giant wind turbines. The thunder rumble grew louder and louder. And more consistent, like contractions of a mother in labor, getting closer together.

Seconds later, the rain started. It hammered down in the distance and the thunder rumbled again, until it turned to roaring. Giant bolts of white lightning spider-webbed across the clouds' underbelly.

It was only a matter of seconds until the rain came down on top of me. Now, fingerprints really didn't matter. The whole crime scene was about to be drenched. All the fingerprints, DNA, and tracks were going to get washed away.

I unclipped the radio, reversed it, and stuffed it all the way down into my pocket to stop it from getting wet. Moments later, the cloudy, starry night turned into a freefall of rain and bursts of lightning and raging thunder.

# CHAPTER 18

Voss and Oliver were coming to me. I didn't know when or how many, but so were the bad guys.

I was wet from the sudden rain. The truck's leather seats squeaked under me as I shifted my weight around. I wasn't drenched, just wet. I had jumped into the truck right after the rain started.

The storm would slow the bad guys down, but I didn't know how far away they were. I had no idea which direction they were coming from. From the east, it would've slowed them down, but from the west, back toward Angel Rock, not that bad. It was as if the storm stayed right over my position. A bad omen. A dark cloud. My own little storm cloud.

I sat back and stared out the windshield at the rain and the blur of the dead cops' police car, thinking about how the forensic evidence was being washed away right before my eyes. Which wasn't good for Voss, as she was the one who had been obligated to call this thing in much earlier. I couldn't think about that now. It wasn't my concern. My concern was Janey Saunt.

What was I missing?

There was nothing for me to do but sit and wait and go over the evidence I had already been over several times before. I recapped everything in my mind. And I couldn't help but feel like I had missed something.

I watched the rain through the Silverado's windshield. It soaked everything. It pounded on the truck's hood. It blurred the headlight beams. The rain puddled in the footprints left in the dirt. Some of the shell casings floated away in rivers of rainwater. They were carried off and away into the darkness. The nearest wind turbines became invisible from the trunk up. The blade tips spun and became visible on the down-swing. They came out of the darkness, fast, and swung up and vanished, like giant pendulums.

Watching the rain and the ground got me thinking. I leaned forward in the driver's seat and stared outward. My eyes squinted, and I focused on the blurred cop cruiser. I thought about the trunk. Two grimy shovels, two pairs of dirty mud boots. What were they digging?

I shuffled around in the seat, to give myself more room to sift into my pocket. I reached down and scooped the radio out and called Voss. I clicked the *talk* button, and said, "Voss? Come in."

Static.

I clicked the *talk* button again, and said, "Voss?"

More static, and then a click, and Voss's voice. She said, "Widow?"

"Here. Where are you?"

"We're on our way. It's coming down pretty hard."

"Where are you, exactly? Right now? What's your twenty?"

"We're just pulling onto the highway. Why?"

"Which highway?"

"The one you're on. The crime scene one."

I said, "I'm headed your way. Meet me on the road."

"Why? What's up?"

"Just do it."

I dropped the radio on the passenger seat and put the gear into reverse and hit the pedal. I no longer cared about messing up the crime scene because the rain would do that anyway. It was too late to worry about it now.

I shoved the gear back into drive and slammed on the gas. The truck skidded in the wet mud and the tires kicked and bounced up onto the track. Seconds later, I was back on the two-lane highway. Driving faster than I should've been in these conditions.

I drove fast, keeping the high beams on so I could see Voss's cruiser whenever it came into view.

I drove fast, because I knew where Janey was.

# CHAPTER 19

The Silverado bucked and dipped and splashed mud and water under the tires on the two-lane highway, going back toward Angel Rock.

Voss's police cruiser came into view up ahead. The blue light bar flashed. The headlights were turned up to high beams. The high beams flicked twice—a signal. Voss saw me. She saw the truck's headlights. She switched her high beams down to regular. I followed suit and turned mine down. I drove fast a little farther. Then I slowed the truck about a quarter of a mile from her. I took my foot off the gas and let the Silverado coast. The speed slowed to thirty miles an hour, then twenty, until I stepped on the brake, and came to a stop. Dead center of the road.

Voss's police cruiser skidded to a violent stop twenty feet away. The rain looked distorted in the blue lights. Voss waited for me to make a move first. I jumped out. I called from over the open Silverado door at Voss. She threw the cruiser's gear into park, stepped off the brakes, and hopped out. Rain washed over her body. Her uniform was dark and wet in the rainy moonlight. The rainwater slicked her hair back in seconds. A man got out of the passenger side. He was tall and lean, like a nameless cowboy who just rode in from out of town. I guessed he was Oliver, the FBI agent. They stood outside the cruiser and stared at me.

I said, "I know where Janey is!"

Voss asked, "Where?"

Lightning crashed far off behind her and lit up the sky and the road. And thunder rumbled, shaking the sky, vibrating a nearby derelict power line pole. The underbelly of the clouds lit up in flashes of pure white.

I called back to her. "Take me to where you first followed them!"

"What?"

I raised my voice and shouted, "You said you kept losing them at a certain spot. Remember? You said near an old windmill. Take me there! Where they ditched you!"

"Why there?"

"That's where Janey is."

"Inside the windmill?"

"No. That's just a land marker. They had dirty shovels and mud boots in their trunk. They must have a buried cellar there somewhere."

Voss's face lit up. She called out, "Bunkers. The people who lived around the old mill had bunkers, from the cold war. Everybody had them."

I nodded, and said, "That's where she is. The images we saw. The room looked like a cellar or basement, but it was a bunker."

Oliver spoke for the first time. He cupped his hands around his mouth and shouted, "Are you certain?"

I ignored him, and said, "Let's go!"

Voss nodded and hopped back in her cruiser and Oliver followed. Then she circled around me and hit the gas.

I reversed the Silverado, punched the gas, and followed behind them. I started a good way behind. The Silverado wasn't built for speed, not when compared to a police cruiser with an expensive police package. Not even close. But the Silverado was better in mud and rain. Eventually, I gained speed and traction and came up close behind them. We drove in a tight line, like a special forces convoy on a rainy Afghanistan road, back when I first started my NCIS and SEAL career.

We continued for a long time. Part of it was the rain. Part of it was the darkness. We drove until Voss pumped the brakes and slowed. I slowed behind her, doing the same, pumping the brakes because of the wet road. Voss stopped pumping and let the tires roll. She leaned forward all the way over the steering wheel. She moved her head closer to the windshield, and looked up, like she was trying to find something. Which she was. She was searching for the old windmill.

I sat in the truck in silence. There was no noise but the rain pounding on the roof.

Voss saw the old dairy windmill. It was small compared to the giant wind turbines. It looked like a relic from ancient times. It was built with old, sturdy wood. The propeller blades were old and rusted. Some were missing. The wheel turned slowly and whined in the heavy wind. The tower stretched pretty high, higher than I expected, but nothing compared to the wind turbine giants. A ladder spanned from the base up to the top. Several rungs were missing.

Voss stopped and looked down at the computer screen in her cruiser. She punched some keys on the computer and waited. Exhaust pooled out of her cruiser's tailpipe. I stared at it and waited. She was checking her GPS logs to see which way to go. She must've got an answer, because she hit the gas and went to the left of the windmill. She turned, and I followed. We went off-road. The truck bucked and bounced, like a wild horse. We were going fast. The tires hugged the terrain well for the bad weather.

We drove for five to ten minutes, darting one way and ducking the next. Most of the terrain off the track was too rocky to be our target. The dead cops couldn't have dug into the rock. I hoped Voss knew where to go, where the bunker might be. She led me down an obvious off-road path. A moment later, the path shrank and narrowed. The rocks grew larger. Both sides of the track became impassable for a road vehicle. Within seconds, the rain hammered down worse than before. It became harder to see out of the windshield. The wipers blasted hard, like they were in overdrive. I struggled to see twenty feet in front of the truck's grille.

Voss slowed and turned onto a sharp, rocky patch of wet gravel and dirt. And we drove some more. We drove until a clearing appeared ahead. It was a circular clearing that butted right up to the edge of a rocky mountain. There was an old structure still standing from long ago. There were a couple of walls and concrete front steps and the foundation of an old, abandoned house. There was a cluster of them, like an old family dairy farm. Which is what it had once been. The front side of an old barn still stood. It leaned in the wind but stayed standing.

Voss drove into the clearing and around the ruins of the old family house. She led me around back about a hundred feet from the back of the ruins. We came right up to the butt of a rock wall, the edge of the mountain. There was no place farther to go. So Voss slammed on her brakes and threw her cruiser into park. I parked behind her and left the engine running. The relentless rain engulfed the windshield. It was blinding now.

I hoped we were at the right place. And we were, because Voss honked her horn and jumped out.

Oliver stayed inside the car.

Voss ducked her chin in to help her see. She turned sharply and jogged to the trunk of the cruiser. The lid came up. Her hand gripped over the top, and she ducked into the trunk and grabbed something and came out with a thick police rain poncho. She slipped it on over herself and raised the hood and put it on. Then she dipped back in her trunk and pulled out another one. She lowered the trunk lid but left it cracked. She ran away from the cruiser, around the Silverado's grille and hood, and made it to my door. I dashed it open. She came up and stopped and stared at me from under the hood of her poncho. Her face was drenched.

The rain pounded so hard that we had to yell at each other, even close up. I asked, "Is this the place?"

"What?" Voss asked. The rain pounded against the hood of her poncho. It was hard for her to hear me. I didn't repeat myself. And she handed me the extra rain poncho, and said, "Here. Take this."

I took it, slipped it on. It was a size XXL, and it fit. Voss stood there, shaking in the cold rain. So I said, "Go around and hop in."

"Okay," Voss said, and glanced back at her car, back at Oliver, who sat there in the passenger seat, one arm stretched out, hand on the top of Voss's seat. He stared back over his shoulder at us, like he was trying to decipher what we were saying.

Voss darted away and back around the Silverado's hood and grille. She stopped at the passenger side door, jerked it open, and hopped in. More lightning flashed in the distance, followed by the same angry thunder—like the night was against us.

Voss slammed the passenger door shut and shivered. I tapped the touchscreen and pressed the heat icon. The vents blasted her with hot air. She said, "*Phhh*. This rain is crazy!"

"I know. It came out of nowhere. Where's the bunker?"

"Right here is where the bunker should be. I looked it up. The family that used to run this dairy farm had lived here during the Great Depression, but they wouldn't have had a bomb shelter. Not till the fifties. And back then, the county code on bomb shelters would've been a hundred feet or more from any other structure. So it should be here," she said, and pointed ahead in the rain, past her cruiser.

I said, "That's *if* they built a shelter to code."

"They did. Don't worry. Dairy farms were pretty regulated back then. It was a big enterprise here. I promise. If there's a bomb shelter, it'll be here. What made you think this is our spot? I mean, other than them losing me out here?"

I said, "In the trunk of their police car."

"Yeah?"

"There was everything you'd expect."

"Okay."

"But one thing bothered me."

"What's that?"

I said, "The shovels and the boots."

"Shovels are standard. I've got a shovel in my car."

"Yeah, but they had two shovels. Both covered in dirt and grime as if they had been used—and recently. Plus, they had two pairs of mud boots, also covered in dirt like they'd been used a lot."

Voss nodded, and said, "And the pictures. How everything looked dank. The piping was on the ceiling. The way they had the lighting rigged. The floor was concrete. That looks like an old bunker. Makes sense. I'm going to grab my shovel. Let's get to it!"

"Damn! I should've taken the ones from the bad guys' trunk!"

"Not worth it now. The entrance to the bunker won't be buried that deep."

"You're right."

"So where do we dig?"

I stayed quiet and leaned forward, tried to look out over the clearing, past her car. I scanned the ground as best I could until I saw it. I reached out and pointed. I said, "There. See them?"

Voss turned and looked at where I pointed. She leaned forward and squinted her eyes to see through the drenching downpour. She said, "Yes."

If the clearing was a clockface, there was a mound between the one and the two. Protruding out of it was a cluster of pipes and machines.

Voss said, "That must be a ventilation system."

"It is," I said, and paused a quick beat. "One more thing. "

"What?"

I thought for a moment. I was about to tell her about my phone conversation with Mister Man, but I thought twice. Instead, I shrugged, and said, "Never mind. I'll tell you later."

She said nothing to that.

I thought about what these guys had done, and I wasn't sure if they deserved the kind of justice they would get from Voss. She would arrest them. They'd go to jail, then court, and prison. But would they? I knew two of them were cops. Mister Man had already said they were powerful. Maybe the regular way wasn't the right way? Not in this case.

Fair trials and bookings and witness testimony and bail and a jury of their peers may not be the right way. Months and months of evidence and lawyers and being presumed innocent until proven guilty might be more than they deserve. I needed more intel before I told her.

So I stayed quiet.

# CHAPTER 20

Oliver stepped out of Voss's car, and the three of us stood out in the pouring rain. Oliver seemed okay to me, so I didn't press him. He and I took turns hacking Voss's shovel in the mud at the spot we figured would be the buried hatch to the bunker. It was a mound of mud, higher than the rest of the area, and it was close to the ventilation system. It seemed like the best guess.

Oliver wore Voss's rain poncho, and she walked back to wait in the police cruiser with the car facing us with the headlights on so we could see the mud. The rain battered the windshield. She had the wipers on full blast. The wiper blades flung back and forth, fighting the rain, like out-of-control clock hands.

I called out to Janey every couple of minutes on the off chance she could hear me. I hoped she'd scream back at us. If she was alive, which was another lingering question.

I felt the rain thumping down on my back. My muscles ached, and my head hurt from the relentless rain and thunder roaring. The rainfall made the poncho feel so heavy. Every time I stabbed into the mud, the shovel became heavier and heavier.

Oliver was a fit, lean guy for an FBI agent. He had a good build, and he was young too. He didn't appear to be one of those pencil-pusher, desk types. He looked pretty sturdy, more like a Secret Service agent, only humbler and less intimidating. He was less than forty, but barely over thirty-five.

We poked and prodded all over the area, which wasn't a massive space but big enough. And the rain and darkness made it slow-going and burdensome. Maybe the whole area was about a couple thousand square feet. We ruled out a lot of the area as a place to bury a hatch because it was all ditches and dips and rock walls. It made no sense to bury a door under terrain like that. It would've been too hard to uncover the hatch every time they wanted to get in. It was most likely on flat ground.

For the first forty-five minutes, I cursed the rain because it was making it hard to move. That changed when Oliver was dredging along near a low hill and hit something beneath the dirt. The rain was so harsh and powerful that it pummeled the ground into muddy dirt. It caused a thick top layer of the dirt that covered the hatch to liquify and slide off.

Oliver said, "Here! I found it!"

I went over and looked. The adrenaline kicked in for both of us. Oliver shoveled like a madman. He slung the mud and dirt to the side as fast as he could. Our boots sank into the wet mud. Within moments, I saw what he was yelling about. He hit a metal object under the mud. He shoveled faster and faster. Wet mud slung everywhere. He got it on my pant legs. I didn't care. He got it on my boots. I didn't care.

Minutes of intense digging passed, and finally, I saw the metal that the shovel hit. It was a steel padlock. It was new. The muddy metal still glimmered. This must be it. They used this underground bunker to hide their victims. I was horrified at what we might find down there, but I hoped it was a living, breathing Janey Saunt.

Oliver kept shoveling mud out of the way until a square outline was exposed. He stopped shoveling and tossed the shovel aside. We both dropped to our knees in the mud and started wiping the grime and slush off the surface of the square object. It was only seconds until we found an old, rusted metal hatch. It nestled neatly into the ground.

Voss witnessed our demeanor change from tired to excited. She saw us drop to our knees, and she jumped out of the cruiser and ran to us through the rain. With no raincoat, she shivered. The rain drenched her uniform. Her clothes clung to her form under the bulletproof vest. She was too excited to care. She asked, "You found it?"

I jumped up and stepped back to her. I said, "It looks like it."

The rainfall was so intense it washed the mud off my clothes within moments. Oliver stood up, and the rain washed the mud off his clothes too. He said, "We gotta get in there."

I said, "Shoot the lock."

Oliver nodded and handed me the shovel. He said, "Back away."

Voss grabbed my arm and pulled me back several feet. We backed away from Oliver. He drew his service weapon, which was a Glock 22, a .40 caliber firearm. He took aim. Voss moved close to me for warmth and shelter from the deluge. I opened the raincoat and wrapped it over her. I put one arm around her and pulled her close. Which was partially to keep her dry and warm, but also, because I wanted to. I wanted to all night. She wrapped her arms around my midsection and squeezed me back.

Oliver squeezed the trigger and fired twice—*bang, bang*. The muzzle flash was quick but bright in the rain and the darkness. The first shot hit the padlock, but didn't break it. Not all the way. The second bullet did the trick. The padlock exploded into several shards of metal, along with one lumpy piece left over. All that was left was the hatch and a long handle.

Voss let go of me and started for the hatch door.

Oliver said, "Wait!"

She paused.

He said, "We should clear it first."

Voss nodded and drew her gun.

"I'll get the door," I said, and I stepped forward, grabbed the hatch door's handle, and counted to three and wrenched it open. It was heavy, like a hatch on a submarine. It was built more than a half century ago. It was designed to withstand nuclear fallout, and it was built to specification.

The door creaked on its ancient hinges. Rain battered all around me. It poured into the darkness beyond the hatch. I pulled the hatch all the way open and dropped it on its handle against the mud. I stepped back. Immediately, a stench wafted out of the hole. It was horrible, like a shipping container filled with dead refuges who failed to survive a secret cross-ocean escape to a better life.

The three of us all gagged at the smell.

Voss drew her gun and went in first. She took a deep breath to stop herself from smelling the stench. She brandished her flashlight and led the way with it out front. She took it slow. First, she peeked down into the darkness, and then she dove in full throttle, like an experienced point man. Except for the flashlight beam, the blackness swallowed her up like the mouth of an underground monster.

Oliver covered his nose and mouth with one hand, held his gun out with the other, and followed Voss into the blackness. I waited at the mouth.

I glanced back at Voss's police car and saw her police shotgun locked in place near the front console. If I had to, I could run back to her car and grab it. If I had to and if it wasn't locked in place, but knowing her it probably was.

I waited, regretting that I didn't have a weapon.

Down the hatch, I heard nothing but silence. Then a light came on and the dark tunnel below lit up, bright, and Voss's head came into view. She stepped into the doorway. Her face was ghostly white. There was a look in her eyes like she had seen a nightmare. She said, "Widow. Get down here. Look at this."

# CHAPTER 21

The bunker was a pit straight out of hell.

I had seen a lot of things in my life, a lot of unimaginable things, but this was up there with the most disturbing. It wasn't something I'd forget soon. The sights in that bunker would plague my nightmares. It was Dante's vision of hell, on steroids. It was the devil's playpen. It was pure evil.

The bunker was much, much larger than I imagined. It was tall enough for me to stand up straight, but not by much. There was a long hallway that looked like something out of a horror movie where a bunch of teenagers get hacked to bits. I couldn't tell what the interior was made of because water trickled in from a leaky roof, but it wasn't brick or wood. Part of the floor was concrete and part was just dirt with long wooden planks laid out for us to walk across, like a dinosaur dig site. There was electricity, which must've been powered by a generator somewhere, or the whole thing was tied into some old underground power cables.

The lights were small bulbs scattered about in clusters, but they were bright in the windowless space.

There was a conflict of smells. The first was awful like the smell of a morgue. The second was weird. It was new car smell. Instantly, I knew where the second came from. Dangling from pipes, wires, and any other surface on the walls and roof, were hundreds of air freshener car trees. The spun and twirled and dangled from little strings.

I counted three rooms total, including the hallway. The first room had no door and was wide open. It was the room that scared Voss so badly. It gave her the expression of horror on her face.

The room was large. Several patches of darkness and shadows hid things I didn't want to see. The place was a dungeon. The first thing I saw was an open barrel. I stepped closer to it and peeked in. Immediately, I regretted it. It was filled with bones. They looked human. The smell was almost as bad as the sight of them. Some were fragmented and broken. Some were charred like they were burned in a fire. There were no remains of flesh at all. I hated to imagine what they did with the skin and organs.

Against one wall, there was a demented handyman's table. A pair of bloody handcuffs dangled from it. There was a rack lined with tools hanging from it. They were rusted from old blood stains and other fragments that I couldn't identify, not without a crime lab and a forensic background, which I didn't have.

I grimaced at everything. It looked like a torture chamber. Suddenly, I realized I had no idea how many other bunkers there were out there. Maybe Broome and Aragon, and Mister Man, had them stashed all over the state.

Off to the left, there was another bucket. This one didn't have human remains or bones. This one was filled with old wallets, driver's licenses, passports, car keys, and jewelry.

There were three digital cameras in the room. The first laid on the demented handyman's table. It was small and looked like any other digital camera, like the one we found in Saunt's room. The other was a huge, old-style camcorder. It hung on the rack with the tools, like it had always been there. And the third was a newer camera set up on a tripod. The nose faced down.

I could only imagine what took place here. The horrors would give me nightmares.

Oliver was down the hall, trying to get into the last room. He kicked the door repeatedly, like a desperate man trying to save his daughter—like Saunt would've done.

Oliver screamed at me. He shouted, "Widow. Come here!"

I backed out of the room of horrors and into the hall. I wanted to forget what I had seen. I turned slowly and saw Agent Oliver banging on a door at the end of the hall. I jogged over to him. The walls were made of dirt, held up by old wooden beams. And there wasn't much room to maneuver for a guy my size.

I made it to the door, and asked, "Is she in there?"

He said, "Someone is! But it's locked or barred from the inside. I don't want to fire into the room. Might hit someone."

I said, "Got it. Move back."

Oliver stepped to the side. Voss was back at the entrance, crouched and watching us.

There was a tiny hole in the door. I peered in. It was very dark, like the inside of a whale's stomach. I heard something. It was faint, very faint. But something or *someone* inside made some noise.

I concentrated and listened hard. The rain pummeled the ground above us, making it hard to hear. Water leaked and dripped from the ceiling. It dripped everywhere. Another roll of thunder *boomed* overhead. Then it faded away and my ears adjusted back to the sounds of leaking water and rainfall. I tried hard to drown them out so I could hear inside the last room. And then, I heard it. It was breathing, low and ambient, but it was breathing. Something or someone was alive in that dark room.

I reached my hand out and pushed Oliver gently back, farther away from the door. He moved as far back to the wall as he could. I reared all the way back against the wall as far as I could next to him. I looked down at the door handle and the lock and gauged the thickness of the door's wood. The lock was a simple deadbolt.

I exploded from the back of my heels up through my shoulders and charged at the door. There wasn't much space between the wall and the door, but I was a big guy with a lot of power and a lot of force. I charged full force into the door. It exploded and splintered open, like weak bones shattering from brute force.

Inside, I heard whimpering and scattered sounds and rusted springs and chains scratching against metal. Then the smell hit me. It was awful, even worse than the next room with the barrel full of human bones.

I fumbled around on the left wall for a light switch, but Voss came in behind me with her flashlight. She swept the room fast.

The flashlight beam stopped dead on something that made her retch in horror. There was an old bed with a rickety mattress on top. No sheet. No covers. On top of the mattress were two figures sitting next to each other.

The first was the dead girl from the camera we'd found in Saunt's motel room. No question. It was her. She had the same face, piercing, and hair. There was a look of horror on her face—a look I would never forget.

Her rotting corpse was the smell that rivaled the barrel of human bones. She had been dead and decomposing in that room for God knew how long.

Next, we all must've felt the same rush of speechlessness—because we saw Janey Saunt. Alive, but barely. She was terrified. She hid behind the dead girl's body, clinging to it like a shield, a dead human shield. She was shaking and cringing, and she was staring right at me. I realized the sight of me in the darkness, bursting through her door, must've been pretty terrifying for her.

With my voice low and friendly, I said, "Janey? I'm here to help you."

Voss came into the room and holstered her gun. She walked toward Janey with her hands out, offering them to her like they were long-lost friends. She said, "Janey. We're the police."

Janey tried to scream, but it came out like a high-pitched shriek of a dying animal.

I whispered to Voss, "She probably lost her voice from screaming over and over for help."

Voss shone the flashlight on her, and then, at me and at herself. The beam went from face to face to show Janey that we weren't the bad cops. Voss said, "We're the good guys, Janey."

Voss kept the flashlight out of Janey's face and walked to her slowly, almost in a crouch, like she might do when approaching a stray dog to show it she was friendly. She said,

"We've got your father, Janey. He's in Angel Rock, the nearest town. We're going to take you to him."

I glanced back over my shoulder quickly and saw Agent Oliver was staying back in the hall. He watched with real concern on his face. Voss finally reached Janey and grabbed her. Janey reached out and latched on to her tightly and squeezed her close, like Voss was an angel from out of the white light at the end of the tunnel. That's when I saw Janey was handcuffed to the dead girl.

Those bastards left her here, locked up for days on end, hand-cuffed to the dead girl. I stared at her corpse. The dead cops handcuffed the girls together as a sick and twisted warning or an evil prelude to what would happen to Janey next.

Rage filled me. A sudden lump came up in my throat. I started breathing heavy. I caught Oliver leaning in closer to me in the doorway. He reached up and put a hand on my shoulder. He asked, "You okay?"

"Yeah. Couldn't be better. We got her alive."

"Yeah. Thanks to you."

I turned and stepped out in the hall. I asked, "Shouldn't you call the cavalry in?"

"I texted them. They know I'm here."

"Why are you here?"

"To help find her."

I said, "I mean before. What're the odds that you'd be here at the same time as this whole thing?"

He paused a beat. He said, "I was here because of Ryan."

"Saunt? Why?"

"We started investigating him about two months ago for financial crimes. It was really just a dead end. We picked his company because they had some questionable dealings. It was all on suspicion. And it was just about to end until—"

"Until he emptied his bank accounts," I said.

"Yeah. He emptied his personal accounts and then his business accounts. I thought he had gotten scared and was trying to run. His kid stopped going to school. The guy emptied his accounts and abandoned his house. One day I was questioning him about his finances. He complied, and then, just when I was about to close the investigation, just when I figured him to be innocent, he up and vanished. It was a real anomaly. He went from a boy scout type to a guilty criminal. I thought he was trying to run. He looked guilty as sin. Why else would he run?"

"So he really was paying off a ransom?"

Oliver nodded, and said, "Trying to save his little girl."

"Life's full of anomalies."

"Poor girl. She must've been locked in here for weeks and the only friend she had was a dead girl. She must've been terrified every time they came back. Every time they brought her water or food, she probably thought they were going to kill her."

I stayed quiet. But I clenched both of my fists.

*I would've killed them both myself. Given the chance*, I thought.

We stood there in silence for a long moment, watching Voss hug Janey, watching Janey sob uncontrollably into Voss's chest. Voss stroked her matted hair, like she might her own daughter, if she had a daughter. But she didn't. She had a son. Still, I'm sure she understood how Saunt felt seeing those photos more than I did. I have no children.

The moment grew longer and longer. The room was filled with the sound of Janey's sobs. Sobs, and the rain hammering the ground above. Another thunderclap roared across the sky, and lightning crashed. The white light flashed from the trapdoor above and filled the bunker with light. The light bulbs buzzed and flickered.

Finally, I spoke. I said, "Better get those cuffs off her and get her to the hospital. To her father."

Oliver nodded and entered the room. He approached them slowly so as not to startle Janey. He slipped a hand inside the raincoat and into his pocket and took out a set of handcuff keys. He approached Janey and tried to unlock her, but his keys didn't work. Voss slid away from Janey's embrace and dug her key out and tried it. It worked. Police departments often buy the same kinds of handcuffs, and sometimes the same key will work across an entire state.

The two dead cops had been state cops, so they used the same handcuffs and the same keys to match.

Suddenly, a smile crept across my face. Voss saw it. She asked, "Widow, why the smile?"

*Because I think I know who Mister Man is,* I thought.

# CHAPTER 22

Janey wouldn't leave the bunker or the room. Not at first. And I was the reason. She feared me. She didn't trust me. I had burst through the door, and it shook her, more than she was already shook. It took twenty minutes for Voss to convince Janey that I was on her side. I took no offense. She was in shock. She wasn't her normal self.

Voss finally convinced Janey that we were the good guys. I offered Janey my rain poncho, but Voss insisted I keep it. She gave Janey hers instead. Voss seemed angry. But it wasn't at me. She was angry because she had followed Broome and Aragon around for weeks with no idea what they were up to.

I didn't argue about it because I had a plan of my own, a plan where I would need the rain poncho.

Janey had been locked down in that hole for weeks, maybe longer. She wasn't giving a lot of answers. And Voss wasn't pushing. Janey needed time. She was malnourished and dehydrated and terrified. I figured that the dead cops had to have fed her and brought her water, but it had only been enough to keep her alive. She'd had little exercise and moved slowly. Voss and Oliver had to lift her up out of the hole and into the pouring rain. I stayed out of the way and watched.

They tried putting her on her feet, but she stumbled and moved slow. And they wanted to get her out of the rain as fast as possible. The last thing they would've wanted was to give her pneumonia on top of whatever else she might've gotten from being down in that hole. Possibilities that I didn't want to think about.

Oliver and Voss carried her to Voss's police cruiser and placed her in the backseat and bundled her up in the rain poncho.

By this point, the rain was coming down harder than before. If that was possible. It was unreal, like a monsoon. It fell like it was being dumped in buckets. The rainwater was up to the tops of the soles of my boots, and in some places it was over an inch deep. I stood in between the two vehicles, out in the rain, waiting.

Voss didn't come over to me like I expected. Instead, Oliver ran over to me with his hand up over his head to shield his vision from the rain. He got about ten feet from me, stopped, and shouted over the rain at me. He shouted, "We're going to the hospital! Follow us!"

I shouted, "Go ahead! I'll be right behind you!"

He nodded, turned, and ran back to Voss's car on the front passenger side. Janey was in the back. Voss was back in the driver's seat. She put her foot on the brakes. The red lights lit up my face. The second Oliver closed his door, Voss took the car out of park. She reversed the cruiser all the way back and then straightened it. The tires splashed water and mud all over the place. She stopped for a second, parallel with me. She glanced at me and gave a quick nod, like she knew I was planning something. I nodded back and beckoned her to go ahead. Voss nodded and inched the cruiser past me.

Janey finally looked at me. She stared at me through the window. Her face was pale white. She had been through something awful. That part I knew. But I could only imagine the horrors she had faced. There was probably years of therapy and psychiatrists and pills in her future. The therapy would help her forget. The pills would suppress her night-mares. And none of that took into consideration whether her father would live or die.

Once Voss had the cruiser's tires on the highway, she flicked on the blue lights, accelerated, and sped off as fast as she could in the rainstorm.

I stood in the rain and walked out behind them to the road. I stayed there and watched as the police cruiser's taillights and the blue strobing lights faded into the night.

I would go to the hospital like I told them, but later. Not now. Now, I had something else to do.

# CHAPTER 23

The Silverado's engine hummed. The rain battered the windshield. The wiper blades were off. The headlamps and the interior lights were off. I sat in the truck in silence, letting the heater blast me with warm air. I waited for two things—to dry off and for the phone to ring. The only lights on in the vehicle were the ones emitted from the instrument gauges on the dash. The dash screen was dark, some kind of screensaver mode.

After several minutes, I pulled the Angel Rock Police Department's radio out of my pocket and tossed it on the dash. Then I fished Broome's phone out of another pocket. I stared at the home screen. I couldn't call out because I didn't know the guy's passcode. For now, I had to wait. So I sat behind the steering wheel and let the warm air keep me comfortable until then.

Thirty-seven minutes later, the phone vibrated on the dash. Aerosmith's song played again. It was loud over the hum of the Silverado's engine and the ambient rain. I leaned forward over the steering wheel and looked at the phone. I let it ring a few times before I grabbed it. I wanted Mister Man to think he might lose me, lose my interest in his proposition. The worst thing to do was make it seem like I was eager to get paid. That'd look like a trap.

On the third ring of the Aerosmith song, I swallowed hard, not because I was nervous, but because I was still angry. I glanced at myself in the rearview. My hair was wet. My beard was wet. I looked like a dirty hobo caught in the rain, like an old dog left out. I smiled at myself. Smiling in the mirror was a simple technique to help raise one's mood. It worked. The anger subsided. My normal calm composure resurfaced. Then I clicked the *talk* button and answered the call. I said, "Hello?"

Mister Man's voice came over the phone. He said, "It's me again. Where are you?"

"Still here. The same place. Where are you?" I said, and closed my eyes and listened carefully. I heard the rain behind his voice. I heard road sounds behind him. He was driving, or being driven. Thunder roared in the background on the phone line, and then, it roared high above me, to the north. He was coming from the north.

"On the freeway. We're about twenty minutes from Angel Rock now."

That was fast. I glanced at the truck's dash screen, reached over, and tapped it. The dash screen woke up. It displayed the time. It was later than I thought. It had been a long and eventful evening. No wonder I lost track of the time.

Twenty minutes from Angel Rock? That was the last place I wanted them. I didn't want them near Angel Rock or the hospital or, especially, near Janey or her father. Or Voss. I wanted nothing to happen to her. Not that I doubted her skills. But these guys were something different. They could've been out of her league. From what Mister Man had said earlier, I had to assume they were out of Agent Oliver's league, too. At least on his own. If he had listened to us earlier and called in the cavalry, then maybe we'd stand a chance against them. But he hadn't done that. And I had no clue what we were up against.

The one thing I knew for sure was there were two dead cops involved. We're talking state detectives. They were a part of a special unit, according to Voss's intel.

They were two dead cops, which made them dangerous. But they weren't the top of the food chain, which told me more than that. It told me they were just cogs in a wheel of death and terror. I couldn't be sure how high this went or how big the machine was. I had to assume the worst. Assuming the worst was how I stayed alive. *Always hope for the best, but plan for the worst.* An Army motto, not a SEAL one, but a good one. This wasn't an opportunity to blow, as much as it wasn't one to get complacent. I needed to know what I was up against. Mister Man wasn't going to tell me, not exactly. But he had told me enough to know to expect more highly skilled, highly trained guys. He made it seem like he was a part of a bigger organization. How many members were there? I had no idea. It could be two more. It could be a hundred. There was only one way to find out. I had to bring them to me.

"Don't stop there. Not in Angel Rock. That's too far from me. I got the money. Plus, some more evidence I found at the scene," I lied.

"What evidence?"

"A camera. I found it on the other guy. I've been sifting through it. There's a lot of damning photos here."

Mister Man stayed quiet.

I said, "There's more than just cops and crooks here. There're photos of dead girls? Plus one who looks alive. It looks to me like you guys are up to some horrible stuff. Abduction and ransom games? Is that what's happening?"

Silence.

I said, "This'll cost you a lot more than whatever you're offering me."

Mister Man said, "What more do you want?"

I smiled. He was falling for it. I said, "We can talk details face-to-face. And try nothing funny. I hid the camera. No one knows but me."

Silence on the line.

I said, "So if you want it. You'll come to me directly."

It was quiet for a beat, then Mister Man said, "So, where are you? Tell me. We'll pick you up."

"No, I don't think so. What, do you think I'm an idiot?"

"Of course not. I'm just trying to get you your money. Plus, find my guys before the cops get there. That's all. We gotta clean this up. Contain it. If the local cops find the dead ones, the jig is up. There'll be questions. What's bad for me is bad for you. Okay? We're partners here."

I stayed quiet, let him think I was getting skittish, like I was mulling it over.

Mister Man said, "I want what you want. Believe me. We're on the same page here. I want to cover this thing up as quickly as possible. Where are my guys? Why don't you tell me?"

GPS was an exceptional tool for law enforcement. They had GPS in their cars, surely. They had it in their phones. But was Mister Man in law enforcement? I didn't know for sure. Even if he was, he may not be able to access their car's GPS. And their phones were a whole different set of problems. Plus, GPS works best in more urban areas with cell phone towers. If we were in Roswell or Albuquerque, it would work great. But out here, GPS wouldn't lead them within five miles of the dead cops. In this rain, they'd be searching the plains all night long before they found anything.

"Not yet. I'll lead you to them once you show me the money," I said, then grinned as I realized I saw it in a movie somewhere.

"Yeah. I got it."

"Okay. Bring it to me. Then I'll take you to them."

The phone went silent. Mister Man said nothing for a long minute. I waited, listening to the water pouring across the truck's windshield. I heard the same sounds of rain on his side of the line, but also, there was road noise. Mister Man asked, "Where do we meet you?"

I smiled because I knew just the place, not the site of the dead cops. I wanted to ambush these guys, if possible. Ambushing them depended on how many there were and how much fire-power they brought. I didn't know how many there were, but I would soon enough. I said, "Do you know the town of El Demonio?"

Silence, like Mister Man was looking it up on his phone. Mister Man said, "Yeah. I see it."

"Good. It's an abandoned ghost town now. No one lives there anymore."

"Okay."

"Meet me there."

"Where exactly?"

I thought back to what I had seen passing through. Which was at night, but it was less than six hours ago. And it hadn't been raining like this then. I remembered all the crumbling buildings and overgrown grass and broken traffic lights. I also remembered there was an abandoned police station. It was still intact. I said, "Meet me at the El Demonio police station."

"How will I know where that is?"

"You'll know. Trust me."

"Okay. I'll be there in thirty minutes."

"Call me when you get close or if you get lost."

He said, "See you soon."

I clicked off the phone. Now, I needed a gun. Luckily, I knew just the place to get one.

# CHAPTER 24

I drove back toward El Demonio, but I had to make a quick stop. I pulled the truck up slowly to the scene of the dead cops. The rain continued to pummel the landscape. Lightning sparked and crackled beneath the heavy clouds. Thunder rumbled all around me. The weather showed no signs of subsiding soon. Which could give me an advantage in case things went south. I expected they would. It was harder to battle in storm conditions for the untrained. But I was not untrained. I'm highly trained and skilled. I welcomed the weather. It could prove to be the difference between winning and dying. The rain and the darkness could suppress any sounds I might make, like footsteps. The thunder could provide suppression for the weapon I hoped to use, which was the Remington 870 locked up in the center console of the dead cops' unmarked car.

I pulled the Silverado close to the bumper of the dead cops' car and left the engine on and the driver's side door open and hopped out. The door-open alert dinged every few seconds. Wearing Voss's spare rain slicker, I rounded the truck's hood and grille, cut through the headlamp beams, and jogged to the cop car. The dead cops were still there. They were still dead. The bodies clumped there like husks.

The weather had pummeled the cop car so much that the doors had sealed tightly shut. It took some force, but I wrenched the driver's side door open, ducked down, grabbed the dead driver's legs, and lifted them. I shoved the dead cop, legs first, over the center console, as far as I could, like a sack of potatoes. I shoved him into the other dead cop. The driver's torso pressed against the other dead cop, like hunks of meat slabbed together.

The rain battered my poncho. The sound echoed in my hood. I forced myself into the front seat of the cop car the best I could.

I reached over and shoved the driver as hard as I could into the passenger side. Then I fired up the engine. The headlamps clicked on, illuminating the rainfall in front of the car's grille. I closed the door, put the gear into reverse, and drove back-wards. I went at a medium pace because I wanted to get out of the car as fast as possible. I drove it about forty yards over low hills and dips and back into one nice-sized crater. I drove it until I couldn't see the road any longer, which meant that anyone on the road wouldn't be able to see me. That's what I was going for. I wanted Mister Man and his guys to drive right past their dead friends. It was a precaution, in case they stumbled upon it like I had.

After I was satisfied with where I hid the vehicle, I killed the engine, took out the keys, and unlocked the Remington 870 and removed it.

Before hopping back out, I reached over and stripped the dead cops of their sidearms, which were both Glock 22s. Both .40 caliber, both magazines held fifteen bullets. Both weighed 22.75 ounces, 34.39 with a loaded magazine.

Then I kicked open the door and stepped out into the downpour. I walked back up over the dips and the hills. I trampled through wet grass, through the thick mud, and made it back to the Silverado. I dipped into the truck and laid the Remington 870 across the seat, and tossed the two Glocks in near it.

A lightning bolt crackled the sky and struck a nearby tree. A huge tree branch splintered apart and fell to the ground. I ignored it, grabbed the roof handle, and hauled myself up and into the truck. I shut the door, threw the gear into reverse, and then drive. The truck spilled back out onto the road. I stepped on the gas, accelerated, and headed to El Demonio.

# CHAPTER 25

El Demonio was cold. It seemed colder than Angel Rock, colder than the rest of New Mexico. It was like I crossed over into a different dimension. Maybe it was because the wind picked up and blew in the cold rain. Maybe it was because the wind had no obstacles around to block it from rolling off the low hilly surroundings. Or maybe it was ghosts of the derelict, abandoned town, returning to haunt their forgotten homes.

Before coming into El Demonio, I drove through Angel Rock. I passed the hospital, saw Voss's cruiser in the lot near the emergency room entrance where we entered earlier. There was a gas station on the other edge of town. I stopped there before heading farther. There were a few items I needed. They were paramount to the success of my ambush. I went in and made three purchases. I bought a gas can, the largest they offered. I filled it with gas. And I bought a tall cup of black coffee. The gas can sat snugly in the truck bed, nestled under a lip near the rear cabin. The coffee cup sat in the cup holder, up front with me. I drank a third of the coffee on the way to El Demonio.

The roads were long since ruined, dried up, and abandoned. Therefore, maneuvering was difficult. The rain turned every ounce of dirt into mud. Streams of rainwater flowed everywhere, like tiny flash floods.

Driving with the high beams on, I took it slow. I drove up and down streets, dodging rubble and old deserted structures. Most had standing walls and doors and half-collapsed frames, but none had everything. Weeds sprouted up over walls. Brown grass burgeoned over the ruins. The windows were almost all gone or turned to dust. Looters had come and gone. The town had probably become a thing of legends and scary bedtime stories for the kids who lived in Angel Rock.

*Don't stay up too late or the ghosts from El Demonio will come and get you.*

I turned onto the main street and searched for the old police station I had seen passing through. It didn't take long until I found it. There was an old police cruiser parked out front—not quite parked, but abandoned and forgotten. It was a relic from another time. The cruiser was under an old carport. It was tall, made of rusted corrugated steel. But it still stood and kept the cruiser relatively dry.

The cruiser used to have those old bulb sirens on top. They were gone now. Stolen, probably. Now the car had no tires and no glass in any of the windows. Any stereo and electronic equipment that used to be there was gone now.

The artifact police cruiser was the perfect thing to get Mister Man's attention. So I parked the truck and got out, leaving the headlights on bright. They shone over the remains of the old cruiser.

I had parked the Silverado close to the front end of the cruiser, outside of the carport's cover. As soon as I cracked open the door, the cold and rain swooshed in. I shivered under the rain poncho. The storm sounds echoed all around me and through the ruined buildings. The only lights were the ones on the truck. Everything else was engulfed in darkness. It was only the lightning crashes and what little starlight and moonlight there was that helped me to see.

I tugged the rain poncho's hood back over my head, swung the door all the way open, and slid out of the truck. I shut the door, grabbed the gas can out of the truck's bed, and carried it over to the abandoned cop car. The poncho's hood kept me dry enough. The offset was my vision was limited to an acute cone of sight, like from the blinders on a horse.

The sound of rain hammering on the top of the hood reverberated through my skull. It intensified under the corrugated steel. The rain pounded loud on the metal.

I circled the car and checked out the interior through the empty holes where windows used to be. The dash was completely ripped apart. Anything of value, not just the electronics, had been stripped away, including the steering wheel and the pedals and the knob to the gear selector. Even the seatbelts were gone.

The seats were shredded, but there was still a good amount of cloth left.

Any metal left over had rusted long ago. The paint had chipped away along with it. There were hints of white left, but most of the car looked rust brown now. The bulb lights were gone. But there was an outline of where they had been fastened to the roof.

I popped the cap off the gas can. The smell of gasoline leaked out and filled my nose. I held it up high and doused the old cruiser in gas. From the roof to the interior to the trunk, I covered the abandoned relic. I kept most of the gas under the carport. Rain still got through the holes in the steel. But that was no problem. Not for what I intended to do. I emptied the gas can until it was bone dry. I tossed it off into the darkness. It bounced and rolled on the crumbling road. It drifted away and out of sight on a stream of fast-flowing rainwater.

I returned to the truck, opened the door, and jumped back in. The seats were already wet from my rain poncho. I popped the cigarette lighter in, closed the door, and shifted the gear to reverse. I backed the truck up to the other side of the street, put it in park, and waited.

After several seconds, the cigarette lighter snapped out. It was ready for use. I pulled it out and glanced at the hot end. It was hot, definitely—no doubt about it. It glowed red.

I hopped back out of the truck quickly, leaving the engine on and the door open. I jogged back across the street, trampling through mud puddles, and back over to the old, relic cop car.

I stopped and turned to scan the horizon, the streets that led into El Demonio. The rain blinded me to a certain degree. It was thick, like a wall of water. But I figured Mister Man and his guys would come from the same direction I had, since they were close to Angel Rock. Plus, they'd use their high beams in this weather. No question. No choice.

So far I saw nothing. I turned back to the cop car, approached, and stopped at the rear. I looked it over to make sure the gas had seeped down it, soaking the whole vehicle. One more glance at the road that led into El Demonio. I saw nothing. No one yet. Mister Man and his guys weren't far behind me. It was time to set the bait. So I took the cigarette lighter and turned it upside down, held it like a rubber stamp, and I jammed it down onto the gas. As soon as I saw a spark, I dropped it into the gas, turned, and ran—full speed—until I was halfway back to the Silverado. I stopped and twisted around and walked backward to the truck, watching the gas flame up. The police cruiser ignited into a mountain of fire. It was fast. A quick burst of fire balled and rounded and erupted into flames and black smoke. One second, the car was long forgotten. The next, it was engulfed in flames.

I kept walking backward to the truck. The ball of fire was magnificent in the wet, dark sky. It would get their attention. No question.

I made it back to the truck. The phone in my pocket rang. Aerosmith hummed and filled the interior of the truck, as I climbed back inside.

I waited until I was completely inside the truck before I slipped the phone out of my pocket and clicked the button to answer the call.

Mister Man said, "There's a fire. Is that you?"

"That's your cue. I'm here."

"Kind of dramatic, don't you think? What if the cops see it?"

"Relax, the town is abandoned. There's no one here. No one will bother us. No one will care," I said, trying to sound as dumb as I could. I wanted Mister Man to hear what I was saying and think: *No witnesses.*

He said, "And what about the cops in Angel Rock? Won't they see fire? Christ! They're probably sending the fire department right now."

"They won't. The weather's no good. The visibility is too poor. The fire will be rained out by the time anyone sees anything. Just get here. The fire will light the way."

"We're about a mile out now. We'll be there shortly."

"Good. Don't make me wait," I said, and clicked off the call.

I put the truck into drive and slipped forward a bit and then drove about a block away and pulled onto a side street, near what looked like an old diner. I parked the truck and grabbed one Glock. I pressed the ejection switch and ejected the clip—fully loaded with .40 caliber rounds. I racked the slide back once, twice, and nothing came out. The gun wasn't chambered. I dry fired it. It worked. Always test an unknown weapon. Then I slipped the magazine back in and chambered a round and set the Glock on the seat next to me.

I picked up the second Glock and ejected the magazine and checked the rounds. I racked the slider, same as before, and nothing came out. I dry-fired the weapon, and it clicked. It worked perfectly. I tossed it onto the other side of the front bench. I wasn't planning on needing it, but I was glad it was in good working order just in case. But I wanted the extra magazine. I might need it.

Next, I grabbed the Remington 870 and pumped it. Nothing came out. No shells discharged out of the ejection port. I racked it again. Still nothing. The weapon was empty. This Remington model was a tactical police special version. It was modified with the Archangel shell holder screwed to the side and a tactical stock that extended, but I left it in the tight position. The shotgun was an eighteen gauge with a black, tactical slide. It ran smooth. I slid a shell out of the holder and loaded it into the tube. The shell was a three-inch Magnum round. There were seven of them. The damage from a Magnum shell was devastating, and that's the best-case scenario for anyone hit with one. A Magnum round will blow a hole through a target made of flesh and tissue and bone the size of a dinner plate. Truly not a round you wanted to get hit with, but definitely one I wanted chambered in my weapon.

I wondered if it was legal for a couple of state police to be using it in their shotguns. Of course, these guys had already blown past the ethics of legal versus illegal. I loaded the Magnum rounds into the gun until it was full and pumped the action.

The most universally powerful sound of the last hundred years echoed into the Silverado's cabin. *Crunch! Crunch!*

I smiled.

I had seven Magnum shells and two full clips for the Glock. I was ready for bears or wolves, or whatever Mister Man was going to bring with him.

# CHAPTER 26

The rain hammered relentlessly against the skin of my poncho as I stood on a crumbling street, watching and waiting for Mister Man and his guys to show up. I didn't have to wait long. A few minutes later I saw them. They drove in from the same direction I had. They rolled up in cop cars, like the one Broome and Aragon had. They flashed blue and red lights embedded in the grilles and rears of the vehicles.

Judging by the guys who rolled up with him, I didn't think they were all cops. They looked more like street guys for some gangster. Maybe they were. Maybe he was in bed with them. Maybe Mister Man recruited them out of prison. *Who knows?* I didn't care. I wasn't looking for answers. I was looking to end them.

How many bad cops he had on his team, I wasn't sure, but I was certain that they would all come tonight to clean up this mess. This was an all-hands-on-deck situation. No way would he leave anyone out of the fray.

They drove up in two unmarked police cars—black Ford Tauruses. It was hard to get a headcount in the rain. They could've numbered anywhere from two to twelve guys, when you factor in twelve could squeeze into the front and rear benches of two Ford Tauruses. Twelve was a tight squeeze, but doable, as long as there was no center console. But it was more likely less than that. I hoped for two guys. I got five—which was better than twelve.

I watched as they drove through the rain. They crept up the roads slowly, like hungry wolves stalking their dinner. Their eyes scanned the abandoned streets and buildings and windows, searching for an ambush. They were probably suspicious that maybe Broome and Aragon got themselves caught instead of killed. What if the whole thing was a ruse to get them out in the open? They were right. They should've listened to that little voice in their heads warning them. But Mister Man couldn't listen to it. He couldn't take the chance. Although the money in the bag was a factor, getting caught was the main reason. I was a loose end that Mister Man had to tie up.

At the first chance, the two cars split and went in opposite directions, driving slowly down different streets, canvassing the town, reconning as best they could before they went to the burning police car. I had parked the Silverado down the street in an alley. If they saw it, I didn't care. If they did a license plate search for it, all they'd find was Saunt's name in the registry. They already knew him. I wasn't concerned.

After several minutes, they came back together. They didn't scan the whole town. Probably because some roads were no longer passable, and they didn't want to get stuck in the mud. They should've brought trucks with four-wheel drive, like I had.

The two cop cars followed one-by-one down the main street until they got to the El Demonio cop car. The fire raged. It was unmistakable, even in the thick rainfall. They stopped and circled the burning police car and the old El Demonio police station—all slowly, all cautiously.

They vanished behind the police station. I waited. They reappeared back on the street that looped around the building. The lead car drove around to the front and parked on the street in front of the old, eroding steps in front of the station. The second car came from around the back and pulled up slowly behind the front car. The second one switched on a searchlight, fixed to the driver's side door pillar. The light was white and bright. The beam washed over everything in all directions. They searched the broken windows and splintered front doors and corners of the building. Every nook and cranny was illuminated and investigated. They searched for me.

I pulled Broome's phone out of my pocket and flicked the switch on its side to silent. I didn't want Mister Man calling me. The last thing I wanted was to die tonight because Aerosmith gave away my position.

I waited across the street inside an old courthouse. It had large, glassless windows. Several concrete pillars remained standing out front, above the entrance steps. They provided a bit of added protection in case I needed it. The courthouse was lined with pews like in a church. The judge's bench was still there. The witness stand was still there. Justice was served here once upon a time. Tonight it would be as well.

Finally, the searchlight went dead. It was easy to spot which one was Mister Man, because he sat in the passenger seat of the front car and gave the orders. I saw him barking at the others, like the head dog.

Mister Man waited in the first car as the other car searched with the light and then stopped. The second driver parked about fifteen feet from the bumper of the first car.

The guys left the engines running and the red and blue lights flashing. The beams flashed across the buildings and bounced through the rain. Then the five guys got out of their respective cars at the same time. Two guys climbed out of the second car and three others climbed out of the first.

I waited.

Mister Man confirmed which guy he was in the group because the passenger from the first car, the one who barked orders, raised a phone to his ear. At that same second, Broome's phone vibrated in my pocket.

I ducked back out of sight, put my back to a wall, and clicked the *answer* button. I put the phone to my ear and listened.

Mister Man said, "We're here. Where are you?"

I stayed quiet, walked back through the courthouse and the courtroom. I stepped to the judge's bench.

Mister Man said, "Hello? Where are you?"

I set the phone down on the judge's bench, near where the gavel once rested. Above the judge's seat, above everything, there was an old, life-size statue embedded into the wall. It was set back in the wall about a foot. It stood on a dusty, marble pedestal.

The statue was Lady Justice. It had the balanced scales, the sword, the blindfold, and everything. Lady Justice, the personification of Justice from Ancient Rome. Iustitia, or Justitia, was a statue representation of the Greek goddess Dike, the goddess over justice and fairness. She represented the spirit of moral order and fair judgment. But not tonight.

There was nothing fair or just about what they did to Janey Saunt, or the unidentified dead girl, or countless others. Nothing would make up for that.

# CHAPTER 27

Mister Man and his men stood in a half circle in front of their cars in the rain, facing the old police station. They each wore New Mexico State Police rain ponchos with: *POLICE* written on the back in yellow.

I imagined they wore police bulletproof tactical vests under the ponchos as well. All five of them wore police rain ponchos, but that didn't mean that all five were police. Then again, maybe they were. Mister Man had mentioned some kind of special unit in the state police department. Broome and Aragon were supposedly a part of it. Maybe this was the rest of the unit. They were all bad. I knew from experience that military units are a tight-knit family. Mostly when a bad apple appears, the Navy will isolate that apple and try to retrain him, make him a good apple. But that doesn't always work. Depending on crimes the bad apple committed, the Navy will either retrain, discharge, or, if the crime was severe enough, punish. In rare cases where the crimes are so egregious, they might even end that apple's entire existence.

Usually the Navy can save a unit when there's one bad apple. They simply pluck out the bad apple. But sometimes one bad apple can ruin the whole bushel. Sometimes, one bad leader can corrupt the whole unit. A unit filled with corrupt members will often be irreparable. And they'd have to be dealt with. That was my job in the NCIS's undercover operation—Unit Ten. My job was to investigate the crimes no one wanted to talk about. The worst of the worst. I was a Navy SEAL too. My secret mission was to investigate the SEALs when necessary. Sometimes I discovered bad actors, corrupted units. Units beyond redemption, beyond repair, beyond justice. I was the guy who investigated and dealt with the darkest evil.

Standing there, staring at Mister Man and the four guys in the rain ponchos, all I saw was a dark evil. I didn't see redemption for them.

They came here looking to kill me. They wore the bulletproof vests, but they weren't bulletproof. Not with Magnum shells. *Bulletproof* only goes so far.

Only one of them had his hood down. It was Mister Man. He wore a black baseball cap. He barked an order, and they hopped to it. Each of them brandished their Glocks at the same time. None of them had shotguns. I saw that they left their Remington 870s locked in their cruisers. It was good for me, bad for them. They had the numbers, but I had superior firepower. Still, I wanted to keep things silent for as long as I could.

So I waited.

Mister Man pointed at the station, barked another order. He stepped out in front and walked up the eroding steps to the front entrance. He told one of the guys to go around to the back, while the others followed him in through the front.

I got up slowly and jogged to the side door of the courthouse. It led to a side street. I eased it open and saw that the street was clear. So I exited the courthouse and scrambled along the building's edge to the main street, stopped at the corner, and waited. I peeked around the corner and scanned the police station across the street. Flashlight beams pierced through the windows on the lower level.

Mister Man and three others searched the main level. The fifth guy stood around the back corner of the building with his back to me. He watched the rear entrance in case I tried to escape, but he wasn't completely stupid either. They weren't sure if I was in there. Every so often the guy spun around and checked back over his shoulder to make sure I wasn't sneaking up on him.

The El Demonio police station wasn't huge. They would clear it in minutes.

Staying low, I jogged over to the unmarked Ford Tauruses. I reached one and crouched near the tire well. I gazed over the trunk lid and checked that none of the men were watching. They weren't. Then I eased over to the driver's side door and opened it just enough for me to reach in. I leaned in and popped the trunk. The lid broached with a little metal noise. It was audible even in the rain. No one heard it but me. I wanted to scope their equipment—see if there was something useful for me. I shut the door and slid along the door panels back to the trunk. I lifted the lid and peeked inside and smiled because there was one bulletproof vest left.

I set the Remington down against the rear bumper and stayed low. I pulled off my poncho—fast. The rain hit me hard and drenched my head and face. I pulled out the bulletproof vest and ducked my head underneath the lid of the trunk to keep my face from getting wetter. I slipped the vest on and fastened the straps and adjusted everything as quickly as I could. Then I peeked back around the car and saw that the cops on the ground floor had moved to the second floor. The flashlight beams tore through the windows and shot out into the night sky, like light signals shot out to sea.

Thunder roared overhead and another lightning bolt fired across the sky above the town. I shut the trunk, pulled the rain poncho back over my head, and pulled the hood up. I scooped up the Remington and pointed it at the side street near the police station's corner, covering it in case the guy in the back popped his head out. I crept silently to the side street, stopped at the corner, and put my back against the wall. The grass beneath my boots was soaked and the soil underneath was slippery. Carefully, I took a quick peek around the corner and saw the lone cop. He faced the other direction.

I waited. It was hard to gauge when he might check behind him. He did it randomly. I crouched and peeked, staying as low as I could, which increased my odds of staying hidden. And I watched. The way they'd parked one of the cars, its headlights shone right down the side street. Which was a pretty good cop technique. It enabled the back entrance to remain lit up. I couldn't approach him from that direction because even in the fierce rain the lights behind me would've cast my shadow all over the place. He would've seen me from fifty feet away. More, probably.

So I backed away from the side street and went back to the cop car. I opened the driver's door again and killed the lights and shut the door. Then I scrambled around the car and around the opposite side of the police station, opposite from the car and the posted guard.

I sprinted clockwise, following the cruiser's path around the building, the back, and down the side street. I passed the entrance, the old cop car still blazing, and past the back corner of the building. The rain splashed under my boots. It sloshed my boots and pants. I stopped near the back entrance, the one the last cop had been guarding. But he wasn't now. I lowered to a crouch, raised the Remington, and circled the corner.

The last cop walked down the side street to his police car to see what happened to the headlights. I stayed in a crouch and aimed down the barrel. His back was in my sights. I wanted to squeeze the trigger and punch a giant hole in his back. Shooting someone in the back wasn't honorable. *But what did honor have to do with it?* These guys didn't deserve honor. They deserved to be dead. But I didn't shoot. Not because of honor. It was because I wanted to keep the element of surprise, and a shotgun blast would be heard. Thunderstorm or not.

The last cop approached the cruiser slow and cautious. I followed, getting within twenty feet of him without him noticing me. There were large gaps in the police station's side where the brick had crumbled and fallen off. There were large chunks of brick on the street. I held the Remington with one hand, knelt, and picked up a loose brick. It was heavy and large. I lowered the Remington, raised the brick, and ran at the guy fast. My footfalls echoed between the buildings. The last cop heard me, spun around, and raised one hand in defense and the other to fire his Glock. But it was too late.

In the sheets of rainfall and darkness, all he saw was a blurry and distorted giant running at him with a brick. Terror, panic, and disorientation broadcasted from his eyes and face. He opened his mouth to scream, but nothing came out. Not in time. I slammed the brick down hard. It smashed him square in the face. The brick was old but sturdy. It slammed so hard into the guy's face, the brick shattered into dust. The impact broke the guy's nose and, probably, most of the bones in his face. He collapsed like a rag doll, hitting the moldered concrete. He dropped the Glock before hitting the ground and reached up with both hands at the bloody mess that used to be his face. Again, he tried to scream, tried to call out for backup, but his mouth had completely concaved. Most of his teeth were shattered, broken, and gone—nowhere to be seen. He probably swallowed the fragments. His lower jaw was smashed inward. I doubted he could even make words. He would need years of surgery to fix the damage done.

I pictured Janey Saunt and the dead girl on the memory card Broome and Aragon gave to Saunt. The thought of stomping this man's face to bits with my boot crossed my mind. One good stomp would kill him. It would be painful, but quick, too quick of a death for him, too merciful. He didn't deserve that. None of them did.

I scooped his Glock off the ground. It was the same as the one I stole from the dead cop. So I ejected the magazine and the chambered bullet. The bullet fell to the ground and bounced and rolled away into a mud puddle. It sank and vanished into the murky water and mud. I pocketed the magazine. Now I had three fully loaded magazines. I tossed his Glock hard into the sky at an angle. It flew through a missing window of the neighboring building and clattered away. I knelt next to him. He tried crawling away, but I popped him in the throat. Not enough to kill him, just enough to get his attention. I spun him over with no more resistance and searched his pockets.

First thing I saw was a pair of handcuffs and I took them out. Then I found his keys and grabbed them too. Next I found his wallet with badge and identification. I studied it. The badge looked real enough, but it wasn't a state police badge. It was a deputized badge. It was one step above a phony tin bought off eBay. Old Steven Seagal had a more real deputy badge than this guy's.

I cuffed the guy's hands behind his back. He fought me at first, but I jabbed him in the spine. It was a hard and quick jab. Not enough to paralyze the guy, but enough to hurt like hell. After cuffing his hands behind his back, I spun him around and laid him on his cuffed hands.

I stared at the guy. His face didn't look good. He spat up blood and wheezed and coughed. Partly from the throat punch and partly from his smashed face. I could've interrogated him. Found out if any of them were real cops, but he wasn't able to speak. And I didn't care what he had to say. I didn't need testimony and official statements. I had all the evidence I needed.

The guy was Hispanic, with a shaved head, and covered in tattoos. His arms, neck, and even his face had tattoos. I looked closer and saw that his tattoos appeared to be gang tattoos. These aren't the fake kind guys get to look tough. These are the real deal—Mexican cartel symbols.

Whatever kind of operation Mister Man, Broome, and Aragon were involved in, I didn't care. I just knew that this arm of the operation was going to be severed.

# CHAPTER 28

ne down, four to go. I left the fake cop handcuffed on his back in the trunk of one of the police cruisers. I didn't kill him, but I didn't spare him either. After this is done, Voss and Oliver might find him there alive. Then again, they might not. He was lucky. He was getting off easy. Better than the dead girl. Better than countless others. I had no idea how long this crew had been up to this nightmare. But I presumed it'd been awhile. More than once was enough for me to consider them dead men walking.

I dusted the brick particles off my hands, returned to the police station's back entrance, stepped back, and looked up at the second-floor windows before I went in. The flashlight beams were still there, peeking out. I counted four beams, meaning they all were searching the top floor. Mister Man probably felt safe with his choice in the sentry he posted at the bottom.

Voss's police cruiser flashed across my mind. The mottos on the door: *To Protect* and *To Serve*. Earlier in the night, I discovered two dead cops and thought about how much I hate cop killers. I thought about how angry I got when the enemy killed one of my SEALs, or Marines or Sailors or Airmen or Soldiers. They all signed up to serve. Each of them sacrificed to protect, defend, and fight for an oath to service, to justice. Not Broome. Not Aragon. Not Mister Man. None of them deserved to be in league with dead service members, with fallen cops.

I realized there was something worse than a cop killer. Worse than an enemy who kills a service member. One of Unit Ten's core tenets was to catch those who betray their oaths, betray their country, betray their brothers. Traitors were worse. And Mister Man was a traitor. All of them were. They betrayed Janey Saunt. They betrayed that dead girl. They betrayed justice. But I was here to make it right.

I walked in through the back entrance and swept the first room I saw with the Remington. I checked the corners, the shadows, and anything someone could hide behind. There was nothing there. No signs of life. The cops were upstairs. I heard them talking. Their footsteps creaked on the old floor-boards above me. They hunted in a spread-out formation like the tip of an arrow. One man was on point. Two walked on each side of him and a step behind. The last one picked up the rear.

Knowing their position from sound was good, but not enough to bet my life on. So I cleared the first floor quietly. No one was down here with me. I found the stairs. There were two directions to go—upstairs to face them or down to the basement. I went down first.

The lower level was pitch black, like a dark pit. I wished I had stolen a flashlight from the guy stuffed in the trunk or from one of their cars. But there was no time to backtrack now. They were finished with the second floor. I heard them stop and turn to approach the top of the second-floor landing. They were about to head back down. Then they would search the basement. I couldn't go back up now. I'd have to make a stand in the basement.

I descended the rest of the staircase. Once I got to the last step, I saw light coming from the far wall. At the end of a long hallway, there was a set of windows along the ceiling. They looked out to the street that ran along the front of the station. Part of it was the carport. The light came from the old police cruiser. It was still on fire. Still raging on. The firelight flickered and danced and illuminated the lower level enough to see, but it left a lot of dark shadows.

At the bottom step, I realized I had made a critical error. Outside the rain hammered and pounded everything, including me and my rain poncho and boots and pants. I was drenched from the rain. Plus, I had trampled through the mud and grime. My boots were wet and muddy. I spun around fast and stared at the stairs. Huge muddy footprints tracked down the stairs and into the basement.

My muddy trail could be traced all the way to the back entrance I came through.

*Shit!* I thought.

The remaining fake cops wouldn't notice the muddy boot prints on the first floor because that level was mostly covered in deteriorating carpet. But they would notice the giant muddy prints on the stairs leading down here because the steps were concrete. All they had to do was use their flashlights.

It was too late to retreat now. Just then, I heard voices. I heard a familiar voice. It was Mister Man. He was barking more orders at the others.

Suddenly, flashlight beams fell on the concrete steps and the muddy boot prints—my boot prints.

They were coming.

# CHAPTER 29

I t was stupid. I was stupid for making such a mistake. I stood at the bottom of the stairs in the police station's basement and stared dumbfounded at my mistake. Rookie mistake. I left muddy boot prints evincing where I had come from and where I was heading.

But when you make a mistake, there's no sense in sticking around thinking about it. No time to dwell on it. No sense in questioning it. None of these things will solve anything. You've got to move on. Move forward. Think about what the next move should be.

*No plan survives first contact with the enemy.* Another SEAL motto. The Navy is full of handy proverbs like that. Another one is *shoot, move, and communicate.* I had communicated that I was there and where I was going. Now, it was time to shoot and move.

I thought about Janey. I thought about the dead girl. I thought about the bones in the barrel. And I moved.

The fire from the police car outside burned bright, even in the rain. Eventually, it would burn out. For now, I was grateful for the light. I saw the basic layout of the basement floor. It was one huge room, bigger than the bunker. There were three large jail cells on one side. They were old, but the bars were still standing in good shape. The doors on all but one cell were closed, and probably rusted shut. I doubted they would open without a tremendous amount of torque and pressure.

The first cell door was wide open. I glanced inside. Shadows flickered and danced from the firelight.

Each cell was crammed with a set of bunk beds, the remains of metal sinks, and broken toilets. The cell closest to me still had a mirror above the sink. Instead of glass, the mirror had reflective metal, to prevent inmates from shattering it and using the shards as weapons.

Across from me, there were overturned desks, flipped on their sides and splintered in places. There was a bench, still upright, and a pair of metal filing cabinets. There were two drawers left. The rest were gone.

I stayed where I was and scanned the floor. At the end of the hall, I spotted another room. It looked like a closet. I stepped forward and peered in, squinting my eyes. There was a thin cage inside, like a locker. The door was wide open. It must've been an evidence locker, or weapons locker, or both.

There weren't a lot of hiding places down there. Not enough for me to hide in and never get found. But there was plenty of square footage. More than I would expect for a small-town police station.

I trudged to the right, toward the overturned desks, nearest the firelight. The fire hissed and crackled. The smell of burning upholstery wafted in through the glassless windows. I stepped with huge, purposeful strides, making sure that my boot prints were big and visible. It took me a few long seconds to finish. I stomped over to the file cabinet side of the hallway and stepped behind the closest desk. I sat down on it and leaned the Remington 870 against the wooden top. The old desk whined under my weight, like it hadn't been touched by a human in decades. Which might've been true. I'd have to ask Voss when I saw her again. *If* I saw her again. My back was to the entrance. I heard their voices. Their footsteps grew louder as they marched down the stairs, towards the first floor. I peeked back over my shoulder and listened.

Mister Man and the fake cops spoke in low voices. But they hadn't noticed my boot prints. Not yet. They stopped on the first floor and peeked around. Maybe seeing if they missed anything. Maybe they were checking on the guard they left behind.

I pulled the rain poncho over my head and stuffed it underneath the desk. Then I slipped off my boots and left my socks on. I hid the boots on the floor behind the desk, returned to the shotgun, and picked it up. In my socks, I crept back the way I had come, making sure not to smear the boot prints I had left. I tiptoed back to the first cell, where the door was unlocked and open. It was the darkest of the three because it was far from the firelight.

I entered the first cell, scrambled to the wall, between the sink and the toilet, and crouched with my back to the wall. I raised the shotgun, jammed the stock into my shoulder, and let the shotgun rest in my hands. It felt like an old friend. I elevated the barrel and took aim at the stairwell and waited.

Mister Man's voice murmured from the first-floor landing. Footsteps echoed on the concrete. All four men were in the stairwell now.

I watched and waited.

Flashlight beams clustered together and shone across the steps. They crossed over each other and moved and shifted along each step as the men descended. Then the beams froze. The voices and the footsteps stopped. The flashlight beams stopped on the muddy boot print trail I left behind.

The four guys saw the boot prints and whispered. Three of the voices spoke Spanish. One of them mentioned he didn't see the fifth guy at the back entrance. Mister Man interrupted them in English. He whispered, "Shut up. He's down here. Get ready."

They eased down each step, silently and carefully, like a scared babysitter checking out a noise from the basement.

I waited.

I saw the flashlight beams get brighter and brighter. My neck muscles flinched, and my arms were growing weary of holding the same position for so long. My hands tightened, and my finger slipped inside the trigger housing.

I waited.

All but one of the flashlight beams clicked off. I watched it move down the steps. As quiet as they tried to be, I heard their footfalls. They moved closer and closer to the bottom step. Suddenly, the last flashlight beam went off completely. I aimed the shotgun, eager to shoot the first guy I saw, but I stayed silent.

The first guy stepped on the bottom step, and then on to the basement floor. He crouched close to the floor and scanned the basement. He held a Glock out in front of him, aiming it at every shadow and flicker of light.

The fire outside the windows flickered and crackled. The rain hammered the walls and the police station's roof. Otherwise, the basement was quiet. I heard my own breathing. Some-where water dripped. It was an old pipe or rainwater leaking from outside. Still, I waited. I wouldn't fire until I had them all lined up.

The first guy looked down the hall, and then to the right, and then the left. Which was the direction I wanted him to look. He looked straight at me. Then he stepped aside, and the second guy came down after. He was loud like noise didn't matter anymore. The first guy shuffled farther to the right, making room for the second guy, like the second guy called the shots.

The second guy stopped and faced my direction. He swiveled slowly in a cone of forty-five degrees. The first guy swiveled to the right. Both held their weapons out. They swept the basement but stayed near the stairs.

The second guy walked out in front. He lowered his weapon. The third and fourth guys came down the stairs after him. They all had Glocks. All the same model. All with interchangeable magazines. The third and fourth guy moved off to the farthest sides of the group. They moved well together, like they were a unit. But they were no elite state police unit. I knew that. Maybe Broome and Aragon and Mister Man were, but not the other four.

As they stepped into the firelight, I saw their faces. Three of them were Hispanic. They were covered in tattoos, like the fifth guy. They all wore police gear, but they weren't cops. They looked more like a kill squad from a Mexican cartel than any American police I'd ever seen. Then there was the guy who came down second. He was a white guy, a little older than fifty. He had thick, fair hair, coiffed like it cost him two hundred bucks a week to get cut. He looked more like a politician running for some fancy office than a cop.

It was Mister Man. He proved it to me by barking orders at the others. He ordered them to take different firing positions. They were good. Cops or not, they had been trained well somewhere. Guys three and four moved toward opposite walls and started inching along them slowly, keeping the wall to their back. The third guy crept closer, coming into my view. He was the easiest target. The fourth guy fell out of my view. The cell wall was between us.

If the entire basement was lit up with the overhead lights that worked in the past, then the third guy would've seen me straightaway. But right now, in the dark, he couldn't see me. None of them saw me, not without their flashlights on. And they kept the flashlights off for now. If they switched them on and pointed them in my direction, I'd open fire on them. For now, I stayed quiet.

Mister Man stepped out farther into the mouth of the hallway, like he wanted me to see him. It was a typical police hostage negotiation tactic. He was doing the good cop part, while the *bad* cops took their positions. The firelight fell across his face and torso. I saw his face clearly. He spoke first. He called out to me. He said, "We know you're down here."

It was Mister Man's voice. No question. I recognized it. He hadn't tried to disguise it. It was him.

I didn't answer.

Mister Man spoke in a calm, cop voice. He wanted me to know he was my friend. They wanted me to feel comfortable, safe. Like nothing bad would happen to me. He said, "We're here. We just want to work it out. Come on out now."

I stayed quiet.

Mister Man's face looked disappointed on purpose. It was all a part of the ruse. He moved his sleeve up and stared at his watch, like he was getting impatient. He said, "Time is running out."

I stayed quiet.

He said, "I don't have all night. Come on out. We just want to get our guys and dispose of them. That's best for all of us here."

Silence.

Mister Man said, "We've got your money. It's upstairs. We can take you to the airport or anywhere you want to go."

The car fire crackled. Water dripped. I said nothing.

Mister Man said, "There's no need to be scared. Just come out. We won't hurt you."

Silence.

Then he said, "Think about it. If we get caught, then you get caught. With the money. We just want to compensate you. Help you along your way. That's going to benefit us, too. Isn't that what you want? Isn't that why you dragged us out here?"

The third guy stared into the first cell, at me, but didn't see me. Not yet. I wore all black. In the shadows, I was about as invisible as I could be. But he didn't move on. He stared like he was trying to adjust his eyes to the dark. He'd probably see me in seconds. His gun was pointed out, halfway between me and down the hall.

Behind me, beyond the concrete walls and past the old burning police cruiser, lightning crashed. It was loud. It boomed across the sky. It bought me time. The third guy glanced over, turning away from me. He stared in the lightning's direction, giving me time to move. I seized the opportunity and inched closer to the cell bars, staying in shadows.

There were four of them and one of me. They knew I was down here. My boot prints and my stupidity had given me away. If I was going to die, I'd make damn sure Mister Man went with me.

I leaned out and saw him. He stared forward in the lightning's direction, same as the third guy. They were all looking that way. I lined Mister Man up in the Remington's sights. Suddenly, like he sensed it, he sidestepped and barked another order. "Lights!"

He ordered his guys to switch their flashlights back on. Once they did, they would see me. I wasn't going to wait for that. So I squeezed the Remington's trigger. It *boomed*. The gunshot was deafening in the silence. It echoed and reverberated. The blast sound bounced off the bars and the concrete walls.

The fourth guy had been standing next to, and behind, Mister Man. He never switched his flashlight on. Nor did he ever fire his gun. He had no chance to because I shot him first. The Magnum shell blasted through the cell. The muzzle flash lit up the cell like huge fireworks on the Fourth of July. The Magnum round traveled through the open cell door and hacked the fourth guy's gun hand clean off. The guy's arm exploded into a mangle of bone and flesh fragments. Blood splattered everywhere. It exploded out, even onto the wall behind me. It splattered across my face.

His bulletproof vest absorbed some of the shot, but not enough to save his life. His hand had been out in front of him, holding the Glock. It was completely gone now. The hand took the brunt of the shot, but not all of it. His torso took the rest. It blew a huge hole in his shoulder and neck. The fourth guy flew backward toward Mister Man. He died before he hit the ground.

Mister Man got his flashlight on in time to see it. He jumped to the left and spun, trying to avoid the dead heap. He was well-trained, but I was better. He was fast, but I was faster. I pumped the action. The shotgun crunched. Even in the aftermath of the loud blast, the crunch was unmistakable. The blast rang in my ears, which meant it rang in theirs as well.

The third guy was no longer staring at the lightning crash. He spun around and saw his friend fall. He pulled up his Glock and aimed it into the cell. He aimed at the shadow that had just blown his friend away. But he was too slow.

I crouched and backed into the cell, putting the wall between myself, Mister Man, and the first guy, but I swung the shotgun around at the same time. I aimed at the third guy. He fired first. But he made the mistake of firing into the darkness with no target. He missed, but he saw me in the Glock's muzzle flash. I fired the Remington. The shotgun *boomed* again. I was the last thing he saw, because the Magnum shell blew off nearly everything from his waist down. His legs tore off. Blood and bone and sinew splattered everywhere. Large chunks of dust and rock exploded off the wall behind him. Red mist filled the air. He never shot his Glock again.

The third guy's torso collapsed, still partially attached to his lower half. It folded over on top of the lower half, landing in a pile of mess. It reminded me of the barrel filled with bones. I didn't give him a second thought. He didn't deserve it. None of them did.

Mister Man wasn't stupid. Not completely. He seized the moment and half stepped in front of the jail cell door. He shone his flashlight into the cell. It blinded me for a moment, but I didn't flinch. Flinching is a form of second guessing. And second guessing will get you killed in a gunfight. Flinching was instinctual, and sometimes instincts can get you killed. Luckily, the SEALs trained out most of my bad instincts.

But Mister Man didn't just have his flashlight out; he also had his Glock out. He blind-fired it into the cell, into the darkness. A Glock fired faster than a shotgun. It didn't require pumping action. It held more bullets. That was just a simple fact.

Everything slowed around me. Time slowed. And Mister Man fired once. Twice. Three times.

The brick on the wall behind me splintered and fragmented. Dust exploded into the air, filling the cell with powder and grime. Pieces of it ricocheted off the back of my head. The second and third bullets got me dead-on center mass. It hurt. My abdomen throbbed and pulsated and thrummed, but I fired back. I pumped and fired. Pumped and fired. It was blind. He stood off to the side of the door. Magnum shells slammed into the opposite wall, exploding more dust and soot into the air.

Mister Man fired again. This bullet slammed into the sink, emitting a metallic sound that echoed into the darkness. I pumped and fired again. The Remington *boomed*, overriding the metallic sounds.

The Magnum shell hit something, because Mister Man's flashlight went dead, and he stopped firing. *Maybe I got him?* I listened and waited. I heard nothing, and fell back against the wall. Tremendous pain shot through my chest and abdomen. It surged through my ribs. My skin felt like it was on fire from the two bullets I took in the chest. My whole torso was on fire.

I couldn't breathe. I lowered the Remington, held it one-handed, and slumped down. I stared at the open cell doorway. No one came. There was silence. The dust and soot hung in the air like lingering old-timey gun smoke. I tried to breathe. It was hard because my chest was aching. I felt dizzy and my heart pounded.

I waited, tried to breathe again, and kept my eye on the hall.

Nothing. No one came out. They were waiting, too.

I tried to breathe in deep, but there was no breath. No air. I couldn't breathe. Then finally, air rushed in through my mouth and I felt the pressure on my lungs subside, slowly. I stayed still and concentrated on breathing.

*In. Out.*

The ringing in my ears slowed to a low humming. I pushed myself back up to my feet and undid the bulletproof vest. I ripped it away from the Velcro straps and jerked it over my head, fast. The vest smoked. Two bullets had smashed into the Kevlar. I tossed the vest into the darkness and patted at my chest and shirt. It hurt to touch. My clothes were soaked.

*Blood*, I thought. I patted my shirt more. It was wet but that could've been from the rain. It didn't mean the bullets got through the vest. It didn't mean I was hit. Not necessarily. I pulled my shirt halfway up and felt my skin and chest. There were no bullet holes. Then I felt around my abdomen and my pelvis. There was nothing but my skin. I had the wind knocked out of me and my chest hurt something fierce, but the bulletproof vest had done what bulletproof vests are designed to do. It saved my life.

There were no bullet holes in me, which was good. I was sure there would be deep bruises, but I couldn't worry about that now. There was still one guy out there, for sure. Maybe two. Mister Man might've survived.

I stood up, picked up the Remington, and pumped it. A shell casing ejected out the port. It bounced and clattered on the cell floor. Before I made another move, I counted in my head. I'd fired seven times, which meant the shotgun was empty. I checked it. It was out. I tossed it back in the cell and brandished the Glock.

My vision was stained with black spots from Mister Man's flashlight. I squeezed them shut, fast and tight, and paused a beat. I breathed in and out. My chest and ribs throbbed with every breath I took. I opened my eyes, and the spots faded away.

I stepped to the doorway and glanced at the hallway floor. There were two heaps of dead fake cops. I raised the Glock, aimed it in Mister Man's direction, and exploded into the hallway, fast. I buried my shoulder into the wall, and saw the first fake cop.

The first fake cop had backed away from the wall and moved to the bottom of the stairs. He set up there and waited for me to poke my head out. He must've expected me to peek out. But that's not what I did. I exploded out of the cell.

I fired the Glock. Three bullets centimeters apart tore through the air and through the first cop's face. He folded backwards onto the stairs like a puppet with the strings cut. He was dead before he hit the steps, just another heap of bones, like his friends.

The ringing in my ears continued, but I could hear well enough. I heard my own panting. Also, I heard heavy breathing, but it wasn't mine. It came from Mister Man's position, from near the wall of the first cell. He was on the floor. The firelight danced and lit the air above him. He lay in shadow, like a dark mound.

The heavy breathing turned to whimpering. I pushed off the jail wall, slowly, not out of a need to be dramatic. I moved slowly because I felt dizzy, and the pain in my chest pounded harder than the rain outside.

Keeping the Glock trained on the dark mound, I stumbled toward him. But I stepped on something. I paused, reached down, and grabbed it. It was Mister Man's flashlight. I picked it up and flicked the switch. It flickered on and lit the room. Part of the lens was fractured and splintered. The beam came out and shone a spider web of cracks, like a broken movie projector.

I pointed it down and surveyed the dead fake cops, just to make sure they were dead and not getting back up. First, I looked over the closest one, which was the guy with his hand missing. I found the hand. It was a bloody thing, still gloved, and still with the fingers gripped on the Glock, but there was no arm attached, only half the wrist, covered in blood.

There was a trail of blood that led back to his torso. I pointed the flashlight on his face. He was dead—no question. He faced up. His face was splattered with blood. His eyes were black and lifeless.

I checked the others the same way, just with fast flicks of the wrist, training the flashlight beam on each of their bodies and faces. They were all dead.

I turned the flashlight back to Mister Man.

He was about five feet farther away from where he had been standing, but his boots weren't. They were still right square where he was standing when I shot him. The force of the Magnum round had removed him from his shoes. He just slipped right out of them, like he had stepped near a landmine.

He was curled up in a ball. Just like the third fake cop, Mister Man had taken the brunt of the Magnum round in his center mass and his bulletproof vest. And like the third cop, there were large holes riddled through him—his upper legs, his pelvis, and the vest. Even though the vest didn't completely stop the Magnum round, it saved him after all because he was still alive.

He stared up at me. Tears puddled in his eyes. He was in immense pain. It strained across his face. His left hand was completely broken. His fingers were spread out and bent in all kinds of awkward directions. None of which were normal. His hand was mangled like the frayed end of a piece of cloth. His right hand was trying to pick up his gun, but he was having trouble.

I walked toward him and saw why as I got closer.

A big chunk of his forearm was missing. Not the entire thing, but a significant portion of it was torn away. Flesh was torn off. Blood vessels were exposed like broken pipes.

I stopped a couple of feet from Mister Man, looked down at him, and stomped my foot down on his gun, trapping it under my weight. Then I slid it back and kicked it away from him. The gun clattered along the floor and vanished into the darkness.

Mister Man twisted his head and looked up at me. He tried to speak, but blood gurgled out of his mouth. He spat it out, and asked, "Who are you? Why?"

I said, "Doesn't matter who I am."

"Why?" he asked again.

I looked at him, into his eyes, and said, "Janey Saunt."

"Who?"

"Your phone. Where is it?"

"Pocket. Right. Pants."

I knelt and lowered the Glock close to his face. Kneeling was tremendously painful, not in my legs, but in my chest. My ribs hurt. I patted Mister Man down quick and fished his phone, wallet, and badge out of his pocket. First, I stared at his badge. It looked real, not like the others. I flipped his wallet open and looked in it. There was a police-issued ID with his name and face on it. I had my suspicions about Mister Man's identity, but it was time to find out the truth. I glanced at his face before reading his name out loud. And it was the name I suspected.

"Detective Joe Crocket of the New Mexico State Police."

He stared back at me and struggled to speak. He said, "That's my name."

My suspicions were confirmed. Mister Man was Crocket, the commanding officer of the two dead state cops. The same guy Voss told me had helped her earlier. That is, the one who *seemed* to help her, but he lied to her. Just one more betrayal in his long list of wrongdoings.

I nodded, closed his wallet, and pocketed it. Then I took out the phone and looked at the screen. I asked, "Passcode?"

He gurgled more blood, and said, "HEATHR. Only with one 'E.' The first one."

*Heather?* Must've been a girlfriend's or wife's name. But I didn't care. I typed the passcode and clicked the messages icon and searched for the dead cops' names in his messages. I found Broome first. It was the fourth message down from the top. I clicked on it and sifted through the messages. Right there on the first scroll down was a picture of Janey Saunt. It was the same as the one from the memory card Broome and Aragon delivered to Ryan Saunt with Janey's bloody finger-print on the envelope. In the photo, Janey was gagged and tied and half naked. Her skin was dirty, and her hair was messed up. She looked terrified, just the way I had found her.

Crocket said, "Please! Take me to a hospital!"

I flipped his phone around and showed him the picture. He stared at it. It took him a long second to see it. I waited for his reaction to her photo. He saw it. And his face turned to horror as the realization set in. He knew I wasn't going to take him to any hospital. He knew why I was there. And he started to protest, to shiver. He was scared now—scared of what I was going to do to him.

"I didn't know her. I don't approve the marks," he begged.

I reversed the phone, stood up, and slipped it into my pocket, and stepped back a foot. I pointed Broome's Glock at Crocket. I thought of Janey, her father, and the dead girl. I wondered how many other victims Crocket and his crooked cops and his fake cops had captured. How many lives were destroyed? How many women did they torture and kill? How many other kill bunkers they had stashed all across the state? I thought about the bones in the barrel and the driver's licenses.

I squeezed the trigger, repeatedly, until the Glock was empty. Twelve bullets. Twelve bullet holes. It wasn't twenty-six, like Saunt had given Broome and Aragon, but I wasn't an amateur either. Crocket died when I wanted him to die, which was on the last bullet, a headshot.

Dust clouds, disturbed by the gunshots, billowed around me. When it cleared, I saw Crocket was dead with the last bullet, which left a hole in the center of his forehead the size of a quarter.

# CHAPTER 30

I put my boots and rain poncho back on. I used my shirt to wipe my prints off of Crocket's phone, badge, and wallet and dropped them on his bullet-ridden remains. Using my shirt again, on my way out of the basement I wiped down the flashlight and everything else I had touched—the back-door knob, the Remington, Broome's Glock, the two magazines, and the spent shell and bullet casings, which I collected and stuffed in my pockets. I took the Remington shotgun with me.

I walked out the back door, turned the corner, and stepped onto the side street, pulling the rain poncho's hood over my head. The rain continued pounding on everything. I carried the wiped shotgun, Glock, magazines, and casings with the sleeves of the poncho, keeping my hands inside the sleeves. So I didn't have to rewipe everything. I dumped them into a giant mud puddle in the middle of the road. The dirty rain-water would cleanse them of any other forensic evidence left on them. Plus the rain wasn't letting up. Not anytime soon. It would continue the job—probably all night.

Craning my head back, I stayed there for a long moment and stared at the sky. The rain washed over my face and poncho, showering away any residue or blood splatter left on me. Eventually, I took off the poncho and my shirt and let the rain wipe everything away.

When I was ready, I slipped the shirt and poncho back on, wet and all. I didn't care.

I turned and went back to the police cruiser with the fake cop in the trunk. I popped the trunk and went back and opened it. I stared down at him. He looked back at me wide-eyed, but there was nothing there. He had died.

The damage to his face was too much. Maybe he bled out. Maybe bone stabbed him internally until he bled out that way. I wasn't sure what killed him, but he was dead. I closed the trunk and wiped the lid with the sleeve of the poncho. And I didn't give him a second thought.

I returned to the Silverado. My chest throbbed the whole time. I plodded. But I made it back to the truck.

Aragon's Glock was still on the front seat. I scooped it up and wiped it and tossed it into the distance, into the rain.

I hopped in the truck, fired it up, and drove back toward Angel Rock.

On my drive back, a memory dawned on me. It was from long ago. There was a Navy sailor's name. A Hospital Corpsman. I never knew him. But I'd never forget him either.

# CHAPTER 31

Back in Angel Rock, I stopped at the hospital. I thought about driving straight through town, continuing on my way. That might've been best. I could've taken Saunt's Silverado as far as Denver and left it somewhere. I could've driven north and been far away before anyone noticed the missing truck. But my chest hurt badly. It was best to stop at the hospital and get checked out. Plus, I had unfinished business with Voss.

Voss sat in the entrance to the emergency room, like she was waiting for me. I parked the Silverado in the lot and walked up a ramp and sidewalk to the emergency room entrance. She saw me and didn't wait for me to get there. She ran straight to me, leapt up, and hugged me tight, like we were long-lost lovers. It was a deep embrace. It reminded me of when she first recognized me several hours earlier. She whispered in my ear, "It's so great!"

I flinched as she hugged me, because the pain in my ribs thrummed. It felt like getting stabbed by the dullest knife ever, but it still hurt. She let go and inched back, but stayed in my arms. We both asked, "What?"

Voss smiled, but I didn't. My ribs hurt too much. I spoke first. I said, "I fell. Slipped in the rain. My chest hurts. I think I broke a rib."

Voss dropped her smile and a genuine concern stretched across her face, like a mother's for her children when they are hurt. It was a look she'd probably had a thousand times in her life, because she was a mother. She said, "Let's get you checked out. Come on."

She turned away and held my hand. She led the way, never letting me go. I didn't resist. We entered the hospital through the same entrance but passed a different security guard from earlier. We passed through corridors and open doors back to the emergency room. Voss pushed me into the emergency room and shoved me into a private area separated from the other cubicles by curtains. She sat me on a bed, and said, "Wait here. I'll get someone."

She left and returned minutes later with the ER doctor I had seen earlier. She pointed at me, and said, "This guy's with us. He's critically important. Check him out and take care of him. His ribs hurt."

The ER doctor nodded and came over to me. Voss stayed in the curtain doorway the whole time.

The doctor said, "Okay. Let me have a look."

He reached out and felt my chest and my upper body. It hurt, and I let him know.

He said, "Yeah. It looks like you got a fractured rib. Possibly broken."

I stayed quiet.

He said, "Let's have a look. Pull up your shirt, please."

I lifted my shirt. Voss stared at me. There were two large, black bruises on the center of my chest and abdomen. They were the size of golf balls.

The doctor poked and prodded them. I winced from the pain. He retracted his fingers, stepped back, and stared at me blankly. He asked, "Were you shot?"

I stayed quiet.

Voss stepped into the room, inched up on her tippy toes, and gazed at my chest over the doctor's shoulder. Then she looked at my face.

I shrugged, smiled, and said, "No. Not shot. I slipped and fell. I'm clumsy."

The doctor nodded slowly. He glanced back at Voss and gave her a suspicious look, but he said nothing.

Voss nodded at him, and said, "Looks like a slip and fall to me."

I said, "That's what happened. I slipped in the rain."

The doctor shrugged, and said, "Okay. We'll need to do some x-rays to be sure."

I nodded.

Voss said, "Do whatever it takes. The department will cover the cost."

The doctor said, "Fine by me."

Voss paused a beat, and said, "And keep it off the books. It's critical to a case we're working. Understand?"

The ER doctor nodded and said nothing else.

I looked at Voss. She looked back at me and smiled.

# CHAPTER 32

One of the bullets had fractured a rib. Nothing too serious according to the doctor, not for taking a bullet in the vest, but he said it was serious for slipping in the rain. He advised me to be more careful. It became a running joke among the nursing staff. They thought it was funny that a guy my size was so frail that a simple fall had fractured a rib. I was fine with them getting laughs at my expense.

They kept me in the ER for an hour, wrapping my torso up with bandages. Then they moved me to a private room.

Voss stayed with me for a while, but she kept getting sleepy. She left for the night and returned the next afternoon. At least, I don't think she returned before then. I wouldn't know, because I slept like a baby for ten hours.

I woke up once before noon and glanced out the window. The rain had stopped.

A nurse came into the room, like she'd been waiting for me to wake up. She changed my bandages. After she finished, she gave me some good painkillers. I popped them, drank a glass of water, and passed out. I slept well.

Voss woke me around two-thirty in the afternoon. She stood over my bed. She wore street clothes—a pair of jeans, cowboy boots tucked under the jean legs, and a red leather jacket with a white t-shirt underneath. The t-shirt was tight, and I saw why her bulletproof vest was so bulky on her. The leather jacket concealed some of what was going on, but there was enough to grab anyone's attention.

Voss smiled and reached out and poked me in the ribs. It was a fast, weak jab, like a single tap on the shoulder.

I grabbed at the bandages one-handed. It didn't hurt, not really. It was somewhere between stubbing a toe and walking into a door. It was more shock and awe than pain. I asked, "Why?"

Voss crossed her arms, and said, "I saw you looking."

"What?"

She uncrossed her arms and raised her hand like she was going to jab me again. Playfully, she asked, "You want another? I can do it harder."

I raised my hands to shield me from another jab and smiled. I said, "No. That's okay. You're right. I couldn't help it."

She lowered her jabbing hand, put both hands on her hips, and said, "I'm kidding with you. I don't mind. Not if you do it, anyway."

I smiled.

She said, "I brought you some clothes."

"I already have clothes," I said, and sat up in the hospital bed. I looked around for my clothes. They weren't in the room. All I had to wear was a hospital gown and my birthday suit.

"No. You don't. They mysteriously vanished. Must've gotten thrown in the trash," Voss said, and paused a beat. "Or maybe someone gathered them up and burned them in a trash can."

"Why would someone do that?"

"I'm not saying someone did that. I'm just saying that if they were destroyed in a fire, then it'd be impossible to study them for any forensic evidence."

I nodded slowly. The painkillers were wearing off. I felt a headache coming on. My mouth was dry from sleeping so long.

Voss said, "On a separate note, there was a fire in El Demonio. Our fire department got calls about it and went out there this morning. You know what they found?"

I looked down at Voss's waist to see if she was carrying. There was no gun. No bulge of a firearm. No holster. No handcuffs. None that I could see. I said, "I got no idea."

"They found a dead cop. And guess who it was?"

I shrugged.

She said, "It was Crocket."

I shrugged again.

She asked, "Recognize that name?"

"Can't say I do."

"Detective Joe Crocket worked for the New Mexico State Police. He's the commander of the unit that Broome and Aragon worked for."

"That's interesting."

"Yeah. And he wasn't alone. We found four dead guys with him."

I asked, "More cops?"

"No. They wore cop clothes and had cop gear, but they weren't cops. We don't know who they are."

"But they're all dead?"

"Yes. It was a bloodbath. Looks like they walked into a trap. Probably killed by five or six other guys."

I stayed quiet.

Voss said, "I was down there all morning."

"You were? Why aren't you still there?"

"It's not my problem. The FBI took over. Oliver's there now with his guys. They're also covering the scene with the two dead cops, and the bunker. Oliver said they think the chain goes beyond Crocket. They've got some leads. Whoever's at the top will get caught. They found the ransom money along with other monies for other jobs. They were stuffed in a safe in the corner of the bunker. Anyway, it's out of my hands now. So I took the rest of the day off."

I stayed quiet.

Voss said, "It's probably a good idea for you to move on today. Oliver's got some kind of fancy FBI forensic team coming in tonight. They're going to be pretty busy with the bones in the barrel and the dead girl and all."

I nodded.

She said, "It's best if you're gone before then."

Silence.

I asked, "Is that what you want?"

"No. But Oliver's a boy scout. It's best for you."

I asked, "What about Janey?"

"Good news. Janey is going to be fine. She's endured a lot of trauma, but she'll recover. I hope."

"What about Saunt?"

"Her father's the really good news. He came out of surgery. The bullet cracked his skull pretty badly, but his brain was mostly unaffected. It bounced off his skull. He's lucky he's such a terrible shot. His inexperience saved his life. He's got a long road ahead of him as far as physical therapy. The doctor says he's got some memory loss issues, but he'll make a full recovery too."

I smiled, and said, "That's great news."

"The FBI will charge him with homicide. Probably. There'll be a trial. Surely."

"He's got a strong defense."

"Temporary insanity is probably reasonable," Voss said, and moved closer to the bed, closer to me. She sat on the edge, reached out, scooped up my hand, and held it. She smiled big, and said, "I'm glad I met you again. Not so much the first time. Which you don't remember."

I said, "Hospital Corpsman Petty Officer Second Class James Maxton."

Voss's smile deflated and her shoulders sank. She went quiet for a long second. Her eyes watered just a little. A single tear streamed out. I reached up and wiped it away.

She said, "You remember?"

"I remember. Twenty years ago—"

"Nineteen years ago," she interrupted.

I cleared my throat, and said, "Right. Nineteen years ago. I was just out of Annapolis. A freshly-minted officer. One of the most memorable assignments I had was a death notification."

Voss stared at me. She looked lost in thought, in the memory of it. She whispered, "Go on."

"I was assigned to deliver a death message to the next of kin of a young man named Maxton. He died in a suicide bombing on the USS Bridgton. It was docked in a port in Yemen. A couple of suicide bombers tricked their way past a guard post. A firefight broke out. They fought their way to the ship and blew themselves and the hull up. Maxton was onboard."

Voss said, "Yes. That's right. What did you call it? A death note?"

"A death notification. They go to the next of kin, sometimes a sailor's mother," I said, paused, and swallowed. "Sometimes to the wife."

Voss slowly reached out and put her palm on my breastplate, right over my heart. She fought back another tear. She said, "James was a good husband. He would've been a good father."

I put one hand on hers and the other on her cheek and smiled at her. I said, "I saw your son in pictures in your office. He's a good-looking kid. You did a damn fine job. James would've been proud."

"You think so?"

"I do," I said, and paused a beat. "He needs a haircut though."

Voss chuckled, and said, "I'm always trying to get him to cut it. But what can I do? He's his own man now."

Not knowing what to say, I said, "Boys will be boys."

"That's a fact."

Voss went silent. I put my arms around her, pulled her in, and hugged her tight. She hugged me back. Her breast pushed up against my chest plate. My rib throbbed from the pressure, but I didn't care. It felt too good to be so close to her. I wasn't going to complain. We stayed like that for several long minutes. She stopped crying, stopped thinking of James. She leaned into me. Her body was warm. Her scent of wild-flowers—orange blossom, tangerine, magnolia, orchids, and Osmanthus—filled my nose again. I loved it.

She spoke first. She said, "Can't believe you forgot me."

"I didn't forget you. At least, not for long."

"You're the man who handed me a folded flag at my husband's funeral."

"It's hanging in your office."

She nodded, and asked, "So you remember me?"

"The last time I saw you was at his funeral in Strafford, New York."

She gazed at me. A measured happiness shone across her face, like she was pleased I remembered her. She said, "It's such a small town. I'm surprised you remembered."

"Strafford. Population around six hundred. I think it's in Fulton County."

"That's pretty good. How do you remember that?"

I tapped my skull, and said, "My noggin holds a bunch of useless facts."

"But you couldn't remember me?"

"Well, you're far from useless. Plus, you're completely different now."

She pulled away, slow, and stared at me. She asked, "In a good way?"

"A very good way."

"After James died, I was broken for a while. Lost. Sad. I didn't know what I was going to do with myself. I was scared. Soon, I was scared all the time. And then I got angry. Angry at the world, at the assholes that murdered him. Anger turned to resolve. It changed me. I moved to Arizona, got a degree in Criminal Justice, and took a job here as a cop, worked my way to chief. Now, I run the whole department," Voss said. She paused and looked down at her body and back to me. "Bet I look different too?"

"Yes. You put on some muscle."

She smiled, and said, "When we met, I was a housewife who baked cookies. Now, I'm—"

"Like the Terminator."

She laughed, and said, "Yes. The Lady T-1000."

"You worked out a bit. Plus, got those tattoos."

"You like tattoos on a woman?"

I held up my arms. She studied the sleeve tattoos I had on both. I asked, "What do you think?"

She didn't answer. Not with words. She leaned in and pulled me close and kissed me. Her lips were wet. Her tongue was warm. It was a good kiss. So good we continued for several minutes, until finally she pulled back, and said, "Get dressed. I'll drive you out of here."

"Where to?"

"It's a surprise. Come on," she said, and stood up off the bed. She signaled to the folded clothes and a new pair of boots she had set down on a chair while I slept.

I looked at them and nodded. I got up out of bed and dressed. Voss never left the room. She stayed and watched. And I didn't complain once.

# CHAPTER 33

Voss drove us in her police cruiser out of Angel Rock and off to the next town, which was to the south. It was Roswell.

We stopped, and she took me on an alien tour. We saw all kinds of local alien stuff. There was a museum, a roadside diner, souvenir shops, bus tours, parks with alien themes, and UFO rides. We went to the famous, supposed-UFO crash site. We did it all.

We ate lunch and drank coffee at an alien-themed diner. At night, we ate dinner and drank coffee at a different alien-themed diner.

We talked and laughed. She told me some of her favorite stories about her husband. She told me about how they met. She told me about her son and how proud she was of him. He was about to graduate high school. He wanted to be a veterinarian. She looked happy the whole day. She smiled a lot. She told me about how her department had a shake-up once, and she was promoted to chief.

Voss told me about her past relationships and how some guys came, and some went, and a few stuck around. But nobody made the cut to stick it out for the long run.

I told her about my life on the road but never talked about my days in the NCIS and SEALs.

Several times, Voss's phone buzzed from a text message or rang with a call. She checked it each time but never answered it.

The day rolled by. It turned into night. After dinner, we had a beer at a local bar. It wasn't alien-themed. It was country-music-themed, but they had a live band. The band played no country songs. They played slow rock songs, mostly. We danced twice.

It got late. It got to be time for Voss to head back. She took me to the alien-themed motel. I got a room. We stood in the door-way, kissing goodnight and goodbye. I joked Voss should stay the night. We laughed, but it turned into more kissing. Voss stayed the night.

We woke up early in the morning to her phone. It rang constantly. Angel Rock wanted her to return. We showered and dressed.

Voss drove me to a truck stop on US Route 285, just before it intersected with US Route 70, in north Roswell. She pulled into the lot and stopped at the pumps. She bought gas and filled her tank. I got us two coffees in Styrofoam cups. She took one and hugged and kissed me one last time. Then she got in her cruiser, started it up, and pulled away slowly, without me. She glanced back at me once. Her brake lights flashed, like she was thinking of coming back, but she didn't.

I watched her drive away and pull onto the service drive, and then, turn onto US 70. She drove away northeast, back to

Angel Rock, back to her life. I watched until she was gone from sight.

I walked to US 285, turned, and walked south. With a coffee in one hand and my other thumb out, hoping for a ride, I figured I could catch one with someone either heading west to California or east to Texas. It didn't matter which.

# THE PROTECTOR: A PREVIEW

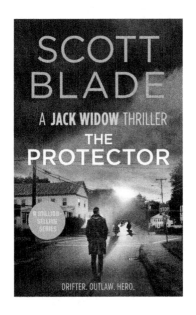

Out Now!

# THE PROTECTOR: A BLURB

**They want her dead.**

**But there's a problem.**

**Jack Widow stands in the way.**

Widow walks the side of the road at night when a pair of headlights is headed his way. It's the first car in hours. With a thumb out, he hopes to get a ride. But when the car drives erratically at high speeds, Widow dodges, nearly being rammed to death. The driver barrels the car into a tree. It turns out the driver had a heart attack. Waiting for help to arrive, the driver enlists Widow's help. The driver is a US Marshal. He was on his way to stop an attack on one of his witnesses. She's been in the witness relocation program, hiding, living a new life. Now, they know who she is. They want her dead. Her only hope is her new protector—Widow.

*Preorder Book 17 in the international bestselling Jack Widow series.*

**Readers are saying about Scott Blade and the Jack Widow series...**

★ ★ ★ ★ ★ Scott Blade and Lee Child are cut from the same cloth! Do yourself a favor and check this series out!

# CHAPTER 1

Out of breath, I sprinted for almost a half-mile, straight out, chasing after a car that barely swerved to miss me. Driving fast, more than sixty-five miles an hour. The car nearly slammed into me. The force would've flung me into the night air, legs flailing about. It would've been a hard landing. At best, I would've ended up in the hospital with two broken legs from crashing into God-knows-what. At worst, the paramedics would've pronounced me dead at the scene. My head could've bounced off a desert rock and busted wide open, spilling out the contents like a split coconut.

Before the car nearly killed me, I walked on the highway shoulder, thumb out, in the middle of a beautiful autumn night. An endless blanket of stars covered the sky. Hulking rock formations and mountains lingered in the distance. A breeze blew off the Arizona desert, chilly but not unpleasant. I welcomed the slight chill in the air. It was a nice change of pace from the blistering heat that swept across North America this past summer.

I tried to get a ride for hours without luck. Honestly, I didn't expect a car to stop for me. Not out here. Even if I hadn't been on this dark, quiet highway, the odds of getting a ride were against me. No one picks up hitchhikers anymore, not at night, not out here, and especially not ones who look like me. On a good day, I wasn't the ideal candidate to offer a lift. I was unkempt on this night, as I was lately. It might be a phase I was going through where I just didn't care how I looked. A two-week beard covered my face and the hair on my head was full and a little bushy. I looked like a caveman who was just thawed out of ice after a hundred-thousand-year nap. The wind blew my hair around like it was at war with it. Strands danced and billowed across my forehead, blotting over my eyes, slightly impairing my vision. But the strands didn't stay still long enough for me to brush it out of my face.

I looked like the sketch artist rendering of the nightmare drifter who'd been killing drivers up and down some dark superhighway and dumping their bodies across state lines. If the FBI was involved in a manhunt for someone like that, they'd arrest me on sight, throw me in a cell, and close the case. No questions asked. And that's only if they didn't shoot me first.

Even if I hadn't looked menacing, hitchhiking was still a dying enterprise. I was surprised I got as many rides as I had this far into the twenty-first century.

I heard of the *good ole days* of hitching for rides from two old timers who hung out together on an interstate cloverleaf back at the foothills of the Rocky Mountains.

They educated me on the ways of the hitchhiker, like older guys did to younger guys. They had that attitude that anyone younger than them knew absolutely nothing about anything and they knew absolutely everything about everything. I don't consider myself young. Not anymore. I think that happens as we age. There comes a point where you think your youth is gone, until you meet someone decades older, and they think you're a newborn baby. These two saw me like that. Apparently, they considered a former Navy SEAL and undercover NCIS agent hovering around forty to be *young* and inexperienced. They acted like it was a miracle that I could tie my shoes.

Some people thought that way. Others didn't. Apparently, they did.

To these two guys, I was a greenhorn, a rookie, a new blood— someone who needed schooling. I've met a lot of interesting people ever since I started wandering around with no clear destination, but these two deserved to be on the most memorable people list.

They were two old guys, one white and one black. Between the two of them, they didn't have a full mouth of teeth. Their faces were dirty, almost soot-covered like two ancient, old west California gold prospectors on their last dime and last shred of reality. They were dressed like California gold prospectors too, only they weren't reclusive. They were friendly, as friendly as any other two old guys would be to a stranger.

They saw me and immediately invited me over to them. Pleasantries were exchanged and conversations took place as the sun descended in the sky, at which point, I said goodbye and hit the road again on my own. They offered to walk with me. I didn't want to be rude, but I felt I had a better chance of scoring a ride with some daylight left—and without the toothless, crazy prospectors on my tail.

Rides for me were scarce enough, but nighttime was ten times scarcer. Getting a ride for me at night was like praying for rain in a years-long drought.

Most people didn't pick up hitchhikers. At least that's true in my case. Then again, maybe they just didn't pick *me* up.

I'm what kids call a *big dude*—six foot four inches in height and two hundred and twenty-five pounds of muscle and bone. I was blessed with good, but half-unknown genetics. My mother was a small-town sheriff. She was tough, the toughest person I ever knew. But she was a tiny thing, meaning I must've gotten my ape-man genetics from my father. He was a drifter, like me, but I never knew him. And I rarely give him a second's thought.

I've got massive arms, the size of caveman clubs, the kind used to crush the skulls of Wooly Mammoth and prehistoric big cats. My biceps are as big as cannonballs fired on the battlefield at Yorktown. And my hands are big, like bear paws, but with long fingers. Both of my arms are covered with sleeve tattoos. Some of which serve meanings for me. Some don't.

People avoided me based on my appearance, which was okay by me ninety-nine percent of the time. I liked not being bothered. If people kept to themselves, I kept to myself. There's always an exception to any rule. That exception for me was when I needed a ride.

But that's how it went sometimes. Often people avoided me when I needed them, and were right there when I didn't.

Usually, I'm surprised whenever anyone stops for me. Even if an exhausted driver, after a long day and night of traversing endless highways, hooking interstates, tolls, and copious bridges, stops for me, I'm surprised. I shouldn't be, because on the surface it all makes sense. It's simple commerce. It's economics. Hitchhikers need rides and some drivers want company. Others need someone to take the wheel for the last leg of their trip. It's fair trade. Road company for a ride. Or free labor for a free ride. You drive for me, and I give you transportation to get where you're going, all in a climate-controlled vehicle. Not a bad exchange. It's a capitalistic approach to a common, everyday problem. It's the old adage of you scratch my back and I'll scratch yours. It's not rocket science.

I knew as the sun went down the odds of someone engaging in this trade with me diminished to nearly zero. In the middle of nowhere, in the middle of the night, on a quiet Arizona highway, I was the last thing someone wanted to see. That goes for any quiet nighttime highway in America. Hardly anyone stops for me under these conditions. Obviously, this isn't always the case. Sometimes people stop for me. It's a matter of numbers. On any day, hundreds or thousands of cars will pass me by without a second glance. But in those numbers, there's bound to be one person who'll stop.

*Statistics.*

So, when I saw car headlights barreling straight at me on a quiet Arizona highway in the middle of the night, in the middle of nowhere, I thought maybe it was going to stop and offer me a ride. I thought it was the exception to the rule. It was the one in a thousand. But I should've known better. My judgement was slightly impaired because I wanted a ride so badly. I wanted to sit in the front passenger seat of a car and get off my feet.

My legs ached and my feet throbbed from standing and walking for a couple of days straight. I haven't stayed for more than a night in a single location in several days. I just felt like moving, with no interest in staying anywhere. My shoulders stung from sleeping on the ground under a tree. The night before, and many miles back, I was tired and the only motel I found was at full capacity. Desperate, I laid up under a tree off the highway, down a hill and out of sight, and slept there. Why not? When I was a SEAL, my team and I slept in worse conditions, outdoors, in rocky terrain, and with enemy combatants hunting us all night. We slept in the cold, in the pouring rain, all while keeping one eye open in case the enemy stumbled upon our camp. Crashing under a tree in Arizona wasn't the end of the world.

But I overestimated how tired I was and overslept the next morning and woke up with my shoulder hurting from laying on it. A large tree root had pressed against it all night. My body cramped up. It was bad for the first part of the morning. It wasn't worst I'd ever felt, but it was still sore.

Moments before I leapt out of the way from being plowed by the car at sixty-five miles an hour, I saw inside the vehicle. It was just a glance, but it was like slow motion, the way time slows when you're being shot at. I couldn't see the driver. I thought I saw two occupants. They looked to be scrambling for the wheel. There was no one in the backseat.

It looked like there were two people in the vehicle's front, fighting over control of the car, maybe? Perhaps the driver was fighting with a passenger, like a carjacking or something. Perhaps it was a friendly conversation turned bad. Conceivably, they fought because the passenger was an unwilling participant on their journey. Maybe it was a kidnapping gone wrong? Or perhaps the driver was victim to a bad hitchhiker, someone with malicious intent. Whatever the reason, I didn't like almost being hit by a car. Maybe I should've let it go. But I wasn't the kind of guy who let things like that go. Not after it almost hit me. Not after I had walked for hours. Not after I had slept on the hard ground the night before.

I saw the car's headlights coming at me. I stayed on the shoulder, watching it, thinking it was coming at me, thinking it was going to slow and stop as it neared me. But it didn't. I leapt out of the way, diving off the shoulder and rolling away in the dirt. The car barreled past me and weaved from lane to lane. It dipped down over a hill, into a valley, and then back up another hill. It ramped up into the air at the apex. The tires came up off the ground and the car landed on the pavement. Sparks flew, and the suspension hissed, but the car kept going. It weaved from shoulder to shoulder, across the highway, until the taillights faded away into the blackness and the car was gone from sight.

I didn't think the car would make it far. Not in the reckless state of driving that it was in. My fear was it would crash into a tree. And that's exactly what it did.

# A WORD FROM SCOTT

Thank you for reading NOTHING LEFT. You got this far—I'm guessing that you liked Widow.

The story continues…

The next book in the series is *THE PROTECTOR*, coming Winter 2021.

To find out more, sign up for the Scott Blade Book Club and get notified of upcoming new releases. See next page.

# THE SCOTT BLADE
# BOOK CLUB

Building a relationship with my readers is the very best thing about writing. I occasionally send newsletters with details on new releases, special offers, and other bits of news relating to the Jack Widow Series.

If you are new to the series, you can join the Scott Blade Book Club and get the starter kit.

Sign up for exclusive free stories, special offers, access to bonus content, and info on the latest releases, and coming-soon Jack Widow novels. Sign up at ScottBlade.com.

# THE NOMADVELIST

NOMAD + NOVELIST = NOMADVELIST

Scott Blade is a Nomadvelist, a drifter and author of the breakout Jack Widow series. Scott travels the world, hitchhiking, drinking coffee, and writing.

Jack Widow has sold over a million copies.

Visit @: ScottBlade.com
Contact @: scott@scottblade.com
Follow @:
Facebook.com/ScottBladeAuthor
Bookbub.com/profile/scott-blade
Amazon.com/Scott-Blade/e/B00AU7ZRS8

# ALSO BY SCOTT BLADE

**The Jack Widow Series**

Gone Forever

Winter Territory

A Reason to Kill

Without Measure

Once Quiet

Name Not Given

The Midnight Caller

Fire Watch

The Last Rainmaker

The Devil's Stop

Black Daylight

The Standoff

Foreign & Domestic

Patriot Lies

The Double Man

Nothing Left

The Protector

Kill Promise

The Shadow Club

Printed in Great Britain
by Amazon